BABA LENKA

AN OCCULT HORROR NOVEL

BY

S. E. ENGLAND

Copyright © S. E. England 2020
Cover illustration by Raven Wood
Cover design by Gina Dickerson: www.rosewolfdesign.co.uk
Editor: Colleen Wagner
All rights reserved.

The right of S. E. England to be identified as the Author of the work has been asserted by her in accordance with the Copyright, Designs and Patents Act 1988. All rights reserved in all media. No part of this book may be used or reproduced in any manner whatsoever without written permission of the author, except for brief quotations used for promotion or in reviews. This is a work of fiction. Names, characters, places and incidents are used fictitiously. Any resemblance to actual persons living or dead, business establishments, events, or locales is entirely coincidental. The only exceptions to this are Hitler and Kaiser Wilhelm 11, who although mentioned here in a fictitious context, did, of course, exist.

ISBN: 979-8-6514-7533-9

1st Edition:
www.sarahenglandauthor.co.uk

DARK FICTION BY SARAH E. ENGLAND

About the author:

Sarah England is a UK author. Originally she trained as a nurse before a career in the pharmaceutical industry specialising in mental health – a theme which creeps into much of her work. She then spent many years writing short stories and serials for magazines before having her first novel published in 2013.

At the fore of Sarah's body of work is the bestselling occult horror trilogy *Father of Lies, Tanners Dell,* and *Magda,* followed by *The Owlmen.* Stand-alone supernatural horror novels include *The Soprano, Hidden Company,* and *Monkspike. Baba Lenka* is her latest.

If you would like to be informed about future releases, there is a newsletter sign-up on Sarah's website. Please feel free to get in touch - it would be great to hear from you!

www.sarahenglandauthor.co.uk

PROLOGUE

ELDERSGATE, YORKSHIRE
May 1979

Nicky Dixon took the parcel from the postman, thanked him and tore it open. Inside was a bound manuscript. Bloody hell, it was from Eva! She hadn't seen her in how long…over a year? Eva Hart had been her best and only friend from the age of eight to sixteen, but one year ago, about a month after Eva's sixteenth birthday, she'd vanished. Totally. No goodbye. No warning. No nothing.

Pulling out hundreds of dog-eared, scruffy handwritten pages, she frowned. It looked as though this had been written in the dark – parts of it scrawled in pencil, others smudged and near illegible with a leaky Biro.

My dearest Nicky, you are the only person I can send this to…

Within the first few minutes of reading, her heartbeat picked up. Some of this Eva had tried to tell her shortly after they first met. She'd recognised then that her friend was battling with the dark side. But the more she read, the more she understood. Goose bumps rose on her skin, and her eyes widened. Many hours passed until soon it was dark.

Forcing herself to take a break, she rubbed her aching

neck. Dear God, poor Eva – what a terrible burden. This was so much worse, so very much more frightening than anything she could ever have imagined.

It wasn't simply Eva who was in trouble, though. It was what Eva had brought with her.

***

Something drops from eyes long blind,
He completes his partial mind,
For an instant stands at ease,
Laughs aloud, his heart at peace...

W.B. Yeats.

PART ONE

EVA HART

CHAPTER ONE

RABENWALD, BAVARIA
February 1970

A raw wind rushed straight from the mountains that day, the kind that whipped skin to ice. Fresh from the snowcaps, it whistled down the slopes and howled through the trees.

The small procession of mourners trailing Baba Lenka's coffin paused momentarily on the hill to the cemetery, gasping in the fresh onslaught. Ice blew off pines in swirls of white dust. It stuck to eyelashes, peppered lungs and froze faces. There weren't many of us – immediate family, the priest, and six elderly mourners at the helm. The rest of the villagers had hung back and refused to come, their expressions dark and unreadable as they stood watching us leave. But the old folk were different, almost as if they were from a bygone age – the women swathed in long, dark robes and headscarves, the men in trousers cut short at the knee and waistcoats fastened over full-sleeved shirts. Swarthy-skinned, their demeanour was quietly watchful. They did not speak much to those in the village, or indeed to us, but in hushed tones amongst themselves.

Less than an hour before, the two old women in the group had washed and prepared Baba Lenka's body for burial, after which the water used had been carried out to the farm's well and tipped away. They stood out there in the frozen yard, heads bowed, muttering in a foreign tongue that carried on the wind. The men then joined them to form a circle, and with heads thrown back they began a strange kind of ceremony, calling and wailing into the wind.

We'd watched from the farmhouse kitchen window.

"What are they doing?" I asked my mother.

Silently she shook her head, narrowing her eyes at the screeching, cawing birds overhead.

We had arrived the day before. I was seven years old, cold, miserable and hungry. Baba Lenka had been my great-grandmother, but I'd never met her. Nor did I understand why we had to come: spring was about to burgeon back home in England, snowdrops and crocus shivering on roadsides, sunlight chasing clouds across the school playing fields... She was ninety-six, they said. Even my mother had never been to Rabenwald. It was freezing, the air biting, cobbles glistening with ice. And towering over the valley were mountains so huge they stood like giants with their heads in the clouds, the blue light of the snowy slopes ominous, eerie, deadly.

If only this were all over – that we had never come here. Baba Lenka's farmhouse didn't even have running water. We'd arrived late yesterday afternoon to find the kitchen cupboards bare except for mouse droppings, and all the mirrors and windows had been covered with black cloths. It had the feel of a church crypt, and if it had ever been a welcoming home, it would be difficult to picture that. In the grim half-light, with the wind rattling the windows and whining down the chimney, my dad tried to get a fire going, and my mother chipped at packed ice outside to get water for the kettle. There was an all-pervading chill in that house, which once experienced could not be shaken, the kind that gripped the bones and iced the marrow. Mould spotted the wallpaper, damp coated the woodwork, and frost glazed the glass.

As evening plunged into the black of night, my mother's footsteps creaked up the old staircase to where we would have to sleep, the wind screaming like banshees around the eaves, candlelight flickering over the walls. I trailed behind her, shivering. But on reaching the landing, she caught her breath, and we both stopped to stare. Baba Lenka's bedroom door was ajar. We saw then what we didn't want to see – the deathbed soiled and sagging where her body had lain decaying for weeks and weeks on end.

The room had been stripped of all possessions. Tidemarks left by her bodily fluids had stained the sheets dark yellow, and the sour stench of terminal disease cloyed the air. As we stood on the threshold, the sound of howling wolves echoed from the woods, and the noise of the wind intensified to violent and insistent. It seemed so very much louder up here, as if it was gaining in strength. Hypnotised, I couldn't look away, the Alpine coldness seeping under my skin…

Suddenly, catching me totally off guard, I was in the old lady's mind – lying there in the bed, dying in my own filth with a throat caked dry. Silvery light streaked through the curtains, and a murderous vixen screech rent the night air. The whole room was rumbling and juddering. The house seemed to shake on its very foundations, the floor tipping sideways... A burst of crippling pain ripped through my chest, the heart muscle squeezing and twisting...

I think I blacked out at that point, stumbling backwards, because the next thing I knew, my mother grabbed my arm and shut the door behind us.

"Come on, Eva – let's make the back bedroom nice and warm. We'll bunk up together in there. Thank God it's only for a couple of nights."

The vision had lasted for a second at most, but the effect lingered. My great-grandma had endured a terrible death.

Downstairs, her body lay in the parlour, where it had been wrapped in a coarse blanket and awaited preparation. It was our job as family, said my mother, to make sure all Baba Lenka's personal things were located and put into the casket, ready for burial. As such, she set me the task of checking drawers and cupboards for jewellery, photographs and trinkets. Nothing must be taken. Everything must go with her to the grave.

There was nothing left in the house, though. Every cupboard and drawer lay empty apart from a few old and very dirty books, which my mother kept.

Earlier, not long after we'd arrived, while Dad was still getting the fire going, I had heard Mum shouting with someone at the door. It had turned out to be one of the old women who'd come to prepare the body. My mother's German was halting, but she seemed to thank them, after which she came in to tell my dad what it had been about.

"I think she was saying no one would tend to Lenka

while she was ill. Those in the village say she was a *Bluthexe* and wouldn't come, so they contacted the old ones. She said they've travelled a long way, and by the time they got here, the storm had blown over. That's how they knew she was already dead. She doesn't seem to speak much German. I don't know what it is they're speaking, but it's like nothing I've ever 'eard in my life. Anyway, I think that's the gist of it."

"Bluthexe?"

"Blood witch."

"For crying out loud – the woman was dying!"

"I know. She was saying the storm went on the whole time Baba Lenka was ill, that it raged and raged as she tried to send her demons to someone else on the wind—"

"What a load of old codswallop."

"Aye, well, that's as maybe, but…" She sighed. "The locals were scared daft, Pete. She was very much alone, I think."

"Apart from these old folk?"

"She said they'd been travelling for days—"

"Bloody hell, poor old baggage with no one to look after her. Managed to strip the house, though, haven't they – the locals?"

"No, I don't think so. It looks like her things have been piled into the casket; it's stuffed with—"

"You've looked inside, then?"

"Only to check all's as it should be. You don't take anything out of a coffin, you know? To be honest, it's a good thing we came or I don't think she'd 'ave been given a proper burial. They really are scared out of their wits of her round 'ere, you know? From what I can gather, the villagers wanted to tip her down the well. Thank God for Jakub and Vanda, that's all I can say."

"Good thing you kept in touch. Who are these old folk anyway? The ones who don't speak German very well and travelled for days? Where did they come from?"

She shook her head. "Further back in my family than Baba Lenka. I don't know, but I'm grateful to them. Anyway, I think they want to come tomorrow to wash the body, and good, frankly, because it's in a terrible mess."

"You looked?"

"Her hand had poked through the blanket…" She lowered her voice, but I heard well enough. "God, Pete, her skin's turned an 'orrible shade of greeny yellow, and the tissue's so thin it's split apart over the bones. I only pulled the top part back, and I wish I 'adn't, because the eyes are still open. I nearly had a bloody heart attack."

They fell into numb silence for a while, watching the flames spark into life and rubbing their hands to get warm.

"She's got no hair, either. And there's this strange silver ring on her thumb, kind of like runes all the way round the band, and a little black sun sign etched into it."

"Maybe she'd want you to have it?"

"God, no! You can't take anything off a dead body!"

"I just thought maybe she'd have given it to you if she could have done?"

"No, Pete. No. It's not something you'd want."

"Okay, okay… I were only saying!"

Around about then, it began to filter through that something about all this was a bit off. My mother had never said much about her upbringing, nor had I known my maternal grandparents. Orphaned, she'd been brought up in various foster homes and remembered nothing much before that. But she could speak German and quite well, too. I'd never heard her use it before, so that was something new. And I also learned there was a huge and possibly terrible secret surrounding Baba Lenka, which no one was going to explain. I mean, I'd hardly heard of her despite the fact she was my great-grandma. We had birthday cards from Jakub and Vanda in Munich, described only as 'distant cousins we ought to keep in touch with', but that was the only connection ever mentioned.

"It's best you don't know," my mother had said on the flight over.

"But why don't they want to bury her like normal people? What did you mean?"

She and my father had exchanged a charged look over my head. The plane had been a jet propeller. And in between each peak of the Alps, it plunged as heavily as a whale before climbing noisily upwards to scale the next. My stomach was all screwed up. I found myself praying when the nose pointed skywards like a rocket.

That flight was the first part of the nightmare – the first recurring dream I'd have for decades afterwards, although it paled in comparison to the second part; and when the final part of the nightmare arrived, it might have been better if the plane had never made it at all. I often think it's a blessing we don't know, or some of us don't know, what is to come or we would not be able to face it. Yet somehow we do. We do face things and adjust, finding a strength and courage we never knew we had.

"It's something to do with the War," Dad shouted

above the drone of the engine.

Please, God, don't let those propellers stop turning…

"You've heard about the Iron Curtain, haven't you, Eva – the divide between east and west Europe? Well, before the Second World War, there was a country called Bohemia just east of the German border. But the Germans who lived there – the Sudetens – were exiled after the Second World War to Bavaria in southern Germany. So, in effect, where Baba Lenka used to live doesn't exist anymore. It looks the same, but the villages are all Czech."

"Why did they have to leave?"

"Because a lot of people died there, Eva. So now there's a line between the two countries, and Bohemia's been incorporated into the Czech Republic."

"Why did Baba Lenka go to Germany and not stay in the Czech Republic? Was she a Nazi?"

Beside me my mother stiffened, her glance flicking around the cabin to see if anyone had heard.

"Where the hell did you get that from? None of our family were Nazis," she hissed. "They were just innocent people caught up in something they didn't understand, shunted from pillar to bloody post."

"So why can't she be buried like a normal German person, then? I don't understand."

"Oh, Eva! Because…" My mother, who spoke with a broad Yorkshire accent and had never even been to Germany, sighed heavily. "It's just as it is, Eva. Baba Lenka wasn't liked, and there's an end to it. Some say she's more Czech than German, others say she was a double agent, a traitor, whatever you call it."

"And some say she was an old witch," said Dad.

My mother shot him a look, and I sensed the conversation was closed. Besides, I was focusing intently on a prayer to God that the plane wouldn't crash. A monumental spike of black rock loomed perilously close. There was a small hut at the top of it, jutting out from an overhanging crag, and I wondered very briefly who had built it and why and how. Out of the tiny porthole windows, surreal white-tipped mountains dazzled in distant sunlight as the jet slowly climbed and the engines screamed. Finally, it tipped over the apex. There was a collective, silent exhalation of relief – before, with a stomach-lurching plunge, it dropped through an air lock. People screamed and overhead lockers flew open, drinks were spilled and shaking hands re-lit cigarettes. The journey was interminable, sickly sweet with smoke, and heady with whisky and wine.

There was no choice – we had to go to this funeral, and there, as my mother was fond of saying, was an end to it. Two days. Three at most. It would soon be over.

The cemetery was quite a way out of the village, perched high on the hill and well away from the church. The priest had not been happy about burying her, either. There had been a loud exchange of words at the farm door about it this morning.

I didn't understand German, but, fortunately, neither did my dad, so Mum had been forced to explain. She sounded weary. "He'll do the ceremony, he says. But not in the churchyard because she weren't a Christian. It's to be in the cemetery outside the village. We'll 'ave to settle for it, at any rate, and we've to pay him."

Now, as we began to climb the hill once more, the old women stood like wizened crows watching our slow ascent.

We'd already been walking for a good twenty minutes by the time a particularly ferocious blast of icy wind hit the procession. Everyone dipped their heads, turning away from it, eyes streaming. It froze your lungs; you couldn't breathe at all.

In the distance the higgledy-piggledy crosses of the old cemetery finally came into view, with what looked like wishing wells – but were actually carefully constructed gables or little houses – over the graves. Ribbons and garlands, scarves and mementoes clanked and danced in the wind. It looked like, what did my dad say...*heathen* was the word...like something for gypsies.

"We take food and drink into the graveyard and leave it there," my mother had explained when we'd set off from the house. The old ones had handed out round parcels for us to give. "It's part of the special ceremony and must be left for the deceased. Nothing must be removed after it's been taken in and offered. Not the flowers from the grave, the water, even the ropes used to lower the coffin into the ground – or they could be used to bring greater power to a curse."

She fed my imagination with talk of superstition and bad luck. If the flowers strewn at the funeral were picked up, you risked transferring the disease of the dead one to yourself; you must not bring any dirt back on your hands or shoes from the cemetery, and never drink from the cup meant for the deceased. The table where the casket had rested back at the farmhouse would be turned over, an axe would be placed on the deathbed, and candles burned on water and salt instead of in candlesticks, the contents later tipped away and blessed. All of these precautions were to prevent illness and harm for the forty days following a funeral when the soul was transcending. Most of all, the bindings used on the body of the deceased must remain there at the site. And buried.

I had never considered being partly German would mean all this.

My mother read my mind. "The people here, the old ones, are from a different age, Eva. They came from a different place. These are very old Slavic traditions and something they wanted to preserve. It's dying out now, though. So we do this for Baba Lenka and for our ancestors, okay?"

She looked away quickly, and for the first time a layer of doubt crawled in and wedged between us. First she didn't know who these old people were and couldn't understand them. Now she knew a whole lot more. And what did *Slavic* mean?

On the brow of the hill, the four elderly men set down the coffin while the rest of us caught up, the wooden cart they'd been pushing like a barrow now resting at an angle on the snowy ground. But as we neared, the men moved into position – one on each of the four sides of the cart, facing outwards. And the two women who had washed Baba Lenka's body turned and stepped closer to it.

"What are they doing now?"

"It's a crossroads," my mother said, as if that should make sense.

With their backs to the coffin, the men stared outwardly ahead, grim-faced and expressionless, in the directions of the four winds while the women began to mumble and wail as they had earlier at the well. Those raggedy birds overhead circled and cawed, and the women's cries, not those of sadness, quickly became frenzied. They stamped their feet and began to swirl around and around in a dance ritual. In an instant the bizarre scene became sinister, the women clapping, stamping and shrieking.

The priest pushed past us, marching forwards. "*Nein! Nein...Achtung...*"

I had a really bad feeling then in the pit of my stomach, something deeply foreboding. And no sooner had that thought consolidated when the day darkened as abruptly as if a switch had been flicked. The sun was no longer a hazy, wintry sun but that of a bright moon, all colours ebbing away in a tide. There was an intense feeling of being trapped in a place of impending doom, of being unable to move forwards in time or space, of things coming to an end. A skyline of withered trees seared onto my mind's eye in a crackle of black and white, every bit as violently imprinted as the looming view of the glacier from the plane, with its tiny hut clinging to a precipice.

My mother's grip tightened. Three sharp jabs. I wasn't to speak but to stay put. She seemed to know something, to anticipate it, and by the time the vision of doom ended, she was already running uphill fast on the heels of the priest.

Just as suddenly as they'd started the tribal dance, however, the two old women fell silent and the four men turned back around to face the coffin. Events happened simultaneously. As the priest and my mother drew level, without any warning, the old ones picked up the coffin and began to rotate it, spinning it around and around and around – before flipping it upside down.

The corpse tipped over inside.
The lid gave way. And Baba Lenka's body fell out.

***

CHAPTER TWO

Amid all the gasps and shouts, a tiny object came hurtling down the hill with all the alacrity of a Catherine wheel flying off a wall.

At first it looked like a scrap of tumbleweed billowing down the lane, only taking form when it finally bumped the toe of my shoe – a strange little bundle of straw and feathers in the shape of a scarecrow.

To you…

Bending down, I quickly picked it up and pocketed it before anyone saw. They'd be bound to ask what it was and maybe snatch it away, so a cursory glance was all there was time for. Enough only to note the hooked beak and tiny crow-like skull, to feel the crepuscular rustle of its feathery arms in my fingers and the strongly bound cord of its hemp body. No one else had noticed it. Maybe my mother was quick enough to catch the guilty look on my face when she swung around a second later, but she didn't see the poppet. No, she hadn't seen…

As it turned out, the momentary distraction was a blessing. In fact, it would have been far preferable had I carried on staring at the straw dolly and thus never seen the contents of the overturned coffin. Instead, immediately after secreting the poppet, I glanced up. And the full impact of the tragedy struck with a force I would never forget to my dying day.

Baba Lenka had fallen badly. In their apparent haste

to wash and inter the body, the old women had not bound the corpse properly or disguised the mutilation, let alone fastened the shroud securely enough. She lay at a distorted angle in the snow, the stem of her twig neck clearly snapped in two, her hands bent backwards in rictus claws, one blind opaque eye staring directly at me. The muslin shroud she was wrapped in had hitched up to expose where the backs of her ankles had been hacked to the bone, the heels stuffed with coarse black hair before being crudely sewn back together.

Everyone stared in freeze-framed horror. Baba Lenka's meagre possessions lay strewn across the crossroads – smashed earthenware, shattered glass, a wooden hairbrush netted with a few wisps of grey hair, grainy photographs scooting across the snowy fields.

How could the nails have given way? How could the bindings holding her legs and arms together have come untied and flown high into the ether? They should have been buried, my mother had said so… And the cross that had been put underneath her body…how could it have pierced her spine like that?

It's possible that my young mind blanked out what followed because I don't remember a thing. I don't even recall the flight home. All I remember and all I will ever remember is that the watery sun had turned into a bright moon, the whistling wind died on a whisper, and the day became unnaturally still. And I remember the old folk. I see their backs to this day, bent and black, as they threw themselves to the floor, wailing and hitting themselves with sticks and chains.

To you…to you…

***

CHAPTER THREE

ELDERSGATE, YORKSHIRE

When we returned home, my perspective on the world changed. I looked at my hands and felt they were not mine. The eyes reflected in the mirror were stormy, troubled and knowing. And there was the strangest, creepiest feeling that someone else was in my head. I know there is therapy for traumatised children now, but there wasn't then. Not where I came from, anyway – you were either loony or you just got on with it. Besides, it was the Winter of Discontent, the age of the three-day week and power cuts – people had more on their minds. That my great-grandma's funeral casket had tipped over somewhere in Germany was of little interest to anyone. It's a pity, though, because maybe if there had been help, what happened shortly after we got back might not have done?

Eldersgate sounds nice, doesn't it? It isn't. It's an ex-mining village southwest of Leeds; the mine had closed, and the people were angry. The women stood hard-faced in doorways, with their arms folded. Without exception, they were big, wielded slaps harder than men, and meted out judgements more confidently and mercilessly than any judge on earth. They queued for fish 'n' chips in their slippers and saved up Green Shield stamps for little luxuries like a new floor mop. Most of the secondary schoolkids bunked off school to loiter in the park, smoking Silk Cut and terrorising people, and the majority of working-age men rolled out of bed and into the pub the minute it opened. There were three shops in the middle of the estate – a butcher's, a co-op, and a chippie – and on the corner near the main road was the pub – The Greyhound – along with a betting shop and a working men's club.

My dad was one of the few who worked full-time. He was the postman, and prior to the trip to Bavaria, 'Postman Pat' had been the main chant behind me on the walk to and from school: 'Postman Pat' along with 'Gingernut'. Only now it had been replaced with 'Achtung', 'Nazi!' and 'Heil Hitler!' along with goose steps and salutes.

One of the gossiping mothers had found it necessary to spread the news Mum was German. She knew no details other than what my mother had told her in the Co-op one morning, that we had to go to a funeral and Deidre from Number Seven was looking after the cat.

So now I was a Nazi.

It seemed nothing from that ill-fated trip could be forgotten. Even the Alpine winter had followed us home. Eldersgate, never pretty, was now coated in grimy snow. Piles of slush lined the roads, the pithead wheel starkly silhouetted against the bleak and distant moors. The estate's pebble-dashed semis hunkered beneath a dismal wash of sleet as evenings set in early, televisions flickered through unlined curtains, and drunken rows thudded through the walls. When the power grid cut out, it always came as a shock, a collective groan when televisions died and everyone was plunged once more into icy darkness.

We walked to school through the slush, faces pink and stinging. The classrooms were gloomy and unheated, each desk lit with one candle. We sat in wet gabardines and sopping gloves, citing times tables while squeezing fingers and toes together to keep the blood pumping. My ears hurt with a deep ache... Well, that's what I remember – the cold, the candles, the dark. And that terrible morning when my life, and that of my family, changed forever.

We hadn't been home long, maybe a week, but the odd, disconnected feeling persisted as if a sheet of glass separated me from the outside world. And it was impossible to shake the cold – it shivered like an icy breeze inside of me – or the feeling that day was night. And the strangest thing of all was that the girls who'd been my best friends before the trip were now whispering behind my back. A band of evil little Machiavellians, they exchanged significant looks or pulled faces whenever I spoke.

Well, that particular morning, while it was still dark and candles were flickering on the wooden desks, we were instructed to split into groups for a reading project. Expectantly I turned to my trusted set of friends – Sharon, Jill, Lizzie, and a girl called Maxine Street, already gathering up books – when Maxine gave the others that significant look, and the four of them shot off without me. They actually linked arms, moving fast and purposefully towards the reading corner. It had been planned; of that there was no doubt. And the air of daring excitement about them confirmed it.

The instigation, of course, had come from Maxine. Maxine was the cool girl – the one whose straight black hair had been cut into a pageboy style while the rest of us still had pigtails. She was the first to have a cheesecloth blouse to wear at weekends, and white boots that laced up the front. She told us to like T-Rex and dump the Osmonds.

Yes, she was the one. And when that knowledge hit me and I saw what she had done, I hated her to murder pitch.

Without further thought, as the giggling girls ran past – leaving me alone, stunned and humiliated – I unzipped my pencil case, took out the geometry compass and, with wildly shaking hands, hurried after them. Adrenalin obliterated all further thought and I fair flew into the reading room.

As I approached, Lizzie turned. The room was unlit save for a few slats of light through the blinds and buttery flicks of candlelight, but a flash of horror registered on her face…

Just before my hand plunged the compass needle into the back of Maxine Street's calf muscle. I stabbed her hard, over and over and over, and I meant to do it.

***

Afterwards, there was a missing jigsaw piece in my memory, only this vague recollection of howling hysterically in class later on that day. The teacher, young and pregnant in a flowery smock, with a topknot on her head, snapped, "For God's sake, Eva, shut up!"

Her words were like a slap, and the misery stuck in my throat un-sobbed. How did I get home? I don't know. What happened to Maxine? Again, I don't know. I think she had to have stitches, and so did Lizzie because she'd put out her hand to protect Maxine. Oh God, yes, I can see her hand now – splayed over the other girl's leg…and all the blood…gushing into her white ankle sock.

Mum and Dad found out from the headmaster because I sure as hell wasn't telling. A stone of fear dropped into the cold pond of my stomach at the look on my mother's face. I was drifting away…a small figure clutching on to a balloon as it caught on the wind and lifted off… She changed towards me, too. Even her voice changed – her entire demeanour. "We'll have to go to the police. Or a psychiatrist! God only knows, because I bloody don't."

What actually happened was I never attended that school again. The ensuing months became a blur, spent lying on my bed in a stupor. I think a man came to ask questions. All that remains of that time is the view from the bedroom window of the distant pit wheel and the moors, and the sound of tinny bursts of laughter emanating from the black-and-white television set downstairs. The only companion I had was Sooty the cat, named after Sooty out of 'Sooty and Sweep'. He slept on my bed, came in through the bedroom window, and exited the same way. Mum even took to leaving his food out at night because he never came in the house except to my room.

Sometimes I'd take out the strange little straw dolly with its beak head and feather arms, a prize kept hidden since the day it had rolled down the lane to bump against my shoe...*To you*... The little creature was endlessly fascinating and not at all frightening, just the opposite, in fact, for on the day of the funeral, it had offered both distraction and consolation, and I clung to it – my secret – the one good thing to have come out of that horrible trip. Someone had fashioned it with such care and skill. It was quite a work of art: a small half-bird, half-man had been moulded from clay, the chest bound with hemp, glossy black feathers stretching outwards in the shape of a cross to resemble a scarecrow. Closer inspection revealed engravings on the neck and forehead, little nicks of a knife, tiny symbols.

Had some other child lost it? It seemed like something that would be made for a child, for a girl...or what else could it be?

As the months drifted on, I lay watching clouds scud across the sky. Occasionally the sound of other children's shouts carried on the wind, or the clunk of a cricket bat on willow. But I never went back to that school or saw any of those girls again. One day, it occurred to me the sun seemed lower in the sky; a soft haze hovered over the purple moors, and the leaves had become tinged with gold.

In walked my dad. "We're moving house, Eva."

My words sounded syrupy and slow. "What, now?"

He laughed, "Well, not right this minute."

"Before my birthday?"

"You had your birthday six months ago, love. Don't you remember?"

Six months? I'd missed my birthday? I must be eight!

"You've been poorly, love." He sat on the edge of my bed and stroked my hair from my face. "Thing is, we reckon a move will do us all the power of good – you know, a fresh start?"

"Where are we going?"

"A fantastic place we've found in Leeds. Needs a bit of doing up, but you're going to love it – it's huge, and it backs onto the woods. And best of all, you'll be going to a new school – a much better one an' all. We're going to see it tomorrow. You up for it?"

He had such an air of optimism about him as he faded in and out of focus that it seemed mean not to smile and nod. But the truth was, it frightened me very much. Waking up, that is.

***

CHAPTER FOUR

It was like being beamed into an alien landscape, standing there on a tree-lined pavement with cars whizzing past. And the new house was far bigger than the last. We got out of my dad's Cortina and stared up at a large Victorian four-bed detached. Set well back from the road, it had an air of hollow neglect about it, the window frames ragged with flaking paint, a crazy paved driveway tufted with weeds, and a badly overgrown garden tangled with nettles and brambles.

It was the only way we could afford to live in a posh area like this, Dad explained as we walked up the drive. He planned to renovate it all himself.

"Call it an investment – a chance for your old dad to make some proper money!"

A man in a suit stood on the porch, clutching a folder. "Mr and Mrs Hart? I'm from Bradock and Bradock. If you'd like to follow me."

My dad was practically bowing; it was embarrassing. Somewhere underneath all the ivy and weeds, there was a stone bird bath and a tiny pond coated with emerald algae. I had the feeling the garden had once been loved, that a tiny wren had flapped its wings and sprayed the air in a fountain of diamonds… Someone had caught that joy…

"Come on, Eva. Wake up, love."

I trailed after them as the man walked briskly around to the side of the house and let us in.

"The price is for a quick sale," he was saying. "The owner passed away, and her son's put it on the market. This is a great chance to do the place up and make a profit, or of course"—he smiled at my mother—"it would make a wonderful family home."

Thing is, while he was talking, I was staring open-mouthed at the scene behind him. There, still on the kitchen table, was a layer of pastry half rolled out and a pie dish partly lined. Had the old lady dropped dead right there, then? Is that where she'd died? No one asked the question. Instead, they walked right past the flour scattered on the floor and the rolling pin under the chair to admire the view from the kitchen window.

"Ooh, isn't it lovely, Pete? Look at them woods!"

Dad smiled and put his arm around her shoulders.

Shit! We'd be moving in.

So that was how we came to buy a big old house that someone had just died in. A big old house with a big old back bedroom looking out onto a wooded copse that screeched with crows. And it came ready-made with bloodstains that trailed up the wooden staircase and across the landing floorboards, all the way to the back bedroom – drips, streaks and splotches.

This was our fresh start, though.

"This is where you're going to get better, Eva," Mum said. The mess was nothing to worry about, and old people died at home all the time – there wouldn't be a house in Britain that hadn't had someone die in it, so it didn't do to dwell. "We're going to get you off those drowsy tablets, too. And then you can go to the all-girls' school down the road. It's got lovely navy-blue uniforms. Come on, love. Be a bit excited, eh?"

The move seemed to be the next day. Of course, it wasn't, but it seemed that way to me. So fast. A jump. And immediately Dad set about knocking the old-fashioned pantry and coal house out of the kitchen. He had a red bandana round his head, and Mum had the Carpenters playing on the record player. Cement dust coated every imaginable surface as he went at it with a sledgehammer, and two days later, there was a huge gaping hole in the outside wall.

They stood back and looked at it.

"Don't worry, love," he said to my mother. "I'll get some plastic sheeting over it, just 'til I've got hold of a brickie."

She laughed, and they started kissing again.

Next day, he got down to the next job, steaming off years of layered-on wallpaper in the lounge. Ah, this was going to be such a transformation! I never saw him as happy as he was then, with the radio on, smoking and hammering, nailing, steaming, sandpapering, and painting.

But the following week, my mother lost her job, and everything changed. She'd been an evening cleaner at the secondary school in Eldersgate and had a nasty row with one of the other women.

I knew all this because the doctor was reducing the dosage of my drowsy tablets and I'd taken to sitting on the stairs, listening through the bannisters.

"I'm not bloody 'aving it," Mum was saying. "I'm taking this to a tribunal."

"Oh, Alex—"

"Don't 'Oh, Alex' me! That bloody bitch called me a Nazi, Pete!"

"You didn't 'ave to belt her one."

In the end, Dad persuaded her to leave it, advising she channel her energy into looking for another evening job – he'd do double shifts, and she could look after me full-time until I started school. By then the year was tipping into November, so it meant we'd have to go through winter with nothing but plastic sheeting between us and the outside world, running the constant risk of burglars. It also meant putting up with exposed bloodstains on the floorboards and the horrible dark green bathroom with its rust-spotted mirror. The unpredictable, clunking boiler would have to stay, so, too, the oppressive oak panelling in the hall downstairs. Ditto the heavy oak wardrobe in my bedroom – the back bedroom looking onto the woods, the one with peeling flock wallpaper and a whistling fireplace choked with birds' nests and soot.

That old lady had died in here, in this very room, I was sure of it – could picture the stained sheets where she'd stewed in her own body fluids, the yellow tidemarks just like the one in Baba Lenka's bedroom… Someone had lifted her up and put her here, where she had decomposed, staring out at the same barren treetops I was staring at now, but with unseeing opaque eyes…her flesh festering in pee and pus and old blood…

I'm not sure exactly when the night terrors started. And I don't mean nightmares but night *terrors* – paralysing, heart-stopping visions meant to cause maximum fear. They became so bad I ended up in hospital with suspected heart failure. Sometimes they started with the plane flying into the side of a mountain, but the bad ones, the ones when something unimaginably terrible and unstoppable was coming, something unspeakably horrific, would always start the same way. That was how I knew they weren't dreams or memories or anything else…but visions. I was meant to see them.

Around this time, the sedative effect of the drugs was wearing off, with the result that every sight, smell, and sound hit me with hyper-surreal, almost psychedelic impact. And the more it wore off, the more the feeling of disconnection and alienation crept back in. Once again, I was floating away. Just like when we'd first returned from Bavaria, the world seemed strange and so did the human race – as if everything had simply been put on hold. My eight-year-old mind tried desperately to make sense of it but could not. And back came that same feeling of impending doom, of something about to happen – just like at the funeral before the casket had been tipped over and the morning before I'd stabbed Maxine Street.

Those night terrors would start the minute my bedroom door was shut and the landing light turned off at seven in the evening. By then, Dad was counting every penny, and no light was ever left on if it didn't need to be. Downstairs, the sound of murmuring voices on the television would drift up the stairs, and Mum and Dad would come up around ten. Which meant three hours up there on my own. Sooty would always leave at dusk. As soon as the light faded, he stood up, stretched, then leapt onto the windowsill to be let out. Looking back, I realised he wasn't ever with me at night and only returned at dawn.

The first time it happened was about two weeks after

we'd moved in. I was probably on about half the dose of the blue tablets by then and had trouble getting off to sleep. Dad had shut the bedroom door and clomped back downstairs. Initially it was more of a feeling that something was off, that my stomach was prickling and my pulse points ached. I lay there, eyes wide open. It was far darker than usual. It's hard to explain except the blackness was total and seemed to breathe, hiss, be alive. The sense of foreboding racked up rapidly, exactly as it had on the hill to the cemetery in Bavaria, and all at once, the need to get out became overwhelming. Every nerve was firing. I imagine it's the same kind of panic as being trapped underground or buried alive. All I knew was I had to get out.

This is our fresh start; this is where you get well…fresh start…fresh start…

I sat up, hot, breathing hard.

Mustn't scream, mustn't cry out…mustn't ruin it… This is me being silly, causing problems for them…

But the atmosphere was electric. Someone else was here in the room – they were breathing, loudly, the rasping gasps of one old and sickly. Who was here? Who? A feeling of menace crawled up my back; pressure pounded on the top of my head. Someone was going to arise out of nothing, out of the air, and materialise in front of me. What was coming?

My eyes burned into the void. A face would appear, or eyes…something horrible… And then what? I couldn't scream, could not even breathe…my throat had constricted. I was going to see eyes in the darkness, and I thought my heart would stop.

There was a lull, a moment.

Before what sounded like the dull, rolling roar of a strong wind whipping up. Not from outside, not thunder, but from inside the room – to be precise, from inside the wardrobe! This had to be a dream. But here I was, sitting up, ramrod straight with my eyes wide open. And the wind was not imagined, either – it was icy, blowing the hair back from my forehead, whistling as it had that day in Bavaria, racing down from the mountains and through the trees. The cries of crows carried on the air along with the wailing cries of the ancients. Every detail of the funeral procession then began to replay, as if we were still standing there on the hill to the cemetery, as sharp and clear as the day it had happened. The wintry blast nipped my face, and the smell of smoke and pine filled the air.

My breath had lodged like an iron nut in my chest, and I could neither breathe in nor out. My lungs had set to stone. In desperation I tried to move my arm, to knock something onto the floor so someone would come; I was in bed at home, not here on this hill in the freezing cold. I was not on this mountainside but trapped in a waking nightmare. Yet even as I told myself that, the daylight of the scene switched to night, and the sun became a brilliant full moon, starlight glittering on the snow.

The shock of what happened next caused my breath to come back with such force it left me gasping as frantically as a person half drowned and given the kiss of life. Something was walking out of the wardrobe. And taking form.

I shut my eyes, opened them again. She was still there. Only much, much closer.

Wake up, Eva! Wake up...wake up!

Baba Lenka, with her twisted, broken neck, was almost level with the end of the bed, ankle bones cracking and crunching with every step, that one staring eye fixed directly on me just as it had the day she'd fallen out of the casket.

I screamed so loudly that Dad thundered up the stairs two at a time.

"What the hell's happened? Has someone broken in?"

He had the light on, was scanning the room, his face ashen.

"Baba Lenka's in the wardrobe!"

"You what?"

"She's in the wardrobe," I wailed, sobs hitching in my throat. "The door opened, and she came out."

He sat down on the edge of the bed, shouting down to Mum that it was just a nightmare.

"Sweetie, she's not in the wardrobe, okay? It's just a bad dream."

"But I wasn't asleep.

"You were, chicken. You'd nodded off and had a bad dream. It's understandable considering what happened, but it was just an old lady's funeral, and it was eight months ago now. She's dead and gone. And when people die, they go to heaven. They go to be with God. It's over. They definitely don't come back and open little girls' wardrobes. It's not possible." He walked over to the wardrobe and yanked open each of the doors. "Look – just your clothes in there, see?" He parted the new little school pinafores and dresses to show the solid wood at the back. "That's it. It's just a lump of wood, and there is nothing in it other than your things."

I bought it. I believed him. I wanted to so badly.

He smoothed back my hair. "Maybe those drowsy tablets delayed the reaction. But it's all over, all right? We should never have taken you, but we'd no one to leave you with – we couldn't tell your grandparents we were going, you see? Not with how me dad is about Germany. Listen, it were a bad experience for you, but you're home now and you're quite safe. So go back to sleep, there's a good girl, and let us grown-ups have a bit of peace – I've to get up at four in t' morning."

"Okay. Sorry, Daddy."

"That's all right. You just call me if you're frightened, chicken. But remember this – only human beings can hurt you. If a big fella comes to take you away, then you scream your lungs out, all right? But nothing else can hurt you – no old ladies coming out of wardrobes, and there are no ghosts."

I smiled.

He got up, walked to the door and turned out the light.

But as the door clicked shut and I turned over to go to sleep, doing what he'd told me to do, Baba Lenka was staring right back. Up close. With her head on the pillow next to mine.

***

CHAPTER FIVE

"She'll 'ave to see a psychiatrist, Pete."

My parents stood over me, faces bobbing like white balloons, voices disembodied.

By then, the night terrors had been going on for weeks. After the first few episodes of bloodcurdling screams, my parents had stopped running upstairs and decided instead on a tactic of ignoring me. Maybe that would work? Maybe it was attention-seeking and would stop?

Only it didn't. As soon as the bedroom door shut, the blackness thickened and crackled. It pulsated, hissed, watched and breathed. She knew I was alone. Knew I'd be lying there fixating on that wardrobe, never wavering, waiting for the key to turn in the lock and the door to nudge ajar…until the creak sounded as it eased away from the hinges, followed by a rush of icy air fresh from the snow-topped mountains.

Baba Lenka was as starkly vivid to the eye as anyone else, the rotting stench gag-inducing as she hobbled out, bones and joints cracking and splintering with every step. I could not face what was coming, my small heart banging so hard it hurt. I screwed up my eyes, repeating over and over that she was not, could not, be real. But when I opened them again, she was inches away from my face. And my throat was raw from screaming. But like I said, after the first few nights, my mum and dad didn't come running anymore, didn't switch on the light or say it was a dream. They left me screaming – screaming with my hands over my ears until I began banging my head on the walls to get her out of it.

"This will end when you let me—"

"No, no, no, go away! Go away!"

I took to holding on to the crow poppet, which once again offered comfort, a silken balm to the raw terror. I held it like a nun holds a cross. When Baba Lenka appeared, I would reach into the pillowcase for the doll and hold on fast, whimpering, sobbing, begging, "Leave me alone, go away, leave me alone, please! Oh, please!"

And every time, the room grew cold. The shivering that began in the dorsal spine would ripple up my back and across my arms like a breeze across a pond, making my teeth chatter and skin goose. The smell, too, was something I'd only ever encountered once before in my young life, that of rank, diseased flesh mixed with human excreta and black mould, the stench that had pervaded the farmhouse in Rabenwald.

So, I knew when she was coming.

And that she wanted something.

When you let me…when you let me…

She wasn't going to stop, was she? The more I begged her to leave me alone – the more I tried to pretend it wasn't happening, the more I screamed – the more that fact became clear. It was going to go on and on and on…until what? Until I let her what…?

The courage to not screw up my eyes and scream anymore, to open them and keep breathing while looking her in the face, came nearly two weeks after my parents had left me to scream myself hoarse. Maybe not courage. Maybe it was exhaustion?

Baba Lenka was lying on the bed. Right next to me. Her head on the same pillow.

Look at me…look at me…

The breath stuck hard in my chest, my stomach clenched in a tight knot, and my heart slammed like a hammer into my ribs.

Don't scream, don't scream, see what she wants…breathe…breathe…

Slowly, very slowly, she turned towards me. A bone cracked as she did so. Fetid breath wafted into my face. And then one long, gnarled finger traced down the side of my cheek. I shut my eyes fast.

Oh God, oh God, oh God…

Opened them.

Holy hell! She was suspended over me, floating a matter of inches above my face.

The white muslin shroud, stained and dirty, dropped in folds around her, and the tissue flesh of her cadaverous face hung from shiny white cartilage. It was impossible to resist, to not look, to not see what was in those hollowed eyes boring into mine. Mesmerised, I stared right into them.

At which point there was such an almighty bang in my chest, it nearly stopped my heart. My reflection in her eyes was upside down.

***

Hands reached down and shook me. Someone was patting my face, more than patting – slapping. "Call the doctor, Alex! Tell him she's got a pulse but not much of one. Christ, what's wrong with 'er? What the bleedin' hell's happened?"

Brushstrokes of weak light fanned across the far wall, and a wood pigeon cooed from a nearby tree. Where was this?

"Eva, wake up, love! It's seven o'clock in the morning. Can you 'ear me?" His voice was breaking, this man whose face swirled in mist. "We're going to get the doctor to you, love. Your mum's on the phone now. Christ, I think you've frightened yourself to bloody death. We should have got you more help, but we didn't know what to do. We thought the memory of that place would fade, that you'd eventually forget…"

The doctor came in the next flutter of my eyelashes. Listened to my chest with a stethoscope. Did the pulse and temperature routine. "Nightmares, you say?"

This was a new doctor, not the one who'd taken me off the blue drowsy tablets.

"She had tablets earlier this year from the doctors in Eldersgate," my mother told him. "For anxiety." She then told him a pack of lies about what had happened at infant school last February and how a family funeral had upset me. I heard the word *amitriptyline* and saw him frown and shake his head.

"All right, well, the good news is I don't think there's much to worry about. She's having withdrawal symptoms – hallucinations, by the sound of it – so I'll prescribe a mild sedative to help her come off the amitriptyline and suggest she stays home from school a while longer. Meantime, she'll need some tests to check out her cardiac function, dot the i's and cross the t's, as it were. Let's give her a full MOT."

The days blurred. And later, from the back seat of the car, petrol stations and streetlamps whizzed by in the indigo of November dusk. Our footsteps echoed along fluorescent hospital corridors, and the smell of fear and disinfectant tainted the air. My heart was okay, they told Mum and Dad while I stared up at the ceiling at cartoons of Mickey and Minnie Mouse. The whole thing was due to a panic attack caused by hallucinations, just as the family doctor had said. All was perfectly normal, and there was no need to worry. Meanwhile, it would be wise to ease the withdrawal from amitriptyline by continuing with the mild sedative prescribed. Just for a while.

It made sense. Everyone was nodding and agreeing.

Mum stayed home, clacking knitting needles at the end of my bed while I drifted in and out of a sedated sleep. I'd get over this. It would pass, all come out in the wash...

And while she was there, Baba Lenka didn't come.

The minute she left, however, as soon as dusk fell and the soft hoot of the owls blew like panpipes in the woods, that wardrobe key turned, the door groaned on its hinges, and the spirit of Baba Lenka blew over on the cold, cold wind.

Sedated now, I could no longer call out. Instead, fear washed over me in dull expectation. Paralysed, my eyes looked into pupils reflecting my upside-down face, and like pins to a magnet, the draw to look into them was unstoppable.

You must take the gift, Eva... Accept this or it will kill you!

***

CHAPTER SIX

A heated exchange drifted up from the lounge.

My eyes flicked open. The conversation was yet again about me. You could tell by all the heavy sighing.

Had a day passed since we'd got back from the hospital? Or two, maybe three? Curious, I pushed back the covers and crept to the top of the stairs to listen. The afternoon had set to a foggy drizzle, and every few seconds, car headlights lit the oak-panelled stairway in a ghostly sheen. The bloodstains on these floorboards were no longer a puzzle. The scene had played out a few times now: an elderly lady had been dragged up the stairs by her hair, having been hit hard on the side of her neck with a rolling pin. Blood drooled from the side of her mouth and out of her nose, every step jolting the bones of her spine. I saw, too, the tall man who had done it, the thin strands of greying hair that barely covered his pasty scalp. Grim-lipped, he had the gleam of self-righteousness, of entitlement, in pale eyes behind wire-rimmed glasses. 'Mother', he called her – never 'Mum', always 'Mother'.

"Well, we can't go on like this, can we? It's been the best part of a year, and nothing's worked. She's just not right, is she? And we're broke, Pete – I have to get some work. That plastic sheet covering the wall isn't safe, and come winter it'll be bloody freezing. I can't sit home all day every day doing bloody nothing."

"I agree. It'd be better if you could work, then I'd 'ave time to try and brick it up meself. As it is, I'm on double shifts."

"Chicken and the bloody egg, though, isn't it? I can't get out for interviews and leave her, can I?"

"Well, do you think she's well enough to go to school, then?"

"You know she isn't. Anyway, the doctors all say she's perfectly normal. No, I think what we need here is a priest."

"You what? You mean a bloody vicar? Are you joking? It's mental illness—"

Silence hissed.

"This isn't something a doctor can fix, though, is it? All they've done is zonk her out with drugs that've given her hallucinations and made it so she can barely get herself to the bathroom. Listen to me, there's something unnatural about this. There's an energy here even you can't deny. You must have noticed how many lightbulbs keep blowing? That one in Eva's room won't work at all. Replace it and it sparks out instantly. And how when I come down in the morning, the television's on? We switch it off at night, yet there it is – buzzing with static the next day! And then there are drawers left open when I know I shut them. I've had glasses leap out of the kitchen cupboards and smash on the floor. Even the cat won't come inside anymore."

"What are you saying? That we've got a poltergeist?"

"I don't know—"

"Well, I don't think we can blame all that on Eva."

"Children pick up these things, though, don't they? I

mean, she had that horrible experience, followed by strong medication. Then we bring her to an old house that's fed her imagination. It's no wonder she's disturbed. She told me the house is haunted, by the way – by the old lady who died here, apparently – and that Baba Lenka lives in the wardrobe. I think there's something really wrong, and I think it's supernatural—"

"You're a superstitious lot, where you come from—"

"What do you mean, 'a superstitious lot'? I was brought up in the same country as you."

I could feel my dad squirming. "I just meant your history. You knew all that stuff when we were in Bavaria about Slavic customs—"

"Well, of course I did. My mother told me things when I was a child, before she died. And I've read about the place; I wanted to know where my family came from. It's natural!"

"Don't take on, love. I didn't mean anything by it, only that we don't believe in all that mumbo-jumbo in our family, that's all."

Whoa! He was on dangerous territory there. My mother's eyes must have been flashing a storm. He'd stopped short of calling her a Russian harpy like he'd done before, which was something I'd never understood. She was hardly Russian. Although she did have high cheekbones, as I did, along with flame hair. And she sure as hell had a temper.

"Right, well thanks for that. So 'ave you got a better suggestion, then, fucking Einstein? Isn't it at least worth trying? I take it you do agree there's a problem?"

"Of course I do. We both want what's best for Eva."

She sighed heavily. "Right. Good. Well then, that's

something."

There was another long pause.

Then she said, "Okay, well, can we at least get the house blessed? Let's say Eva's right and the house *is* haunted? I mean, when push comes to shove, you've got to admit she's not getting any better, is she? She used to be a lively little girl, and now she walks around in a trance. Her eyes are unfocused, and she's hearing and seeing things that no one else can. So I vote we ask someone at the church for help, at least get someone to come and talk to her."

The church…

I slammed a hand to my mouth. They were going to bring someone from the church to sprinkle holy water around. Didn't they know it was far too late for that?

***

When the vicar arrived, a rotund man of around forty, with a mass of thick chestnut-coloured hair and a matching beard, he sat in the lounge drinking tea with my mother. For a while they exchanged pleasantries and a few lies, while I sat on the stairs with my ears pressed against the bannisters.

First, Mum told him exactly the same story she'd told all the doctors – that I'd been upset at a funeral, had unfortunately looked into the coffin, seen a dead body and had nightmares ever since. I'd been picked on at my last school, and there had been a fight. Following that, we'd come here to what I was convinced was a haunted house. She told him about the smashed glasses, the television coming on in the middle of the night, and my screaming conviction that the wardrobe door was opening. I was a frightened little girl, she told him. Terrified. And, as such, was now under sedation and unable to go to school. She was half out of her mind with worry, couldn't leave me to go to work, and, well…look, she told him, we needed to fix up the house and were broke. "We really are at our wits' end, Father."

"I'm Church of England, Mrs Hart," he corrected her. "And please, call me Colin."

There was an awkward silence. My parents had never been to his church.

After a moment, during which he let that mutual knowledge sit uncomfortably between them, he said, "All right, let's start at the beginning, shall we? So when exactly did the disturbances begin – the wardrobe door opening, television set coming on of its own accord and so on?"

Quickly she brought him up to speed, her voice somewhat sharper following the rebuke. "Any road," she finished. "We were wondering if you'd bless the house? My husband thinks it's a poltergeist we've got."

Their voices murmured on, with him assuring her there was no such thing. Then, finally, a cup clattered onto a saucer, and the big man's shadow filled the gap in the lounge doorway. "However, I will of course bless the house, Mrs Hart. I did actually know the old lady who lived here very well, you know. Marlene was a regular attendee, never missed a service and often did the flowers. If ever you feel you would like to be on our roster, we'd be delighted to welcome you. And your husband and daughter."

"Thank you, Vicar. I'll bear it in mind. I've a bit on at

the minute, though, like I said."

"Of course, well, whenever you're ready. God's house is always open."

"Right." She pushed open the lounge door. "Have you brought the holy water? To do the blessing with?"

"Of course."

They stepped into the hallway, and I shrank back, scrambled back into bed and pulled up the covers.

He did my room last, murmuring words he did not believe. He might as well have been sprinkling vodka onto concrete for all the good it was doing. Then, when he'd completed the task, he sat on the edge of my bed, his weight causing the mattress to seesaw alarmingly. He slid almost to the floor.

Adopting a cheery 'let's talk to a child' voice, he said, "Hello, Eva? I'm Colin. How are you feeling today?"

Everything about him was repulsive, from the wiry black hairs poking out of his cheeks to the speckles of grease on the lens of his glasses.

"All right."

"Your mummy's been telling me you've had some nightmares?"

I closed my eyes. Maybe he would just go away?

"But there's nothing to worry about, you know. There's no such thing as ghosts."

What a twit! Hadn't he just been uttering the words 'In the name of the Father, the Son, and the Holy Ghost'?

"And I can assure you that the lady who died here has gone to heaven. I knew her very well. She used to come to my church and arrange flowers. I know it's hard to understand the concept of death, but—"

"She isn't in heaven. She was murdered, and her

blood's on the landing floorboards. Her son did it, and she's mad as all hell. You should dig up the grave and find all the bones he broke—"

He reeled back as if he'd been slapped. "Pardon? Oh dear, no. I think someone's imagination is running away with her."

"He hit her in the neck with a rolling pin, then dragged her up the stairs by the hair while she was still alive—"

"Eva, stop it!" My mother's voice. "I'm so sorry, Father—"

Colin the Vicar's voice was harder now, too. And louder. "You are a very disturbed little girl indeed, aren't you? I knew the old lady who lived here, and I also knew her son. He's a church-going man, a doctor. Well, not exactly a doctor, a radiographer, I think – but a caring, good man. His mother fell in the kitchen. Bernard lifted her upstairs and put her into bed, where she passed peacefully in her sleep. He lived here, too, and doted on her, took care of her. So you can't say things like that, Eva. It's wrong – very, very wrong."

While he was full monologue, my body began to twitch and then jerk alarmingly. Flour was all over my hands, and a blinding pain shot down the side of my neck… Strong hands grabbed my hair and began to drag me along the floor. The roots were being yanked out of my head. I tried to reach up, but my skull cracked against the foot of the stairs, then, oh God, the pain…bump, bump, bump…every metal ridge of those stairs slammed into each vertebra. My leg twisted, and screams rent the air. Blood was pouring down my nose…the back of my head pounding…

"What's she doing?" Colin stood up and began to back towards the door. "It looks like a fit!"

"Oh, bloody 'ell. Call the doctors, tell them it's an emergency – hurry up!" My mother ran over and slapped my face repeatedly. "Eva! Eva! Can you hear me?"

I think she must have held me down until the doctor came, the same one who'd prescribed mild sedatives. He wacked up the dose and injected a syringe full of something for good measure. "Well, she's calm enough now, but I think we might need to consider epilepsy. That could be it."

"Epilepsy? Oh, bleedin' Nora. What's that when it's at home?"

After that incident, the days grew shorter. The beech trees in the woods shone silvery in the moonlight, and fog crept in at dawn, muffling the smoky air with damp, grey mizzle. Sooty took to watching me until the light faded and the moon rose, his yellow eyes steady, purr hypnotic. Sometimes he sat on my chest, creeping in as close as he could, as if drawing fear itself from my breath.

And then one day, my mother must have felt secure, or desperate, enough to leave the house. Why not? I slept soundly all day and all night. It was just after lunch. She said she had an interview for a waitressing job in a local steakhouse. It would mean Dad wouldn't have to do double shifts and could mend the hole in the wall. She wanted to surprise him with the good news.

"Just carry on sleeping, princess. I won't be long."

Her words floated on the air.

She was gone for two hours.

And when she came back, her screams ricocheted around the whole street. During that short period of time, someone had slashed through the plastic sheeting at the side of the house and burgled us. We didn't have much, but they'd taken the television set and Dad's whisky. Most of the glassware had gone and my mother's pearls and engagement ring. The only room that hadn't been touched was mine.

She bounded upstairs. "Eva! Wake up! Eva – oh, thank God."

"What?"

"Well, didn't you hear anything?"

"What? No, nothing apart from you screaming just now."

"Eva, we've been burgled. The bloody television's gone. My jewellery… Are you telling me you didn't hear a thing?"

"No, I swear. I'm sorry, Mum."

She sat on the edge of my bed then and cried, just put her head in her hands and howled. "I can't take any more of this, I just can't."

I reached out through a misty haze to touch her. "I'm sorry, Mum."

"I'm at the end of my tether, Eva."

"I'm sorry."

"So you keep bloody saying!"

The harshness of her tone was a painful jar. My face screwed up, and tears burst out.

"Oh, don't start, Eva. Just don't."

I cried harder.

Her anger was a rabid dog unleashed. Pacing the room, she stomped back and forth, the skin taut across those glass cheekbones, every sinew tight in her face. She wanted to hit someone very badly indeed. The flame red of her hair glinted like fire in the low winter sun, and then she swung around to face me.

"I've tried not to dwell on this Eva, I really have. But I can't help thinking this is all down to you. Ever since the funeral, you changed. The day before, you were perfectly all right – a nice, normal child – but something happened, didn't it? I can almost see the moment. It's on the edge of my mind…"

I stared at her.

To you…

"We took such a bloody risk even going, but I were told she'd left us the 'ouse, and even that were a bloody lie…" Her eyes, so like mine – dark grey, slanted upwards – sparked with a sudden flash of understanding. "You didn't take owt, did you? Remember when I told you how important it was not to take anything away? Either from the house or the coffin?"

I shook my head.

"But you took something, didn't you? You must 'ave."

"No."

"It's there on the edge of my mind, something. What am I missing?"

"I didn't take anything, Mum. The only thing—"

"What? What only thing?"

"Well, there was something on the lane…" I so badly didn't want her to take the poppet away. It was a good thing, not a bad thing, and had nothing to do with Baba Lenka or her coffin. I started to cry again. "It was just a toy on the lane. I found it. I didn't take it from the house or the coffin, and it wasn't Baba Lenka's. It was just a doll."

All her colour washed away. She lunged over and

gripped my shoulders "What doll?"

I turned my face to one side.

She shook me. "What doll, Eva?"

Tearfully I reached inside the pillowcase for the little thing that had brought me comfort night after night, and took out the crow poppet.

"Flamin' 'ell!" She whipped it off me. "So that's it! I knew there were summat! Right, well, this little fucker's gonna get burned to high hell."

"No, please! It's just a doll."

"It is not just a doll, Eva, it's a witch's poppet, and don't you dare tell your dad about this. It's what's called an alraun. And because of this, you've brought a curse home with you. I expressly told you not to an' all. I said, did I not, 'do not take anything away'? And now look – see how ill you are, and look what's 'appened to us all! Think about it if you don't believe me. And think hard an' all. You either invite this stuff in or you accept it…either way, it comes through you!"

I was bawling my eyes out by then, afraid of my mother's anger yet more afraid still of the consequences of burning the alraun. It was part of me.

"Right, I'm getting rid of this, and it's got to be done before your dad gets home. Pray to God it's not too late. Now where are those bloody books…it'll be in there…what to do to reverse what you've done and banish this thing to high hell."

Books? The ones she took from Baba Lenka's house? She'd told me not to take anything, yet she had!

The tears dried on my cheeks. Why would she have books that would banish things to hell? What did she mean? And how come she knew so much about a witch's poppet? Everyone had been telling me it was all in my imagination – the illness, the wardrobe door, the visions. Yet now Mum was going to do some kind of spell. Fear gripped my stomach. This was all real, wasn't it? Not my imagination, not mental illness, not brought on by trauma or tablets – but real, and that was why my mother was so frightened. Deep inside, I think I knew that all along.

My voice caught in my throat. "Please give it back to me. You can't hurt it or bad things will happen—"

Alas, she was already pulling down the loft ladder, fully intent on locating Baba Lenka's books.

***

CHAPTER SEVEN

I couldn't even watch from the window. Instead, I lay on the bed as flames crackled and rose from the garden below. Dirty smoke and cinders billowed in on the breeze, along with my mother's alien chants. It coiled down my throat and infused my lungs, the very essence of the alraun transferring the spirit of another on the current of a burning wind.

Swallowing and coughing, a cage of incineration now surrounded me, the sizzle and spit of melting flesh and muscles became mine, and scorching pain roared down my throat, the ferocious ignition of hair and clothing an enveloping inferno... Gulping down the smoke, my mind blanked into a tunnel of darkness as consciousness slipped away amid loud cries of 'Burn Witch!' and 'Go to hell!' Thrashing around, clutching my head, kicking and lunging for air, I was burning to death.

When I woke up, it was to find both parents sitting on the bed, their faces ashen. By the look of it, they could hardly bear to be in the same room as each other.

There's been a row.

"You're going to Grandma Hart's for a bit, love," said my mother, thumping pillows into shape. "Here, come on, sit up and drink this tea or it'll get cold."

I swallowed a tepid mouthful. "Why?"

"Never mind that now," my dad said. "It's just for a few weeks until your mum and I can get the house fixed up. It were stupid to leave that plastic sheeting as it was and you here alone."

My mother was glaring at him. Yes, they'd had a right old humdinger.

"It's for the best, Eva," she said. "It won't be for long. And maybe you won't get nightmares there about the house being haunted. It'll do us all the power of good, you'll see. Give us a bit of breathing space, bit of a rest."

"By Christmas we'll be in better shape," Dad said in a false chirpy voice. "We'll have this hole in the wall bricked up, and then with your mum working and you back at school, we can crack on with carpets, maybe even have a new bathroom. What colour wallpaper would you like in your room?"

"Purple."

My mother's smile faltered.

Dad grinned. "Purple it is, then."

"And pink."

"You're to be good at Grandma Hart's, mind," said Mum. "No going on about dead people in the wardrobes and stuff like that. I don't want them upset. They're old, and they've been very good about this."

"I want to stay with you and Dad."

She sighed. "I know, love, and believe me, this is a last resort, but we're in a bit of a pickle at the minute. We'll both have to work all hours, and you're not well enough to be left on your own. It won't be for long."

"We have to have you safe," Dad said.

It made sense. At that time they really did think they

were doing the right thing.

"Oh, and like I told you before," Mum said, "don't tell your grandparents you went to Germany, all right? Do not mention Baba Lenka, and do not tell them you went to the funeral. You know how Grandad Hart feels about Germany, and we don't want him upset. He fought in the War and lost a lot of his friends and family, so it's very hurtful."

"His brother," said Dad. "My Uncle Seth died."

My mother nodded. "I mean it, Eva. Don't say a bloody word or there'll be no Christmas presents, do you hear? It's extremely important. Promise me!"

"Yes, I promise."

"Good, right, then. We wouldn't do this if we weren't forced to, so I'm going to have to trust you."

"All right," I said, watching their anxiety drain away...*please don't make this any harder for us*...like water down a plughole. "I'll go."

"You won't have to go back to that school, neither," Dad assured me, warming to their success. "And me dad's a great one for 'aving your back. No one will mess with Earl Hart's granddaughter, believe me."

"Aye, there'll be no name-calling, that's for sure. If anyone calls Earl's granddaughter a Nazi, he'll knock them into the middle of next week."

"He were a boxer, me dad – used to have bare-knuckle fights. He earned a fair bit of money back in the day."

I looked from one to the other. "And I'm definitely not going back to that school? Definitely? Not ever?"

"No, you're doing schoolwork at home, where your gran can keep an eye on you. Then you'll come back here after Christmas and go to the girls' school at the end of the road. Like we said, it's not for long, love."

There was no point arguing. Besides, they were desperate, and it was all my fault. I was the one who'd brought the poppet home and with it the ghost of Baba Lenka. And that ghost was mine to deal with, no matter where I went. Moving me from one place to another was not going to 'make me better', I saw that now. So it was best for all concerned if they were left to mend the house and make it safe and get on their feet financially.

But after they left me at my grandparents in Eldersgate, said their goodbyes and drove off, the sense of abandonment was overwhelming.

Gran and Grandad Hart lived on the row of terraces closest to the pit, and, believe me, it looked its grimy worst on that miserable, foggy morning in late November. Earl, my grandad, had worked as a miner all his life until the pit had closed last year. Now he headed up the local union. It was Arthur Scargill this and Arthur Scargill that. Whenever we went to visit, he and Dad would get pretty het up about pit closures and trade union dictates. Either that or it would be the War. Earl had fought in the Second World War and wanted to go over and over it, often with the same stories and always ending with how much he hated the Jerries or the Krauts, as he called them. Odd he didn't seem to notice my mother was German.

"Mum was one," I said once.

He turned and fixed me with a cold blue stare. "She were only a lass; she knows nowt about it."

There was an air of severity in their house. It was dark and narrow with a downstairs bathroom reached by walking through the galley kitchen at the back. Only a frosted glass door separated this bathroom from the corridor, which had a corrugated iron roof and adjoined the coalhouse. Unheated, this was where Grandad Hart had washed when he'd come in through the yard from the mine. You could still see ingrained soot in the paint.

The house was a miasma of brown and green, the staircase as steep as a roof ladder and so narrow my gran's shoulders touched both walls as she led the way up to my new room. Tears filled my eyes. Everyone else had trendy parents who wore flares and platform boots and drove Capris. Grandad Hart had a bottle-green Škoda and wore a flat cap. The place smelled of soot and boiled vegetables. It was out of another age.

"You're going to be with us for a bit, Eva, love," said Grandma Hart. We were gazing out at the colliery through my bedroom window. It was so close you could see the rust on the railings. She was smoking a Senior Service and wore a hairnet with curlers underneath. "It's just while your mum and dad get back on their feet," she said, flicking ash out of the open window. "Then when the 'ouse is done up and you're well enough to go to school, you can go back."

It was coming into winter, and I'd been off school for nearly a year. Various officials had been here and left textbooks 'to be getting on with', but it was expected I'd go to the all-girls' school in Leeds after Christmas. The one with the lovely navy uniforms.

"You're to get on with your reading and sums, love. Now, if there's nowt else you need, I'll get tea on. You can put your clothes in them drawers over there and come down when you've unpacked."

After she shut the door behind her, I sat on the bed

and cried.

This was all my fault.

If only I hadn't picked up the poppet – that's what had brought the evil witch, Baba Lenka, home with us. At least that was clear now; I wasn't imagining things like everyone had said. She had followed us home and she'd come out of that wardrobe and she'd spoken to me – my mother knew it, too. Why else would she have brought Baba Lenka's old spell books back with her? She knew things, believed in them, and was terrified of admitting it. Why? Was she ashamed? Hiding something?

I begged her to tell me more about the alraun and the books, but all she would say was "No, Eva. Because once you know, you can never un-know. Trust me."

Know what, though? Dad said it was all hocus-pocus. The vicar said there were no ghosts. The doctors said it was hallucinations. So what was it she knew that everyone else did not? Why wouldn't she tell me? Was it preferable to have her daughter branded insane?

The closest she ever got to disclosing anything had been on the plane over to Bavaria, when Dad had been talking about the Sudetens fleeing Bohemia after the Second World War. She'd said the reason for the rising unrest was something about roots being ripped out, about more witches being murdered in Germany and Eastern Europe than anywhere else in the world, that fury with the church would be eternal. I think she regretted the outburst instantly – the sinews of her face had tightened, and the words had been terse, almost spat out. I didn't understand any of it, really. But the term *witch* had been synonymous with Baba Lenka in one too many sentences.

One more thing I didn't understand – if the poppet

had brought the curse home as my mother had said, then how come it had only ever felt good? Amid all the night terrors and visions, the only thing that had softened the edges of my fear and provided something to hold on to was that doll.

And now she'd burned it.

After a while my tears dried. It seemed time to pick a side. My mother had both deceived and rejected me. But Baba Lenka had not. In fact, she was only too keen to reveal her journey, promised it would help 'when the time came'. I could not have known, of course, how dark that journey would be, how unutterably black...not then...and by the time I did, it would be too late.

You must take the gift, Eva...accept it or it will kill you...

Miserably, I nodded to the voice in my head. Okay, then. If I didn't, I would be destroyed like she said. And if I did, the night terrors would stop.

The conclusion gained strength. By day I could be Eva Hart, a normal little girl who went to school and had friends. And at night Lenka would show me her world. I would not go mad; my life would not be ruined. All I had to do was listen to her story. Isn't that what most ghosts want – just to be heard?

So I dried my face with the back of my hand and lifted up the small pink valise my mother had packed. As I did so, a cold wind whipped up outside, smattering sleet against the windowpane, and the shadow of the pit wheel fell across the bedroom wall.

I clicked the case open.

On top of the neatly folded layers of cardigans and pinafores was the crow poppet. Not burned. Not even

singed.
To you…

***

CHAPTER EIGHT

Every detail of the poppet was intact – from the soft feather wings and the little beaked head to the cleanly bound hemp.

How the hell...? This could not be possible. No way! And yet there it was.

Wave after wave of shock hit me in the gut. Backing away from the open case, I sank into the furthest corner of the room, crumpled onto the floorboards where the carpet didn't meet the skirting, and shoved my fist into my mouth to stop the screams. Every beat of my heart was such a thump, it nearly blacked my mind. How could this be? How, how?

Eva, it exists...it exists...look...accept...

Eventually, I'm not sure how long it took, my breathing calmed and the initial panic subsided. My mother had definitely burned the poppet! I'd seen her snap its neck as she'd left the room, heard her strange incantations as the fire had crackled outside, and the heat of the flames had seared my own flesh, dripping off bones like candlewax as the witch was burned to death. On top of that, she'd been determined, furious, and even taken the risk of being caught doing it. Oh, she had absolutely annihilated the doll.

Magic...magic...believe...believe...

A child's laughter reverberated around my head, a tinkling delight all the more sinister for its innocence.

If you don't accept it…you will go mad…completely insane…

Magic or insanity? I chose a side.

With dried tears and a sickly thudding heart, I stood and walked over to the open case. Picked up the poppet. It had a whiff of bonfire about it. Closer examination revealed the markings were unchanged, too, with nothing charred or smudged. Later, these somewhat indecipherable glyphs would mean more, but the only one that always jumped out was the somewhat childish drawing of a shining sun. This was etched into the forehead and resembled a circle with rays sticking out like pins, the middle filled in with black ink. Funny, I'd never really noticed that before despite endless scrutiny. Why black for the sun?

The poppet felt very warm to the touch and seemed to smoke like incense, but there was no doubt it was exactly the same one.

Cutting into my thoughts, Grandma Hart's voice trilled up the stairs. "Eva? Eva, love, your tea's ready."

How long had I been standing there? That was another thing – time just vanished. The light had dimmed, and evening was closing in rapidly. So fast. What happened to all that time? Yanking open the chest of drawers in the corner, I fudged my clothes in, then slipped the poppet inside the pillowcase and ran downstairs.

"Coming!"

"Wash your hands and face in the scullery, love, then come to the table."

Grandma Hart, still in hairnet and rollers, was draining cabbage when I hurried to the sink. The omens weren't good regarding the evening meal. I was not going to like this. The room stank of school dinners and something that hit the back of my throat like an emetic.

"What are we having?"

"Liver and bacon with cabbage and mash. That all right for you, love?"

I almost cried. Oh no, what fresh batch of misery was this? I bloody hated liver and cabbage. She'd put horseradish into something, too, hadn't she? Oh God… If it was in the potato, I couldn't eat that either. But how to tell her I couldn't eat offal and I'd be sick from horseradish? The tablets made me nauseous, and I hardly ate a thing as it was – my body, as it had been pointed out many times, was emaciated, with a stomach the size of a walnut. My mother had only managed to 'get one thing down 'er all day' as she'd said to my grandma earlier, and that had been a Rich Tea biscuit smeared with jam. But how to get out of this? What would happen if my grandparents didn't want me either?

"Sit down at t' table, there's a good lass."

She placed a steaming plate of liver in front of Grandad, who put aside his paper and rubbed his hands together with glee.

"For what we are about to receive, may the Lord make us truly thankful. Amen."

"Tuck in, lass. Tha's got no meat on thee," he said, smearing a wedge of bread with gravy.

Perched on the edge of a chair, I picked up a fork and pushed at a bit of greying liver lumpy with tubes. Even the bacon was ribbed with fat. The smell of it cloyed the sooty air. The clock ticktocked on the mantelpiece, its metronome clicking, winding up each and every nerve along with the sound of steel knives on china plates, the cutting, scraping and chopping greedy and fast. Food slopped and churned in cement-mixer mouths, lips smacked, gravy dripped down chins. One by one, each bundle of nerve fibres began to pop and snap inside my head. Electric tingles travelled the length of both arms, my jaw had clenched, and my fists balled around the knife and fork. And then my grandad did this monstrous thing of plopping potato into the dregs of his teacup, mixing it up and then gulping down the gloop.

That was it.

The room was suddenly too small, too confined, and too hot. Leaping back from the table, I turned and fled.

"What the heck?"

The gravy boat had been knocked over and a plate crashed in my wake. I flew up the stairs with my grandma right behind me, and into the bedroom, backing into the furthest corner to await punishment.

She slammed back the door, beetroot in the face. "What the bleedin' 'ell's the matter with you?" Grandma Hart now looked at me like all the other adults did – with pursed lips and narrowed eyes. "Are you not well or summat?"

"No, I can't eat…I can't—"

"Well that's as maybe, but you can 'ave manners, young lady. You can sit there and ruddy well wait 'til others have finished, do you 'ear me? And you don't leave the table until you're told. Not in my 'ouse, any road."

"I can't eat. I can't eat anything. I'm not well. I'm too hot."

"Aye, well, you will when you're 'ungry enough. I'm going back down or me tea'll get cold. You can get ready for bed, miss. I'll fetch you a glass of water when I've washed up."

Snivelling, I wiped my nose with the back of my hand.

"Don't take on now, Eva. You just need a bit of straightening out. Your mother's been far too slack with you, if you ask me."

Never before had I yearned for nighttime. Other people were another species. I didn't belong and didn't fit in. I wasn't like them. I couldn't even stand to hear them eating, to watch their mouths – hated the food, the smells, the noise. What was wrong with me?

When she finally shut the bedroom door behind her, it was a blessed relief. Her footsteps thudded heavily down the stairs, and the familiar sighs and murmurs of bewilderment drifted up. After a while I moved over to the bed and lay down, staring up at the changing shapes on the ceiling. Their anger would pass. Soon they would turn on the television and watch a sitcom just like my parents did, and later Grandma Hart would come up and peep round the door.

I prayed for sleep. Now that I'd accepted Baba Lenka's request to tell her story, dreams no longer seemed daunting but an escape route – a different world awaited like the open pages of a fairy-tale book, complete with illustrations of castles and snow and forests and mountains. I couldn't wait for the story to start, for this other me to begin the adventure that was Lenka's. Think of it, I told myself, like watching *Fiddler on the Roof* at the picture palace. It would be exciting. It felt as if it might be…

Only it wasn't like going to the pictures at all. It was real. I slipped inside her skin and became her so completely, so perfectly, that it was less a dream sequence and more of a memory. I walked in her footsteps as if they were mine. I breathed the same air and had the same thoughts. Her heart bounced with a powerful joy that infected mine; her body danced, and her mind glittered like diamond dust. Her fingers tingled, and excitement skittered along her veins. It felt as if there were others around her, invisible yet mischievous beings, and as if anything she wanted could be achieved. She knew it, had been born with it, and intended to use it. Lenka was, in short, magical and wonderful, her life so very much more desirable than mine.

As predicted, Gran did come back to check up. Plonking down a glass of water, she swished shut the thin flowery curtains, then kissed my forehead, her breath sour with cigarettes, milk and gravy. I had been falling, falling, falling down the rabbit hole to a sparkling world, about to blossom into beautiful Lenka, when she sat heavily on the side of my bed and shoved me gently on the arm. "Eva, love?"

Please go…

"Your grandad's not best pleased, I 'ave to say, but we'll bring 'im round between us, eh?"

Please go…

"Been a bit of a day, 'asn't it? All right, I'll let you sleep. See you in t' morning. You'll 'ave a boiled egg, won't you?"

Oh God… "Please could I just have toast?"

Her shoulders sagged. "Aye, all right, love. We'll do you some toast over t' fire on a toasting fork. Have you ever had it like that? Nice, thick white bread with butter and treacle? I'll get your appetite back. You leave it to me. Mind you, yer dad were never this fickle. Right greedy little sod, he were!"

Eventually she left me in the darkness again. They always did. Only this time, it was not in terror but in thrilled anticipation of what was to come. The first page of Lenka's storybook was opening, and I plunged back in. Sleep took a while to return, but when it did, a cold wind blew against my face. My heart clenched a little.

Don't be afraid...
No, I won't be...

And then she was standing before me, more than a dream, so real – a voluptuous girl in a long red skirt and billowing white blouse. Around the waist she wore a deep-laced black corset. Flame hair framed a high-cheekboned face with slanted grey eyes. The face was bewitching, mesmerising and twinkling with mischief, but there was something odd about one of her eyes: one was fractionally different from the other – something I was homing in on, trying to work out what it was, when she raised one finger and beckoned.

Come, Eva, let me show you...you must see die Heimat. Komm und sieh!

I followed the call of the piper's tune as eagerly as a Hamlyn rat. Destiny is destiny, after all, particularly if it's ancient sorcery passed down through generations. No rites, no initiations, no studying or covens needed – the knowledge and power is for always and is hereditary. Of course, I had little concept of the kind of force we had aligned with. At the time it seemed like a magical world of make-believe, a Grimms' fairy tale of spectacular colour and infinite fascination. This was my gift, and I was going to accept it.

See, it was easy after all... So much suffering and all for nothing...

Yes, yes, I see that...

Ultimately, the full enlightenment was a process that took many years, but acceptance, as every skilled manipulator knows, is best instilled at the youngest possible age and done gradually, so silkily and surreptitiously that the victim is, in fact, a willing one. This particular point was to be underscored on many levels, as Lenka's terrible story was drip-fed into my subconscious over the best part of a decade. Because of its enormity, the slow feed was crucial in terms of acquiesance, in order to avoid madness or suicide. Had it not been accepted by my growing mind, I realise now that I would not have been able to take the path chosen for me, cross so many bridges of disbelief, or wander so far into the unknown that there would be no way home again.

And she did a good job; she really did. Because when the time came for the most horrific shock imaginable, I was exactly as she had said, primed and ready, and insanity did not come.

***

CHAPTER NINE

It took nine months for Eva Hart, the child, to fully reject mundane life.

The tricky part at the time was managing those around me, protecting them from what was happening inside my mind, concealing what was secret, dangerous, and incredible. In effect I had to become an invisible 'good child' in order not to attract attention. *She. Me.* Strange, I know, but I think now of Eva as someone else, more of a vessel for what was incubating.

Looking back, perhaps ordinary life was supposed to verge on intolerable – perhaps, well, almost certainly to push her ever further into the world of the occult. And it was intolerable. It was Earl, you see? Poor Eva. I see her now as she was, so alone, terror having almost killed her night after night, rejected by her parents, then ultimately forced to fit into the world of Earl and Maud Hart. Every word of Earl's had to be listened to attentively, acknowledged and obeyed, and the painful pretence began at seven every morning with breakfast on the table, seven days a week.

Everyone must have chores, said Earl, and Eva's was to set the table for meals, help with potato peeling, and do the washing-up. She must also keep her room tidy and go to church on Sundays. If Earl Hart was speaking, then she did not interrupt, and if she didn't clean her plate at mealtimes, then there would be nothing more. Anything left on the plate would be reheated and served again next day until she was hungry enough.

On Saturday afternoons Earl and Maud watched the wrestling, both of them yelling and shaking balled fists at the set. Eva was to sit quietly and do a jigsaw or get on with the knitting Maud had set her. And on Sundays after church, Earl would go to the pub and Maud would put on a big Sunday dinner.

"You peel them spuds, Eva, love," she said that first Sunday. The day I found out who or what my grandad really was.

It was all right doing that; I didn't mind. The scullery was cold, and my fingers were numb, but I learned quickly, peeling and chopping while the rain pummelled the corrugated iron roof and Grandma Hart smoked and whisked up batter for the Yorkshire pudding. On the stove, carrots and cabbage simmered, steaming up the windows until they ran with condensation, and a joint of beef roasted in the oven.

She seemed agitated, though, constantly watching the clock. And I wondered why.

I never had to wonder again.

At 'chucking-out time', which was two o'clock, Grandad Hart rolled in through the kitchen door, smashed it back with his elbow and stumbled in. His nose was purple with veins, eyes glassy and unfocused, and the stink of him fair sent you reeling. The smell was new to me, like a jar of pickled onions. He lurched from table to doorway and into the living room, knocked something over and swore loudly. "Why the fuck did yer put that there? Yer stupid cow! I'm hungry. Where's the bloody dinner, woman?"

Grandma Hart's hands were shaking. Stubbing out her cigarette, she finished mashing the potatoes and quickly drained the cabbage. "Coming! Two minutes, love."

He banged the table with his fist, his voice thick and syrupy. "For fuck's sake, what's tha been bloody doing all bloody morning? Fannying about? Gossiping?"

Hell, he was coming back to the kitchen.

She'd been cooking ever since we'd returned from church. Why was she letting him speak to her like this? He seemed like a different man.

"It's nearly ready," she trilled in a light, jovial tone belying the grim look on her face. "Go and sit down. I'm just serving up." Then, turning to me, she hissed, "Hurry up, get them carrots on to t' plates, Eva."

The scullery was as steamy as a chip shop. Frantically she stirred gravy with one hand while taking out of the oven the Yorkshire pudding she'd made with onions in a tin.

"Cut him a slice of that and take it in. Hurry up."

I put the plate in front of him, and he wolfed it down.

The atmosphere was charged like a bomb was about to go off. Gran served the lunch in silence, and then we tentatively joined him and sat down.

"Where's the bleedin' salt? I'm looking for salt, woman! For crying out fucking loud!"

She was the colour of cigarette ash, her great bulk shifting at speed to get the carton of salt.

Noticing my wide eyes, she slightly shook her head. *Don't say a word!*

It wasn't until after he had eaten, though, just before dessert was served, that he finally spoke to her properly. "Right bloody kickoff in t' pub this lunchtime, Maud."

She was clearing the plates away. "Oh, aye?"

On mine she had only put a small piece of beef and a tiny spoonful of mash with two carrot pieces. No gravy. She glanced at the lump of gristle I'd cut away and pushed to one side, pursing her lips, before immediately checking whether Grandad had noticed. Hopefully, she'd slip it into the bin and he wouldn't force me to chew and swallow it.

The purple veins on his nose were darkening to maroon. A rant was coming. "It were Bobby Waller who started it – telling us who've worked down t' pit for twenty year we should accept what's on t' table."

"You mean, for t' redundancy package?"
"Course I flaming do. What the hell did you think I meant?"

"Sorry, love, I—"

He banged his fist on the table so hard the crockery juddered. "I won't bloody 'ave it. I will not have that bloody upstart telling me, Earl Hart, what to accept and what not to accept, do you bloody 'ear me?"

"I should think not. I hope you told him—"

The conversation rapidly moved on to one I did not understand, but it seemed to revolve around pits being closed due to not being profitable and people being cast aside onto the poverty heap without getting paid properly. And I don't know why I said it. I don't. I should have kept quiet.

But out it popped anyway, in a sing-song know-it-all voice, during a lull. "Well, sometimes it's best to go along with things to keep the peace."

I don't know where I'd heard that line before. Maybe it was from my dad. In fact, I'm sure it was something he used to say when my mother lost her temper.

But the hands of time stopped. The bomb had been detonated.

Both my grandparents turned to stare with open mouths.

A good minute seemed to pass before Grandma Hart's head swivelled oh so slowly on its stem, in the direction of Grandad Hart. Who was standing up. His fists were clenched on the table. His chair fell back with a thud.

What happened next was fast as a hurricane. He lunged forwards, picked me up by the elbow, and cracked me hard across the face. I don't recall the words. Only the blast of stars as his iron fist smashed into my eight-year-old skull like a wrecking ball.

***

CHAPTER TEN

The incident was never acknowledged or referred to. It didn't happen.

Earl Hart simply retrieved his chair, sat down again, and began to eat steamed jam pudding with custard. Globs of gloopy yellow clung to his stubbly chin as methodically he chewed and swallowed. And afterwards, he poured tea from his cup into a saucer and noisily slurped it down.

One of them must have lifted me onto the sofa, because I woke to the sound of *Gardener's World*. Tears burned my eyes, the left one so swollen that the sight was temporarily lost. The salty taste of blood trickled down my throat, along with the sensation my head was enlarging on one side, the pressure causing a dull, sickly ache.

"You mustn't speak to him when he gets like that, love," said Grandma Hart when she tucked me up later. "It's only when he's been to t' pub. He's all right most o' t' time."

How was it possible to survive this? When would Mum and Dad come back? How could they have left me here? How could they? Did they know what my grandad was like when he'd been to the pub?

Choking back the sobs, the pillow wet with tears,

Lenka's glittering world pulled me down once more, and willingly I dropped into it, longing for the story to resume. If this was madness, it was preferable to reality. And perhaps insanity would have won out had life continued like that with Earl and Maud, but have you ever noticed how something or someone turns up during the darkest of days? That even during the unhappiest of times, there is a chink of light – just enough to keep you going? Perhaps there is a God? That would depend on who orchestrates the whole, and what do we know?

For me, anyway, that someone was Nicky. She got me through.

Nicky Dixon was the girl who lived next door but one. The same age as me, she was walking up the street with a satchel slung over her shoulder when I first spied her. Her head was down, shoulders stooped.

I was kneeling on the storage chest in the hall, watching the kids walk home from school.

"She looks sad," I said.

"The dark girl? The others call her names; I've heard them," said Grandma Hart.

"Why?"

"Because she's different, I suppose. You know what kids are like."

"Yeah, but why? It's mean."

She stroked my hair, one of the few soft gestures she ever made. "I don't rightly know, love. It's just how it is wi' kids. They can be 'orrible sometimes."

As she spoke, Nicky Dixon looked up and saw me. I suppose she must have spotted the ghost girl in the landing window a few times and wondered who she was. I thought she'd glare angrily or hurry away... But she didn't. The little girl with the ripped blazer and the cut lip raised her hand and waved. And, like a sunbeam striking with iridescence the spray above a waterfall, smiled.

That smile brought with it an explosion of complex emotion – feelings without words, a timeless moment.

We know each other.

I lifted my hand, and her smile widened to one of joy.

"Can I go out and say hello?"

"Aye, go on, then, but mind you don't go further than Mrs Dixon's. I want you back here at five sharp for tea! It's oxtail tonight."

Nicky stood waiting on the street corner. "Don't you go to school, then?" she asked as I approached.

"No."

"Why not?"

"Oh, it's not for long."

"I'm Nicky. Do you want to come and play at our house?"

"Yes, please. I'm Eva Hart."

"Aye, I know. You're the one that stabbed Maxine Street, aren't you? They say you're a Nazi and possessed by the devil."

"I'm not a Nazi; I were born 'ere like you. Anyhow, what happened to you? Your lip's bleeding."

She swiped away the blood. "It happens all t' time. You get used to it."

"Well, you shouldn't get used to it."

"I'll tell you what," she said as we walked to her house. "If I say I'm with Earl Hart's granddaughter, they won't dare touch me."

I wasn't sure if it was a compliment to have a grandad

known as the local hard case or to be thought of as possessed by the devil; all I knew was that I loved her instantly.

"What shall we play?"

Nicky had another go at licking her fingers and wiping away traces of blood before she opened the back door and we went inside her house. "Me mum's gonna kill me with this ripped blazer."

"It weren't your fault."
"Aye, I know, but you don't know me mum."

Her mother's anger was all show, though. She had a laugh inside her that was always bursting to come out, even as she shrieked at the sight of another ruined school blazer. She'd had her back to us when we walked into the kitchen, busy cooking. The whole house was filled with the aroma of exotic spices, several pans bubbling on the hob with chicken and sauces and what looked like green bananas.

She caught me staring.

"Mum, this is my new friend. She's the one that stabbed Maxine Street!"

Mrs Dixon threw back her head and laughed a great belly laugh. "Well, what an introduction. Are you staying for tea, love?"

God, how I wanted to. "What is it?"

Mrs Dixon laughed again. "Oh, so it all depends on what's cooking, does it?" She looked me up and down. "Who's your little friend, Nicky? She's got no meat on 'er."

"Eva. She's Earl Hart's granddaughter, the one that—"

"That's enough talk, Nicky." She bent down so her

warm brown eyes were level with mine. "What's your name, sweet thing?"

"Eva Hart."

"And you don't go to school, that right?"

I nodded. "I've been poorly."

"Well, Eva, we're having chicken and plantain in Cajun sauce. I'll ask Maud if you can stay and eat with us. It's nice for you two girls to have a friend each, Lord knows."

Grandma Hart made a bit of a fuss. We watched the two women through Nicky's bedroom window, their arms folded in the street, both still in aprons and slippers.

"Bet you she says yes, though," said Nicky.

"She won't. I'll be forced to eat rats' tails, you'll see."

"Rats' tails?"

"Dark brown soup with rubbery bits in it."

She screwed up her face for a minute, then the sunshine broke through the clouds and she, like her mother, threw back her head to laugh. "Oh, you mean oxtail soup?"

"Aye, that's it."

Turned out my gran did agree. I knew why, too – because I hadn't eaten a thing save a couple of toast fingers with black treacle on them for nearly a week. Two-day-old kidneys were never going to go down my throat in a month of Sundays, and nor was warmed-up tapioca or sliced tongue. The sound of their eating had become increasingly disgusting with every meal. From the never-ending tinkle of tea stirring, the monotonous ticking of the clock, and the succession of slurps and gulps and swallows, it was going to send me stark staring mad. One day I'd run round the room smashing everything in sight, and then it would be the funny farm for sure – from where there was no release. Everyone knew that. The doctors wore white coats and stuck a needle in you, and that was you done.

Instead, Nicky saved my sanity. And Mrs Dixon put meat on my noodle bones.

It was so different at their house – with constant music and chitchat – and the food was a delight. That first evening, it was white chicken breast pieces in a spicy tomato sauce. We had the strange banana thing, and then Mrs Dixon put records on. Up to then I'd only heard what was on the radio at Mum and Dad's – The Carpenters, Gilbert O'Sullivan, Cat Stevens – and Grandad Hart only played military band music. But after tea at Nicky's, her mother got up and danced. She was a big woman, but her hips swivelled, and the beat was infectious. Initially I sat there, flummoxed and red-faced, stomach swollen with chicken and rice and bananas…but then, well, once you've discovered Tamla Motown, 'Needle in a Haystack', 'Ain't No Mountain High Enough', 'Can I Get a Witness', and the rest, you find what Lenka called *Lebensfreude* – the joy of life. And I never wanted to go back to my grandparents' house ever again. If only it were possible to just move in and stay with the Dixons forever.

Very quickly we became just as close as little girls are wont to be. It still took months, though, before I confessed to anything more serious. Nicky had a way of pressing for information, a real truth-seeker if ever there was one. And she needled away about my illness, what had happened with Maxine, and where my parents were. So I told her a little. Mostly, I related the nightmares. I never told a living soul about the funeral in Bavaria, but the dreams I was having every single night, well, I told her about those. I told her about the haunted house in Leeds and the wardrobe door creaking open. And then I told her about Lenka – that the ghost that had crept out of the wardrobe was slowly revealing her story in dreams.

"It's schizophrenia," she said decisively. "There's them in our family who've got it."

"No, it's not."

"Yes, it's where you hear voices and see things other people can't."

I shook my head. "It's not that."

"Well, what is it, then? You said this lady speaks to you at night and you can see her but no one else can."

"Aye, but it's not like hallucinations. That's what the doctors said, and they gave me pills to stop it happening, but they just knocked me out so I couldn't even move! And it made it worse. It's real, Nicky. I don't expect you to understand, like. But it's real. She's real. It's not madness. I'm not mad, honest."

"Well, what about a split personality, then? I think we've got that in t' family an' all."

"No, it i'n't that. Because I only see her when I'm asleep. It's only when I go to sleep that she appears, right? I mean, like down to every detail. And not only that, but there's a story, a whole life story, and it isn't like a dream where you don't remember much when you wake up – with this, every single bit of it stays with me. It's like it actually happened to me personally and it's a memory not a dream."

"That's right weird, that is."

"She doesn't frighten me anymore, either, not since I

let her tell me her story…"

She was frowning. I'd said too much. She wouldn't want to be my friend anymore now, would she? And the thought of that was unbearable. We'd been together at her house every day since we'd met. I'd put on weight. Gran was saying I could go to school again soon – at the one in the next village. And I'd found something I loved to do and could do well – I could dance. For the first time since Bavaria, life was colourful again, and it was all thanks to Nicky.

She stared for a while, then seemed to make up her mind and put her arm around my shoulders. She smelled of spices and soap. "I'll tell you summat now, but you keep your gob shut about this, Eva, right?"

"Yeah, course."

"I mean it."

"I swear."

"On your mother's life."

"Yes, I swear on my mother's life, and my dad's.

"And Sooty's – you said you thought a lot about that cat."

"Aye, and Sooty's life, then."

"Right, well my mum does voodoo. It's where you get a doll and stick pins in it. And sometimes she dances after drinking this special brew and goes into a trance. She does it with my auntie. I've seen them."

My eyes were out like organ stops. "Bloody 'ell."

"So I know, like, what you're saying about ghosts is true. There are spirits, Eva. But you've got to be right careful because there are bad ones, really bad evil ones."

"How do you mean?"

"Well, you know how you were saying she scared you,

this old woman, when she were coming out o' t' wardrobe? Well, the really bad ones mean to scare you and scare you bad. At first, they pretend to be your friend or a dead person you once knew – to get your trust so you let them in. You can send them to other people an' all and make evil things 'appen to them, but once you work with these evil spirits, you owe them your soul, right? You can't go back, not ever. So you have to decide. And me, I want to be with Jesus. I'm just saying."

I looked back into those chestnut eyes for the longest time. How could I tell her? How could I tell her it was not only far too late to decide, but there had never been a choice? That whatever force was behind Lenka was now channelling through me? That with every drip-fed dream, the story lost a little more *Lebensfreude* – and dipped its quill into a darker pot of ink for the next chapter? *Invited…accepted…*

She took my hand. "I'll always be here for you."

"Thank you." She seemed older than time, far older than me, anyway. But I wondered if she would be if she had any idea what was coming.

Her eyes searched mine, seeing what others could not. "I see the wolf in there, Eva. And I'm still here for you."

Good people did exist, people who saw the darkness in others and still loved them. She was one of them. And I think in that moment a tiny part of my spirit was preserved – a locket buried deeply inside an attic chest, safely stored until the time was right.

My eyes, Eva's eyes, prickled. The only way, the only course ahead, was to live as Eva Hart by day and Lenka by night – the sun and the moon. I could and would keep them separate for as long as possible, at least until the story was told. Then maybe Baba Lenka would leave me alone? I mean, that was what she wanted, right? All she wanted…

But of course, I had no concept of how unspeakable, evil and inconceivably horrific the story would be. If I had, perhaps even at that late stage a different choice might have been made.

***

PART TWO

BABA LENKA

'Weaving spiders, come not here.'

1. Midsummer Night's Dream, Act 2, Scene 2. Shakespeare.
2. Bohemian Grove.

CHAPTER ELEVEN

WOLFSHEULE, BOHEMIA
1890

The day after Lenka Heller turned sixteen, her mother called her into the kitchen.

"Daughter, there are things you need to know. You are now of age." Indicating a seat at the opposite side of the table, she poured them both a cup of honey mead.

Lenka looked over her shoulder at the sweet autumnal day she'd planned to spend with Oskar. Apples weighed down the trees, and the air was heady with ripe fruit and warm earth. He lived in a wooden house on the nearby lake. Known as Teufelssee, the expanse of water was still and dark even in summer, with mountain mists shrouding it for much of the year. In her mind she was already running through the forest to meet him on the shore.

"Sit down!" her mother said again.

Lenka sighed. "Can't it wait? I wanted to—"

"No, it can't. Come, drink some mead with me."

She slumped onto a chair and took a sip. Laced with spices and vodka, the liquor shocked her throat, and she gasped. Her mother had never given her alcohol in her life. This must be serious. "I suppose this is about boys?"

"No."

She took another sip and tried not to cough. "*Mutter*, I know about, you know—"

"Lenka, this is not about boys. This is about your family, where you come from and who you really are. It's time you knew." Clara took a deep breath before downing her own cup of mead in one.

"Who I am? But—"

"You have asked many times about…about your abilities."

Lenka frowned. "And you have always refused to answer."

"Yes, because you were too young to know. I wanted to put it off for as long as possible, to allow you to enjoy your childhood. But now your grandmother is very ill, seriously so, and this cannot be delayed. I'm not sure how much longer she can hold out, and there are things you must be told."

"This grandmother I have never seen? Where is she? What is she dying of? She cannot be so old—"

"Not so old, no. But she is riddled with the worms of disease and weakens by the day." Clara dipped her head. "I am sorry you have never seen her, but there were important reasons. It was not easy to be around one such as her."

"So where is she? How do you know all this if she is not here?"

"So many questions." She poured herself another cup. "Drink yours, Lenka. You will need it."

"Why? Why will I need it?"

"Because I am afraid for you. You have to be prepared—"

"Mutter, I don't understand any of this."

"Your grandmother lives far away, in Romania. That is where I was born. I left because of what my mother carries and because soon it will be what you carry, too – call it a legacy – and it is this you must be prepared for."

Lenka drank the mead, beginning to relish the warmth spreading through her veins. Now her dark grey eyes met her mother's head-on. "Prepared for what?"

"To receive your gift. Some will say gift, others might say curse. But it is an extraordinarily powerful one. A generation, sometimes two, will be skipped depending on the lifespan of the carrier, but it is passed down the female line of our family, and there is nothing that can be done about it. As such, you are to inherit Baba Olga's gift – soon, possibly within days."

"And this gift concerns my abilities? But I already have it – I know things about people without being told, I hear whispers and thoughts and—"

Clara Heller shook her head. "No, no, that's child's play. So you see ghosts, know what's about to happen before it happens, hear a voice telling you someone's inner secrets. So can many a gypsy. Those tricks are easy. Even I—"

"Yet you told me to keep it to myself."

"Yes, because look, Lenka – see what happens to those who admit such things. There are people who can still remember the massacre of witches. Look how they ripped those women from their homes and tortured them in filthy jails. This was the worst-affected area in the whole of Europe – nine hundred just in this country, more than anywhere else in the world. Churchmen accuse us of worshipping the devil. So, yes, keep it to yourself. But know this: what you think you have is nothing, nothing at all to what will soon be yours. We, you and I, are not German like your father. Your father comes from the Black Forest; his father before him made clocks! You and I are from a caravan of wanderers still looking for their place on earth."

"I thought you said you were from Romania."

"Your grandmother gave birth to me there and stayed awhile. The rest of the family settled around her, as they would. It is where the family is at this point in time." She poured them each another cup of mead. "But now your grandma is dying, and so we must go there; this is what I am trying to say. You especially must be there at the end, so she can tell you what you need to know."

"But that will take days, weeks!" Thoughts of Oskar filled her mind, and her eyes widened, the words catching in her throat as the implication set in. "No, I want to stay here. I don't need to know these things, and I don't want to go all that way—"

"Enough. You will go. There are matters that must be directly passed on – this is real, and—"

"I know it's real, Mutter, and I am not the least bit afraid of it, either."

"You know nothing."

"So you keep saying."

"Ach, you cannot imagine how important this is. What you are about to inherit is thousands and thousands of years old, from a force older than human time. At the very least you need to be informed and prepared because the very power of it could kill you if you don't control it. Lenka, I cannot stress enough—"

"I'm not frightened of this. I speak to demons all the

time and get them to do stuff for me. I have the boy I want, I have beauty, and I have power already. I do not need to see my grandma – this woman I have never met. It will take days to get to Romania, and I do not want to go." She stood up.

Clara's voice rose. "Sit down at once. I have not finished. Listen to me! You do not know everything; you are just sixteen, and we are talking about your heritage, your own grandmother. Have respect!"

Reluctantly, Lenka sat down, twiddling her empty cup around and around.

"I shall start again. Your grandmother did not use the powers she was given, and, as such, her body has been unable to withstand the dark energy. She has suffered disease from the age of a child and is tormented day and night. It is not good to be around her. I could tell you things, terrible things, of her tearing out her own hair, shouting at invisible demons day and night, vomiting back all her food, writhing on the floor in terrible agony, and sometimes I would find her, when I was a small child, Lenka, so imagine this…I would find my mother crumpled in a corner, clutching her head and screaming with the pain, covered in running sores, just begging the demons to leave her alone. She said there were not just dozens of them but hundreds around her, waiting for commands she would not give. The pressure would mount and mount, until the family had to hide her for fear she would be locked away in a hospital for the insane."

"This will not happen to me. No, I will not go."

"If you do not go, then the same fate awaits you without doubt. You have to know what you are dealing with. You need the information so you can make your choice. Lenka, I do not know how to help you because, whether you like it or not, this is coming your way."

Lenka hardened her jaw and turned away from her mother's pleading stare.

"How come it missed you out? You see things, you hear things, you have the house filled with herbs, and I see you making spells—"

"Yes, we have second sight, all of us. But the legacy I am talking about is a sorcery of the darkest kind. Sometimes it will be passed on, or received if requested, from a dying sorceress. But the most powerful sorceress is the one who is born with it, a Bluthexe. As soon as a sorceress in the bloodline is dead, the full power must be transferred along with all the demonic servants allocated for her bidding – or it will follow her into the afterlife. You know other realms exist; you know it well. But what we have in our family is a direct channel to the force behind the darkest entity of all."

"Why is this in our family? What is this caravan of people who never settled? We are gypsies, then, yes?"

"Not originally. I believe, from the elders and from my mother, we come from Russia, but that is far back in time. Since then, we have travelled through all of Europe, and now here you and I are in Bohemia. From here I feel we will eventually move west. Yes, much further west—"

"Always on the move, why?"

"Because…because we have to…"

Lenka frowned. "I do not understand. And what is the purpose of these demons that are not invoked? What do they want with us, apart from to torment us to death if we don't work for them?"

"No, it is not to work for *them*. It is they who work for *you*. You are the one who lives – a mighty sorceress with a powerful channel from the dark source directly to humans, to God's creation."

"So what do they want from me?"

"To destroy God's creation, Lenka. That is your fate. To dull the spirit of mankind or, better still, destroy it. This is hatred of God Himself, do you not understand? Evil beyond anything most people could ever comprehend or wish to. Which does not mean it doesn't exist, of course."

Lenka's eyes widened as they sat there in what had felt, until moments ago, like an ordinary day - the farmhouse kitchen scented with wood smoke and the door open to the fragrance of falling fruit.

"So now you see, don't you?" Clara said. "How important it is that you visit your grandma on her deathbed. Why you must know what to do. Or do you choose illness, madness and a lifetime of torment that will surely follow you into the hereafter?"

It was as if the sun had been eclipsed.

"You should not have had children, Mutter."

"And you will see there is no choice in the matter of children. You will see."

"I do not believe this. I tell demons what to do, I tell them to come to me and do my bidding, and then I banish them back to their place in hell. You will see. You will see on this one, Mutter."

"This is about far more than demons. Who do you think is their master?"

Tears pricked the back of her eyes as the horrible task loomed ahead. Thoughts of Oskar with his lithe, tanned and muscular body flitted across her mind…an image of him wading out of the lake, shaking diamond droplets of water from sleek black hair, long lashes sparkling, deep brown eyes bright with desire… So many nights spent fitful and sleepless, dreaming of their limbs entwined beneath a canopy of shimmering leaves…

"Well, I will not go. I will not. It is too far—"

"Pack your things. We will leave tomorrow."

***

CHAPTER TWELVE

Lenka shoved back her chair. Eyes ablaze, she leaned over the table and snarled at the woman before her, the woman whose every word she had obeyed until now. "I will *not* go to Romania. Ever. I'm staying here."

And then she was running from the house towards the lake exactly as planned. Her boots pounded through the misty woodland as she tore along the path. They could not make her go; the thought was unbearable – to be without him now! He filled her mind, her heart, every waking moment. The journey to Romania would take days if not weeks – it would be winter before she returned. This was terrible, the worst thing that had ever happened. None of what her mother had said was true, it just couldn't be.

She and Oskar were destined to be together – the whole thing had been like magic from the very first moment. Out looking for herbs that day, she'd been caught by surprise at the sight of him, and she'd dipped behind a tree to watch. After a while, with the dying light of the afternoon behind her, she plucked up courage to peer around the trunk. Which was when he glanced up. Her hair was like fire, he said later, as if she'd been set alight, the cool regard of her slanted eyes and sculpted cheekbones startlingly glacial by comparison.

"What are you doing?" she'd asked, emerging from her hiding place.

"I don't know," he said.

She indicated the carving he'd just dropped on the floor.

He was flushing to the roots of his hair. "Oh, this! It is just, erm, a thing…I was making…"

"I have not seen you before, not in school."

"I d-d-don't go to the village school – I was s-s-sent to one in Haidmühle. My parents are German. They don't like the school here; my father says it is full of pagans and Czechs."

"Oh!" She sashayed towards him, aware of his slackened jaw and nervous stutter. "Well, my father is German, too."

"What is your name?"

Up close, she gazed directly into his eyes. "Lenka."

"Your hair, it…it…it's enchanting. Like a witch's hair."

She laughed. "You swim, of course?"

"Yes, I—"

"Then I will come back later."

It had been the best three weeks of her life. Tears smarted. Why did it have to end so soon? At all? Why?

On approaching Teufelssee, she slowed her steps. The wooden houses appeared, as always, to float on the black glass surface, the mist hovering in skeins. She calmed her breathing, letting the warmth of the earth pulse into the soles of her feet. Coppery leaves gleamed as the sun burned through the haze and brushed the day with hues of gold, the gentle lap of the water rippling in the reeds.

She narrowed her eyes. *Please be here…please be here,*

Oskar…

If he was not here today, they might never meet again. She was as sure of this as anything, yet there was no basis or reason: if she was forced to go away, would he not wait for her return? What if she was unable to get home again?

Oh please, Oskar.

She scanned the expanse of water. A small fishing boat bobbed at the far end…

And then he appeared from the mist, wading out of the water with a wooden dinghy in tow. Raising a hand in greeting, he swiftly moored the vessel, hurrying to get to her, his white shirt open to the waist. She found she could not look away from the sight of his smooth stomach and the single line of hair travelling down from the navel. Her legs trembled slightly, and all other senses faded away. She would have him. He would marry her, they would be betrothed, and then her mother would have no power. Damn her mother and damn her grandmother and damn them all! She would have him. Rushing towards him, her dress dragged in the lake, and tears streamed down her face.

"Lenka?"

Without words or hesitation, she grabbed his hand, and together they hurried into the forest, heading for their special place that could not be seen by prying eyes and, on reaching it, fell immediately to the ground. Gone all shy, tender kisses and soft banter, now their lips banged urgently against each other's, and fingers beyond caressing ripped at clothes. He pulled her hair back with one hand, forcing her neck to arch forwards, biting and moaning, his breath fast and low. There was nothing but his mouth on hers, his hands on the flesh beneath her dress, his touch where she had never even touched herself. She held his hips and pulled him inside her, deeper and deeper. She needed more and more and more, and even when he climaxed, he did not stop. She dug her nails into his back as he loved her until they both cried out, and the tears came in torrents.

"You are the one, my bride. Mine forever," he whispered.

"Always."

But even as the word tumbled from her lips, she knew it to be a false hope. She would never be his wife. They would not live in bliss on this lake, with children that would be wild and free and beautiful and loved. It would not be like that for them. She rolled onto her side so he could hold her. Perhaps the poignancy of this, the cruelty after such euphoria, made the last few hours of lovemaking all the more painfully exquisite. Hot tears rolled into her hair.

He kissed them away. "You are my bride, you know that. There is only you."

Yet the sadness ached inside at what was not to be. It did not matter what he asked; she saw that now. Her path would be the dark, crooked one her mother had described, and this sweet joy could never be hers. He would have that with some other. She sobbed into her sleeve as he kissed her neck and stroked the curve of her waist. How could she tell him? There were no words. Why could her mother not carry this burden for a few decades as her grandmother had done? At least let her have some life before it was over, before the torment came?

After a while her tears dried, and she rolled over and

let him cradle her in the crook of his arm, both of them drifting into sleep until the light dimmed and the first of the owls hooted. She looked up at the treetops spiking into the sky. How long had they lain here with the sweat cooling on their skin? Hours probably…hours and hours…

A sharp gust of wind rustled through the trees, and goose bumps shivered across her back. At the gilded edge of the forest, the sun was sinking rapidly, and leaves spiralled in crepuscular swirls. Something had changed! She sat up, unaccountably alarmed. It was coming on the wind…and far sooner than expected, too. In fact, it was nearly here. A snapshot vision flashed into her mind…of hooves pounding turf, horses galloping along the plains, swaying wagons along wooded paths, rocking caravans…

They, the horses and caravan of wagons, were travelling in this direction on the easterly wind, and the feeling of impending doom was overwhelming, sickly and claustrophobic. A sense of panic and chaos gripped her.

Oskar was lying flat on his back. She bent to kiss each fringe of sooty lashes, then his gently smiling lips. "I love you," she said.

Taking hold of her hands, he kissed each in turn. "Don't worry, we will meet again."

She did not question his words, instinctively accepting instead that this moment in her life would never be repeated. In order not to spoil it by asking what he meant, she nodded.

"Yes, yes, we will."

His eyes were closing again. "When it is time, we will meet again."

She thought she would die of a broken spirit, a

devastated heart, of the pain. What was he saying? What did he know? Was he leaving? Wasn't it she who was leaving?

"I don't understand," she said.

He reached up to stroke her hair. "You are leaving; that is what you came to tell me."

"But I will come back. I promise."

They lay side by side again, chilly now as a breeze began to whip up but still holding hands and not wanting to let go. Evening was closing in rapidly, and the breeze picked up, bringing with it a veil of rain from across the lake. Static crackled in the air, and blue flashes lit up the mountains. She snuggled into his side, trying to push away the feeling of foreboding – it was just a storm coming – and closed her eyes.

It had been for just one second…one moment was all…but when she woke, it was to splashes of rain on her face. Startled, she leapt to her feet. The rain was coming down hard, dripping from the canopy, and Oskar had gone. Had he just upped and left her here, in the dark and the cold with a storm coming? There were wolves in this forest!

Confused, she ran to the shore and, on reaching the water's edge, was about to call out when she changed her mind. Perhaps this was his way of making it easier to part?

You are leaving; that is what you came to tell me…

Turning away, she nodded to herself. Yes, that would be it. He had left while she slept in order to avoid more upset for them both. Somehow he knew she was leaving, had guessed, no doubt, by her urgency and desire. He was thinking of her… Besides, night had fallen, and it looked as though the storm would be a wild one. Wind whistled off the mountains, and rain was sheeting across the fields. It was time to go home.

That night, the storm raged, slamming the shutters, banging doors, rattling windows and dislodging roof tiles. Branches snapped off trees and sailed past the window. Dozens of apples thundered to the ground. And still the wind screamed around the eaves. It shrieked down the chimney and blew ash across the floors. At times the very fabric of the house shuddered.

Lenka lay wide awake on her bed. These were the winds of change, weren't they? No ordinary storm, this signalled Baba Olga and her demons were on their way. There was no rational thought to this, only a deep knowing. And every time she closed her eyes, the images appeared, so much clearer now as if the veil was lifting. Closer, then? Yes, much closer. A line of carts and wagons had hunkered in a ring, so near that the smell of the campfire and steaming bone broth filled the air. Tarpaulin billowed in the high winds, pegged down at the corners. And a swarthy-skinned old woman with her hair bound in a scarf wiped beads of sweat from the one facing death. Waxy candlelight flickered as she worked, her forearms marked with snaking veins, hands calloused and worn.

Outside the wolves were howling and a lantern bobbed in the yard. Her father's voice was lost somewhere between the noise of the storm and her own reverie, shouting that animals had broken loose.

A fresh wave of grief rolled over her. This was the end. Would she ever see Oskar again? Why was there such a conviction it was all over?

There is no Oskar.

The voice was barely a whisper, but it came as clearly as if the speaker stood directly beside her.

Had she drifted to sleep?

There is no Oskar.

Now Lenka's eyes were wide, and her heart lurched. She clutched the sheets. The voice was stronger and more forceful.

"No!" she said aloud. She had felt him, had known him, had seen, heard, touched, loved… Had something happened to him, then? Was that it? No Oskar! Had he left her sleeping and then drowned in the lake? Was the voice telling her he had died? She had predicted this, had known…

Throwing back the sheets, she rushed to the window. The vortex of the storm had hit Wolfsheule head-on. Her father was stumbling around the yard with a lantern, the dogs running around barking. She pulled on boots and threw on an overcoat on the pretext of going out to help recover the horses, silently acknowledging the truth of the whispers. She should listen to the inner voice – it was always, always right. Oh God, it was unthinkable. Had he foreseen his own death, too? Is that why he'd said they would meet again? In the afterlife?

With her head down against the prevailing wind, baulking at the force of it, she hurried outside, calling for the horses before running across the fields and shooting straight down the forest path to Teufelssee. Desperation spurred her on as she tripped over tree roots in the dark and rain lashed her face. Once at the shore, she held her hands up in a shield against the onslaught of rain. A lamp was on in one of the hut windows.

"Hey!" she shouted, no longer caring if his family

knew she had been seeing their son. "Hey! I am looking for Oskar. I am worried about Oskar! Did he come home?"

The huts out on the water were cracking under the strain of the storm, the lake's level rising alarmingly. A man appeared on the decking, throwing belongings into a boat, scrambling his things together. An almighty bang showed he had made the right decision. With minutes to spare, one of the main beams had broken away, cutting his house in two.

Lenka waded into the water to waist height.

"Get back, you'll be swept away!" he shouted.

She grabbed the rope to help him. "Where is Oskar? I am afraid he became lost in the storm."

He shook his head, hauling the boat through mud. "No Oskar."

"What do you mean, 'no Oskar'?"

He snatched the rope from her, shouting over the howling winds. "There is no Oskar. My son went to Haidmühle and died there of fever. He was buried at the church here just three weeks ago. Did you not know?"

She stared at him aghast and shook her head.

"Of course, people like you are the reason I sent him away from here."

Lenka stepped back. "I don't understand."

He levelled with her. "Pagans," he spat.

"You blame us?"

"That is why I sent him to a church school – a proper school in town, and now look what happens. I had to bury my only son on the last day of summer. I am going far from here – I will leave you to your pagan ways, your anti-church ways, to the devil you worship! At least you did not come around here and get your heathen claws into him. He died pure. At least I saved him from that."

Her heart banged hard against her ribs. Oskar had died three weeks ago? She flailed around in the dark, backing away, her mind reeling... This did not make sense, not in any way. So...who had she spent the last few weeks with? And who had she just made love with and...and...and...oh God...pledged allegiance to?

You are the one, my bride. Mine forever.

***

CHAPTER THIRTEEN

Shortly before first light, an elderly man arrived at the farm gates.

Lenka woke from a violent dream, disturbed by the sound of voices, and peeped between the gap in the curtains. Weathered and bony, the man was dressed in a black suit of knee-length trousers, waistcoat and jacket. His white shirt was collarless, and he wore long boots and a black hat, which he held on to in the gusty wind. Her father, who had been up all night rescuing animals and securing barn doors, took a note from the man's hand, nodded curtly, and headed back inside. It was customary to invite visitors in, especially if they had travelled far, but there had been nothing more than a brief nod. And when she glanced again at the gates, the old man had vanished.

The disturbing dream from which she'd awoken had left her troubled. In it, she and Oskar had been making love, the rhythmic motion of him inside her building and building into blinding euphoria… *I love you…I love you…I love you…* She was lifting her hips to pull him in deeper, wrapping her arms around his neck in total surrender…when all of a sudden, his face had shapeshifted into something hideous.

"Lenka?"

She sat up in bed with a hand over her mouth, trying

desperately to push away the graphic details as they replayed with mortifying clarity. The creature, not human, had laughed at her during the most trusting, loving moment imaginable. At the point where she had been about to climax, it nastily mocked her: 'I love you, oh, oh, oh, I love you…' Gleefully its mouth stretched open to reveal spiky little teeth, its skin scaly and reptilian, the eyes yellow with vertical slits for pupils – the whole a hologram of a man but ultimately reptilian and utterly without a soul.

Badly shaken, she tried to blank out the memory. It was only a dream, brought on without doubt because of the shock of last night. She must say nothing about Oskar to anyone. He had died three weeks ago; that was the truth of it. So who, then, had she been laughing and swimming with all this time – talking to and caressing? And then yesterday afternoon…? She put her head in her hands.

Mad people were taken and locked inside the Stonehouse in Haidmühle. The windows were narrow cracks between heavy stones, and on walking past, the sound of people screaming could be heard from within. It was said they were tied up with rope and left on cold stone floors, their filth swilled away each day like cattle's. No, whatever was happening to her must be kept secret. All of it. Fortunately, she had never confided in her mother.

"Lenka? You must come downstairs at once!"

She found her mother sitting at the kitchen table. The logs in the grate had only just taken hold, and the kitchen was still cold, the morning gloomy. On the stove a pot of oats simmered, and a batch of bread sat in a bowl covered with a cloth, the smell of yeast comfortably familiar. Clara's face was creased in a frown, her lips thin and chapped. She pushed back her now greying hair and motioned for Lenka to sit.

This is about Baba Olga...

"A note about your grandmother has just arrived." She waved a hand in the direction of Lenka's father, who had gone back into the yard. "You and I will go to see her alone and at once. Baba Olga is close by – at the Mooswald crossroads."

"She is here? I thought you said she was in Romania?" The vision – the circle of wagons in the woods – flashed before her.

"I heard two weeks ago that her condition was deteriorating, but it says here the family have been travelling for over a week already. I did not know her end was so close, but it seems the situation is now very urgent. I am ashamed. I thought we could go there, that there was time..." She pressed a handkerchief to her face and dabbed her eyes. "That she has had to come to us, when in such pain, it is shameful."

Lenka saw her then – the old woman lying in bed with both hands stretched high in the air, calling out, pleading, for the pain to be over: *Make it stop! I end this...I end this!*

"No, I have the strongest feeling I must not go."

Clara looked up sharply. "How dare you! This is your grandmother, and you will come with me, you selfish girl. Lenka, you have to grow up and take responsibility now – you are sixteen, not a petulant child. Your father is exhausted, and I cannot and will not go alone. Now pack and be ready in one hour."

Profound dread took hold of her – a feeling of dirt

flushing down a drain and taking her with it, down and down and down into a swirling abyss. "How long will it take to get there, to Mooswald?"

"If we take both horses and the trap, we should arrive before nightfall."

The journey ahead appeared to her immediately – a dirt track cutting through a hilly ravine dense with spruce trees that creaked and groaned in the wind. Streams trickled down from the mountains, tinkling over the stones, but apart from that and the thudding of hooves on the earth, it was eerily quiet, devoid of life. Those woods, they were a place of death… The horses were nervous, and she saw herself gripping the sides of the cart.

"Why did they stop there, in that particular place?"

Clara had stood up and begun to knead the bread for baking. "The note says her time has come and they can go no further; she is in terrible pain. Hurry now – go and tell your father we need the horses and trap. We have much to prepare and a long way to go."

Her mother refused to meet her questioning stare and clearly brooked no opposition.

There was something here that felt ominous, but further clarity did not come. Occasionally, the old lady's face appeared in her third eye, but there was something elusive, too, as shifting as the mountain mists – information well-guarded and far beyond the threshold of her mind.

And so she went outside to speak to her father about the horses, then upstairs to pack. It would be best to get this over with. What choice was there? Perhaps it would not be so bad? But the weak morning sun seemed to hide and darken, and the alpine wind blew icily off the mountains. Steadily she folded her clothes.

She could not have known that once the true nature of the legacy was revealed, her life would be shattered beyond all comprehension and nothing would ever be the same again.

Or that Baba Olga's death was nothing she could have mentally prepared for, not in a million nightmares.

***

CHAPTER FOURTEEN

The journey through the forest ravine was exactly as foreseen, but far colder. The storm had brought with it a freezing wind that permeated clothing and slipped under the skin. It ran in ice-cold rivers through their veins despite the blankets and furs, rendering their hands and feet numb, teeth chattering and faces frozen. It was with relief when they entered the shelter of the woods.

Clara took the reins and kept the horses at a brisk trot for as long as possible until the narrow track became too wet, rocky and steep. The horses picked and stumbled their way uphill. On either side the slopes were densely packed with spruce, the interior gloomy and grey. Overhead the wind soughed in the canopy, and angry clouds scudded across a charcoal sky. The trees shivered, and a high whistle blew down from the mountains, with the occasional crack of splintering wood resounding through the valley.

The horses shied and bucked at the slightest thing, ears pricked, sweat glistening on their shanks. Lenka cast a sidelong glance at her mother, at the set of her jaw and the feverish expression in her steely eyes as she gripped the reins.

"Come on, keep going, it is just a fallen tree. Come

on!"

The urgency in her voice stabbed at Lenka's stomach. Why was she so frantic? Something here was badly amiss, a feeling she could not place except this was a trip she did not want to make and a destination she did not want to reach. The forest appeared to be getting darker, the path narrower, the sides of the ravine steeper. And confusion over Oskar still weighed heavily on her mind. Who was he? Or what? Of course, magic did exist in elemental form. She had experimented with this herself, projecting images into the minds of others. A friend in the village, Erika, had sworn she had seen Lenka standing outside her window one evening, when all the time Lenka had been in bed imagining that she was there, laughing.

"What was I doing in this dream of yours?" she'd asked Erika with a puzzled look on her face, trying not to smile with her knowledge and power.

"Laughing," said Erika. "Just laughing."

But the thing was, she had touched and talked to this boy, had known him and felt him inside her. Had she fallen in love with a ghost? Perhaps his spirit had not left this earth and still lingered in the home he loved? Did he not know he was dead? One thing for sure, her love was real and it hurt. It hurt so badly it was blinding; it kicked in the gut as powerfully as a horse and had sent her half insane. How could a ghost do that? How?

The journey was long and arduous, yet far from wishing to speed up their arrival, the feeling of dread within her was mounting. It sat like a rock in her heart, weighing heavier with every lurch forwards of the cart. Eventually, the incline levelled off, the path opened up to reveal a plateau ahead, and the oppressive overhanging rocks and trees were left behind. But the relief was short-lived. The flat grasslands ahead were open to the full force of the wind and rain. Her mother cracked the whip, and the horses galloped flat out.

Closer and closer to the destination, Lenka gripped the sides of the cart, swallowing the onslaught of the rain as it battered them from all sides. Over and over, her mother whipped the horses on.

"Mutter, slow down. The horses are tired."

Clara had tied her headscarf tightly around the ears and either pretended not to hear or refused to.

"I'm tired as well. We should rest when we get to Mooswald." She tucked her hands inside her cloak. The boards of the cart were rough, and every bone was jolted and bruised. "Please can we stop for something to eat?"

"Soon."

"Mutter!" It had been six hours. "I am hungry, starving."

"No time, we have to hurry." She cracked the whip again until, finally, a thick copse appeared in a blur of rain on the horizon.

"There!" Clara shouted, her face set in grim determination. "Mooswald!"

These woods were infamous. No one ever entered them after dusk or before dawn. Everyone knew they were haunted by those who worshipped Saturn and Hecate, offering blood sacrifices and screams of terror in return for earthly desires. Within living memory, satanic witches had been dragged here and burned alive by local mobs – and many a criminal, or one deemed criminally insane, had been hanged from its branches.

They entered the woods through an arch of holly, and

immediately both the wind and the temperature dropped. The horses' breath steamed on the air, their great shoulders sagging with fatigue. Although calm within the trees, a deep chill emanated from the green-hued interior, a twisted, gnarled wonderland of haunting beauty. Every branch was coated in emerald moss, the lifeless, spiked tentacles fruitless and leafless. It dripped like a cavern, with water from hidden streams that would soon be frozen. But not a single sound of life came from within. Here, there were no owls, prowling foxes, or howling wolves. Occasionally a wolf's call came from a distant mountain, but as soon as the trees closed behind them, it was as silent as a church crypt.

"Can we rest now?"

"Not here," said her mother, passing over a package of bread and cheese as they slowed to a trot. "Eat something if you want."

The horses, however, baulked at going any further into the woods, sidestepping and putting down their heads.

Clara cracked the whip and yanked the reins. "Come on! What is the matter with you?"

Lenka put a piece of bread into her mouth. The animals were shivering, sweat drying on their coats in ripples. "Enough," she said. "Stop a minute. Let me down, and I will walk with them."

Jumping off the cart, she caught the older horse's bridle, stroked his neck and coaxed him on. The younger one followed the elder's lead, and together they walked into Mooswald towards the notorious crossroads, where legend had it scores of witches had been buried with stakes driven through their decapitated bodies, and criminals left hanging. Why in hell's name had they brought her grandmother to die in a place like this?

***

CHAPTER FIFTEEN

Baba Olga's camp was pitched at the crossroads in a small clearing. Here, a level piece of grass by a fast stream had been settled on by a dozen wagons and carts, exactly as foreseen. Unhooking the cart, Lenka led the two horses over to the stream for a drink before securing them to a tree in case they bolted. They shied at the shadows, eyes wide as darkness descended.

"Don't be afraid," she whispered. "We will go home tomorrow."

But the horses, she knew, were right to be afraid. The place had been bled of human spirit. It brooded, dank and lifeless, the mossy trees so gnarled and warped they resembled otherworldly creatures. Long green twigs poked out like fingers, and whorls on the trunks resembled faces. Some bent crookedly away or into each other as if one or other was dominant. Stare long enough, she thought, and you could see people in those trees. Menacing people…

A shout made her jump. "Lenka!"

Her mother was beckoning. Throwing blankets over the horses, she left them under the trees and walked towards the candlelit wagon. Behind, the blackness of night descended with finality, a door slamming shut. A prison door. Her stomach clenched in a fist of iron.

Whatever was coming wasn't good, and there was no way back, no way out.

Inside, a group of old women huddled together in long black robes, scarves covering their hair. On first impression they resembled gypsies who lived a hard, outdoor life. On closer inspection they were nothing like them. Ancient rather than simply old and wrinkled, their skins were of a dark mustard hue and deeply etched with crisscross crevices, their eyes almost totally obscured by drooping lids. Sunken-mouthed and mostly toothless, all possessed unusually long fingers, which grasped at Lenka's flesh and pulled her inside. The dream from last night snagged and lodged, something off, something not quite human about them…and a chill passed through her. The hands and fingers digging into her arms were sharp as claws.

She found herself pushed towards the deathbed.

Baba Olga was clearly very near the end. The stench of smouldering herbs overlaying that of human waste, sepsis and disease hit the back of Lenka's throat, and she tried not to breathe too deeply. Her grandmother was delirious, murmuring and groaning, every now and again shouting, "Stop! No, please wait, not yet…not yet…"

The crone dabbing Baba Olga's forehead turned at Lenka's approach and immediately gripped her wrist, anchoring her to the spot. "You must take the gift now or she cannot leave this earth."

Instinctively, Lenka tried to step back, but the grip cranked tighter.

"Her body, look…" Peeling back the blankets, she revealed the dying woman's emaciated form. Behind, Lenka's mother gasped and clapped a hand to her mouth.

Of course, Lenka reminded herself, Olga was not a particularly old woman. The ones around her were, but Baba Olga could only be in her fifties. Yet she lay here cadaverous, the jaundiced skin puckered and withered, dark purple patches spreading underneath the surface as the tissues bled. Her ribs jutted sharply above the concave hollow of her stomach, tissue skin hanging from the white bones of stick limbs. Olga was a toothless, hairless, living skeleton.

"She is here, Olga!" the crone said, prodding the cadaverous woman. "Wake! She is here."

Baba Olga's mouth worked into a grimace, and her hands flew up in the way Lenka knew they would. Like a bird's wings, they flapped as if drawing the young girl to her on the air.

"Come closer," she croaked. "Closer! Let me see."

Pushed by several pairs of hands, Lenka stumbled onto her knees beside her grandmother, trying not to inhale the fetid breath. "I am sorry you have so much pain," she said, baulking at the sight of her close up. She had to get out of here really quickly, even if it meant bolting through the forest in pitch darkness.

Blindly Olga scrabbled at the air with claw hands. "Clara! Clara! It is your time. You must take your place. Please, do not let me suffer any longer. Take the gift or they will wait for me on the other side."

Lenka shook her head, confused. She turned around. "Mutter, she calls for you!"

Her mother had vanished.

Scanning the room, she tried to see beyond the small crowd, and a pang of alarm shot through her. The old crones were closing in. "Mutter! Mutter, she calls for you!"

Where was her mother?

"Clara, is this you?" Olga had clasped Lenka's hand in her own, pulling her close with surprising strength. "We must prepare at once. I cannot last much longer. You have seen what it has done to me, but you are stronger, you will do better than I. I feel the strength in this young hand."

Aghast, Lenka realised her grandmother was totally blind and had mistaken her for her mother, but the eyes...there was something about them... Mesmerised, steeling herself against the stench of decay, she leaned forwards to take a better look. Olga's eyes were tiny black glints hidden deep inside folds of reptilian skin...black glints, black glass...she peered closer and closer...black mirrors...

"*Heilige Mutter Gottes, bitt' für uns...*"

She leapt back. Her reflection! It was upside down!

In a flash, Olga's hand shot out and grabbed her wrist. Desperately she tried to wrench it free. "No!"

Her grandmother's grip had locked around her wrist in a handcuff. "If I do not pass the legacy to you, I will take this agony into eternity. They will torture me forever. Clara, it is your duty!"

"But I am not—" She tugged hard to get free, shouting over her shoulder. "Mutter! She calls for you, she is confused. She calls for you, not me. Why? Why does she think I am you?"

But the dying woman had begun to chant in a low voice, "Clara, my daughter, I give to you the servants of our Dark Lord."

A low humming broke out behind her, the old ones

swaying and murmuring in tongues.

She tried desperately to wrench free of the cast-iron grip, turning her head to seek out her mother…she had to be there…somewhere… where was she? But Olga yanked it back with such force it could have broken her jaw.

Then, thrusting a small poppet into Lenka's hand, she folded her fingers around her granddaughter's. "Take it. From me. To you."

The instant the transaction happened, the atmosphere changed – the crowd sank back in a hissing recoil, and Baba Olga's body began to fit violently. Her eyes rolled back, her neck jerked, her legs kicked, and then just as quickly as it had begun, the convulsions stopped. Her body slumped, and the life force, the breath from the old woman's lungs, exhaled in a long wolf's howl that echoed throughout the valley.

Then it was over, and the spent, crumpled body collapsed like a rag doll.

"All hail the Master! Lord of the Dark Sun!"

"All hail the Master!"

"All hail the Master!"

Hands reached down and pulled Lenka away. "We were just in time," said her mother. "She has gone."

Lenka turned around, holding out the poppet. "What is this doll? It is for you, I think, she wanted you. Where were you?"

"Ah, that is handed down from the very beginning. You must keep it safe always. There will be a celebration now. It is good. Very good."

Lenka disengaged her hand. "I must keep it safe? She thought I was you – it is for you, Mutter."

"No, she passed the legacy to you."

"But why would you be missed out?"

"I don't know, sometimes this is so. I explained all this."

"Take the poppet, Mutter. She called your name. She wanted it to be yours."

"My dear, it is too late. Whoever takes the gift takes the legacy."

The colour drained from Lenka's face. "What? I don't understand…"

The crone who had been tending Olga shouted, "Where is the girl? Come now, we must prepare you."

Lenka was still glaring at her mother, uncomprehending, stunned. "You said it had to be me – that the gift had missed you out. But she was blind and thought I was you. This was supposed to be you, wasn't it?"

Clara stared down at the deathbed. "You are stronger than I."

***

CHAPTER SIXTEEN

Lenka found herself gripping the poppet so tightly the hemp was cutting into the palms of her hand. Her own mother had tricked her into taking this terrible, horrible legacy.

"Come, child, drink with us," said one of the crones. The German she spoke was like nothing she'd ever heard before, heavily accented and antiquated. "You are tired, and your grandmother has passed. It is a difficult time for you."

The proffered drink, a greenish swill of tea, looked repulsive, and she averted her head despite having a throat as dry as parchment.

The woman smiled encouragingly. "It is a simple herbal tea, calming, good." Over her shoulder she snapped to one of the others, "Fetch food; this child is starving."

A cushion was brought over. She sat down, and a dish of thick yellow soup quickly followed. "Eat, drink, you will feel better, yes?"

None of it tasted nice, but she had to admit that afterwards, her throat was soothed and her stomach quieted.

"Now take off your cross," said the woman as another

reached to unclasp it from around her neck.

She held on to it. It was just a small silver cross given to her at school for winning a reading competition. "Why?"

"Take off the cross. The time has come."

We will meet again when the time comes…

The vision of Oskar came as a shock. Standing there in her third eye as clear as the day before – had it really only been twenty-four hours since they'd been together? – his warm eyes beamed love into hers, feathery eyelashes glinting with tiny beads of water as he waded out of the lake fresh from his morning swim. In a dream state she glided towards him…oh, so woozy and dreamy… On reaching his arms, he spun her around, nuzzling the nape of her neck while unhooking the chain.

Take this off, my beauty, my bride.

Smiling, she helped him remove the cross.

"Oskar?"

Now he turned her around to face him, taking her hands, pulling her down into the water.

"Come, come…"

Deeper and deeper they waded into the cool depths of the lake. A golden breeze rippled across the surface beneath swaying trees, dapples of sunlight warm on her face. In up to their necks, he put his arms around her and kissed her forehead.

"You must renounce God and Christ," he said.

"I do."

"You must renounce family—"

"I do."

"And the sun, the moon and the stars."

"I do, I do."

"Thrice you renounce." He folded her into his nakedness, pressing her against the hardness of him. Nuzzling her neck, he whispered, "You must repeat the words, 'I renounce God and Christ. I renounce my family, and I renounce the sun, the moon and the stars. I renounce all forms of light and follow the Dark Lord with all my heart and soul.'"

She shouted the words into the air high above them, relishing the echo around the valley.

"Again!"

Three times she renounced everything she had ever known and believed in, laughing, exultant, her arms around his neck.

"And now, my bride, we will be together always, in this world and beyond, just as I promised. You must sever all ties with your family and come with me."

"Oh, I definitely do. I never want to see my mother again. I hate my mother."

He threw back his head and laughed, showing the curve of his Adam's apple, the white of his teeth. "And you will slice the throat of the stolen calf, then drink its blood."

"Yes."

"All hail the Master!"

"All hail the Master!"

"All hail the Master!"

When she came out of the water, hand in hand with Oskar, she shook her long, wet hair in the balmy sunshine and triumphantly turned to face her new husband.

The smile died on her face.

The boy she loved was not there. Instead, a dark shadow chased along the deserted shore. And the trees no longer rustled gently but thrashed violently, the rippling water now rising in a froth of white horses.

"We meet again," a deep and distorted voice said. "As promised."

It was as if she had been slapped out of a trance. The chill night air bit into her skin. In the dark and the cold, she spun around. What the hell was this?

She looked down to find her hands splattered with blood, a spreading pool of it around her feet. She was standing in the centre of a circle marked out in the dirt, around the edge of which a masquerade of animal-headed heathens dressed in plain white gowns stood murmuring and swaying. The effect was hypnotic, the evening as black as the underworld, with no stars or moon to cast a single shadow. Within the circle a fire glowed, spitting with blood, fat, and bones.

She wiped a hand across her sticky mouth, noticing a discarded chalice on the ground. What trickery was this? How could her conscious mind have been stolen? How had time passed without her presence? It looked as if a rite had been carried out and blood tipped down her throat. All she had done was dream for a few seconds that she had bathed with a beautiful, handsome boy...*who was dead...*

Those around her began to chant more loudly now, the words gradually becoming distinguishable...*Nema Olam a son arebil des menoitatnet ni sacundi son en te...*

The words drilled into her head, cited over and over and over, numbing, monotonous, invasive.

Then ceased.

There was a lull. Into the silence a bell rang three times from the dark interior of the forest.

"All hail the Dark Lord!"
"All hail the Dark Lord!"
"All hail the Dark Lord!"

Out of the trees a form seemed to rise. She narrowed her eyes as the ring of worshippers fell to the floor facedown in silent homage, trying to work out who or what it was. The shape grew larger, drawing closer. Man or beast? This was a night terror, it had to be, not real, absolutely not real. But as he neared, her heart banged with a sickening lurch and fear consumed her. Her insides turned to liquid, and her mind repeatedly blanked out. She sank to her knees. Cloaked in furs, he was twice the size of the others, his face concealed by the head of a horned goat. And what he was carrying defied the last vestiges of her belief.

He placed the dead, naked body of her grandmother on the ground outside the circle. Standing over her, he then proceeded to remove the furs and lower himself onto the corpse before violating her. After which he severed her head with an axe.

It happened so quickly, her mind had only just comprehended what had happened when he plunged a knife into the old woman's heart and plucked it out like a plum from a pie.

At the sound of her gasp, his head turned. Then, still naked and masked, he walked over to where she stood, the heart held high on the tip of the blade.

"No! No!"

She fell backwards, shocked to find her ankles were tied, that the earth was rolling underneath in a tidal swell. *I've been drugged, bound, am drunk...*

Those who had fallen to the ground now woke and

began to crawl behind him on their bellies, hissing like snakes, long bony fingers reaching out to grab her arms and legs, pinning her down as the goat-headed man stood over her and forcibly stuffed the heart into her mouth. Powerful hands held her jaw fast, making sure there was no choice but to chew and swallow.

A deep bass voice echoed from within the goat's head mask. "Take and digest the magical power of blood from sorceress to sorceress."

The man's nakedness was appalling, the body scaly, the spike between his legs unnatural in shape and size.

He lowered himself onto her.

"No! No!"

She spat out the contents of her mouth, kicking and bucking. But dozens of pairs of wiry hands held her fast as, sitting astride her in a parody of the love she had made with Oskar, he tore off her clothing and slammed her body repeatedly into the dirt, grinding her into the stones. It scraped the skin off her back in sheets, and the pain ripping inside was that of a scorching iron straight from the fire. It was not normal, not normal, not normal at all…that was all she could think…as the light of her being began to eclipse and fade to grey. To nothing.

She surfaced to the sound of clapping. Blood poured out of her, streaming down her legs, the searing pain unbearable.

But the rape was over. One of the crones removed her sheep's head and shook out long grey hair. "Welcome, Lenka," she said, crouching beside her. She dipped a long, bony finger into the cup of Olga's blood and drew a sign on Lenka's forehead. "You are now a sorceress of the highest order. We will serve you always, until the end of your time."

The others took off their masks.

One of them her mother.

Clara raised a chalice. "To you!"

"Hail Lord of the Dark Sun!" cried the ancients.

"Hail Lord of the Dark Sun!" said her mother.

"Hail Lord of the Dark Sun!"

She glared at her mother, with tears streaming down her face.

Cries of 'All hail the Master!' rang through the woods while the discarded and mutilated body of her grandmother lay a matter of feet away, the skull now staring sightlessly at the woods.

"I hate you with every fibre of my soul for what you have done. I will never forgive you, not now, not in all eternity."

Clara shrugged. "Your grandmother knew what would happen. And I am sorry about the boy, about your poor heart. But it is what you will come to recognise as an opportunity presenting itself – the boy had died recently, and the element of him was easy to project into your mind. Don't worry, his image was just a channel, a means to an end."

"You did that?"

"I am sorry your heart was broken."

"This is evil – it's devil worship. And what they made me do and what the man in the goat's head did to me—"

Clara laughed. "Hate, shame and anger are all good, excellent conduits for the demonic... You must have no ego, nothing left to take pride in, do you not see? Come now, we must call up your new servants. Baba Olga is free of torment, but she has to be buried before the sun is up so the power is properly transferred."

"I will not use anything from such hellish servants. I want my life as it was."

"What – that of an ignorant peasant girl? Who prides herself on being the prettiest in the village? What use is that a few years down the line when you have many children and you are poor, living in the dirt? Human life is brief and useless – you are lied to by the church, so you live in fear, and enslaved by landowners, so you live in poverty. Whereas we are the old believers, of magic and other realms. We are free, and we have the kind of power they will never have. Do you not see who you are and what you have been given?"

"No. It is diabolical and sick. I don't want any of it."

"You have no choice. You are a demonic sorceress, and your task is to use the demons given to you in the name of the Dark Lord. It is the highest of honours."

She glanced to where the horses snorted and pawed at the ground under the trees. On the outskirts of the camp, they seemed so far away. Could she run, even now, and take the bareback gallop back to Wolfsheule? But after that where would she go? And what could she tell her father? For sure he would denounce whatever she said as evil lies.

"I do not think that would be wise," said Clara, noticing the direction in which she was looking. "Not after what you have drunk."

There was truth in that. Indeed, everything was fuzzy, the tiredness overwhelming. She sank to the floor.

"See, they are feasting now. The celebration begins, and it is all for you!"

Through the smoky haze, the revellers were gnawing on the flesh of sacrificed animals, masticating bleeding tissue with what few teeth they had. Cups of blood were passed around, from which they guzzled thirstily. And a group of black toads had been released for entertainment. These were scampering in all directions, some leaping into the fire. It seemed a game, to be quick enough to catch one and bite off its head.

She crumpled onto her side, drifting in and out of consciousness, vaguely aware of the beat of drums, a steady thump-thump-thump. Through her eyelashes she watched as robes were discarded and they began to writhe and gyrate in a macabre dance of seduction. The stench of burning flesh and fat was sickly, and the fire, the woods and the dancers loomed in and out of focus. The beat pounded into her head as the party began to whirl and spin. They were dancing themselves into a frenzy, whipping their own bodies with sticks until they bled. Faster and faster they spun around and around until, one by one, they fell to the floor, pawing at each other until the whole became a seething, moaning orgy.

She forced her eyes to see, unable to believe the spectacle of such ancient beings with emaciated bodies, their skin hanging in folds from the bones, committing such… With a stab of understanding, something became clear…they were not having sex at all. They were only simulating it, sucking and licking and gyrating but not actually having intercourse. Because they couldn't.

All the men had been mutilated. In the light of the flames, through the veil of smoke and burning oils, she realised their groins were scarred, deep hollows. Not a single male had genitals.

Except for the one who'd raped her. And he, whoever or whatever he was, had vanished.

***

CHAPTER SEVENTEEN

WOLFSHEULE

The journey home was utterly silent.

Lenka had been woken at dawn with only a blanket covering her naked, bloodied body, the previous night a blur of frenzied dancing, wailing and feasting.

Her head ached, cuts and bruises smarting with every fresh jolt of the cart. And whatever darkness had been invoked now travelled with her in a cloud, along with the strangest feeling of being observed. She pulled up her skirt and looked at the brand mark on the inside of her thigh. At what point had that happened? The sight triggered a vague recollection of a claw hand holding her still, of gritting her teeth, of searing pain. A cloth covered the spot, and she peeled it back. The sigil consisted of a circle, within it an inverted pentagram, and in the very centre, a black spot with what looked like pins sticking out of it – a child's drawing of a sun, but black.

"Don't touch it," her mother said. "Or it will become septic. Keep it dry."

"You are not my mother anymore."

Their silence continued as the cart rocked from side to side along the narrow forest track. Water dripped from the trees and trickled down the steep slopes on either side.

It seemed to Lenka that Mooswald was not as menacing as it had been the night before. Or perhaps her fear had gone? What did she care anymore? Nothing could be worse than last night. Nothing. She sat swaying in the cart, seething with shock, rage and hatred.

Grandma Olga's funeral had been both swift and brutal. At midnight, after the ceremony, when Lenka had lain by the fire drifting in and out of a drugged and exhausted stupor, her grandmother's body was taken to the crossroads. It had been hard to see what was happening – the men were working quickly and in total darkness, the flames from the dying fire picking out shadowy, robed figures.

The most disturbing part had been the sound of a saw cutting through bone. Had Olga not been butchered and violated enough? Something was then hammered, followed by the solid, dismal echo of grave-digging – spades slicing through soil and the cold finality of a lid clamping shut.

"They had to do it," her mother explained as they packed up the cart. "Come on, don't dwell. We must set back."

"Saw her into bits?"

"A sorceress cannot find her way back to earth. For that reason, she must be decapitated and her head buried deep in the forest, separate from the body. The limbs must then be severed and the heels cut and stuffed with hog hair. It is the way. And an aspen stake is hammered through the chest. Is that what you wanted to know? That is what we do or her body could be used."

"Used?"

"By the demons that remain attached. Or anyone who

raises her spirit after she has gone, by means of necromancy."

"And one day that will be my fate, too?"

"Yes, of course."

After they loaded the cart and began the journey home, a great gulf of silence settled between them, broken only with the exchange about the sigil. And it was not until they were on the final leg of the journey, after many hours, that Lenka could bring herself to ask the questions aching inside. In less than an hour, they would arrive back in Wolfsheule.

"I did not see any demons at the ceremony," she said. "Was that not the point of the thing – to hand over these unseen creatures? Well, I can tell you – there was nothing."

"What did you expect to see?"

She shrugged. Her jaw was clenched so hard her teeth were grinding; every sinew in her face was tight and every muscle tense. "I don't know," she snapped. "Devils with red eyes—"

"Ha! All the fearful images fed to you by your Sunday school teacher? Images are so powerful – you should learn this trick quickly, Lenka."

She turned away to hide the loathing contorting her features. "So what did you see, then, Mutter? The demons were summoned, so what did you see?"

"Nothing. But I am not the sorceress. I have some small gifts but not the brilliance, the vibration you possess. I would say that particular place held a great deal of sadness, pain and anger. The blackness will never lift from there – throats cut, witches hanged, the soil drenched in blood, terrible hatred and fear trapped within its confines – such sickness, a place of death. But that is as far as I go. I stop at the door, at the threshold of being able to see further than earthbound spirits. My limits are thought transfer and simple spells. Simple magic. The demons are not interested in my kind of energy. They are far more interested in yours."

"Yet I saw only shadows."

"There were no shadows. There was no moon or stars, no torches or light. Beyond the fire there was nothing but pitch black. So think harder about what you saw."

How she hated her teacher. It was painful even talking to her. "I saw the ring of ancients, the fire—"

"And beyond? Beyond the circle?"

"All black. I could not even see the trees or the horses."

She cast her mind back. There had been more than that, though. Not shadows but shapes far darker than the blackness of night. They had risen en masse and moved closer in a dense, suffocating cloud – one that now surrounded her.

"Try to see. Try harder."

"The air was full of smoke, everything distorted and hazy. But…" She forced herself to remember in detail, to see the unseeable and think the unthinkable. The blackness had come out of those woods and engulfed everything. Drugged and exhausted, she'd floated in and out of dreams, in an infinite space. There'd been sounds like wooden beams groaning in the wind, barking shouts and screeching metal on metal…deep, distorted words that remained unformed…and, yes, he had been with her since then, emerged out of that!

"Come on, Lenka – images? Thoughts? Speak what is coming to you!"

The words burst out: "I think a man came to me. I think he is here inside my mind...very dark brown eyes, glinting eyes, long legs with one crossed over the other...a glass of liquor, golden liquor...I think some kind of college or school—"

It would be, she thought for the briefest moment, easy to dismiss this as madness, to say she had just made that up, although why or how she could not say. The man, though, oh yes, he had come to her on that blackest of clouds.

"When we get home, I will be discussing with your father an idea I have. I think it is a good idea for you to join your uncle in Ingolstadt as soon as possible. You will like it there, I think."

As Wolfsheule came into sight, her heart tugged at the golden memory of a lost life. It all seemed so long ago, but that life was now over, and besides – the company of this woman who had betrayed her so badly was unendurable. It did not interest her enough to ask how her mother was so ready with these plans for Ingolstadt in Germany. The ties with her were severed, and it no longer mattered.

"Yes, I think I will. When can I go?"

"I will tell your father you need better education and discipline. There is no one more suited to that task than his brother. He will not object. You must understand, Lenka, that the world will be very different to you from now on. Few people can see other realms, let alone accept their existence, but you now know there is something more. Those who do not know this and cannot see it are called 'Mundanes'."

"Mundanes?"

"They accept only their own perceptions of the world. They work, rest, eat, have families, chat and pass the time...never knowing what pawns they are. In fact, they are also spirits and have far greater power than they know, but most, well, they have to survive and thus will never push beyond the barrier of what they are told. Your father is one – mundane to the end of his fingertips. And what a Mundane does when he is threatened or does not understand something is to get angry. Ah, the irony. A good Christian, and yet he thinks nothing of beating his wife and daughter should they make him fearful. So you see what you are up against? Take this from me if nothing else – never speak of who you are or what you know. Never. Or you will be destroyed. Look around you, see all the hundreds of graves for women they called witches but probably were not. That is the level of fear we are talking about."

"I wish I were a Mundane. It is easier."
"Yes, it is. But you are not." Clara took a deep breath and slowed the horses on the downward slope into Wolfsheule. "Lenka, we are almost home, and you must take heed. Your father and I will make arrangements for you to travel. Until that time, we must keep him under the illusion that you are a girl in need of tutoring and refinement. This is how we will get you out and not only save your life but fulfil your purpose. Keep your eyes down, and do not defy him or incite his anger. Soon you will be in the town, and your future path will be laid before you. After this, you will not see me again."

Lenka blinked back the tears.

"Once in Ingolstadt, you will be introduced to the person who will take you to the next level, and you should accept his invitation. Do not be afraid. Our family has had this gift for centuries, and we must take care of it. Only remember, you must pass it on before you leave this mortal world or it will go with you into the afterlife."

Each word her mother uttered was the hammering of a nail into her coffin. So it was all decided, it seemed… Yet what was the point in railing against it? When deep in her bones she knew it to be true, that all would transpire precisely as her mother said?

At the sound of horses clattering into the yard, her father appeared, and as clear as the sparkles of dew on grass, she saw how he would walk over and grab the bridle to take them into the stables. Never in her life had she felt so alone or so frightened. What would become of her? How did her mother know about this man who would take her to the next level? What next level?

And what would happen if she refused to do any of this?

As if in answer to the question, a memory surfaced suddenly of her grandmother's body, of the jaundiced, emaciated concave of her stomach and the skin that rose over her abdomen like an opaque egg covered with a spider's web of purple veins. She had been lying in a pool of her own soiled blood, her fingers black and gangrenous, her skeletal body oozing with sores.

Get out of my head!

In response the image expanded, becoming ever more gruesomely detailed, accompanied now by the stench of decomposing flesh and human waste, of stale breath and disease, death and infection. Lenka's inverted reflection stared out of Baba Olga's deep, black eyes, and she tried not to gag.

"Lenka, are you sick?" her father said, lifting her down from the cart.

She ran for the back door, aware of them both watching.

"She was given strong wine at the funeral," her mother said. "She will be fine, don't worry."

"Strong wine?"

Behind Lenka a small disagreement erupted. She filled a cup with water from the jug on the kitchen table and drank deeply. Aware, when she had finished, of a song trilling in her ear. She swung around to find the source. Was there a child in here?

But the house stood empty, and her parents were still in the yard. So who…?

The high, tinkling voice of a small child was clearly singing an old German folksong:

Muss i' denn,
Muss i' denn,
Zum Städtele hinaus,
Städtele hinaus,
Und du, mein Schatz, bleibst hier.

The voice stopped. Replaced now by another – this one a deep male voice, low, echoing and distorted, the same voice that had mocked her in the nightmare about Oskar.

Wenn i' komm,
Wenn i' komm,
Wenn i' wieder, wieder komm,
Wieder, wieder komm…

She stood riveted to the spot. The songster was standing right by her ear, but she was alone. Her eyes bore into thin air. Who was here? Could they see her?

A shudder ran through her to the core, the acknowledgement sharp that this was real and no longer a fun thing to have – all notions of it being a glittering intuition or a romantic notion obliterated.

A child's peal of giggles rang around the kitchen, and a quick, cold breeze blew against her face.

Outside, although barely dusk, the evening dipped suddenly to night, the soft greys of moments ago snuffed to black. And with a stab to the heart, she knew without doubt that the man inside her head would become real very soon.

***

CHAPTER EIGHTEEN

INGOLSTADT, GERMANY

The preparations took less than a month.

At the end of October, Lenka was lying on the bed in her uncle's spare room, wondering if the whole sorceress initiation had been a dream. Had that or the time with Oskar ever happened? What was real anymore? Nothing. The only reminder she wasn't completely insane was the brand mark on her wrist. She turned onto her side. This place was horrible, and she was not going to enjoy it at all. A week here was already a week too long. The year was tipping into late autumn, steely clouds spitting rain onto cobbled streets and pavements. Soon there would be snow.

She shivered. Never before had she felt so ill. Her stomach convulsed in sweat-inducing waves, and her head thudded with the bone ache of concussion. Her mother had always tended to her when sick, with soothing potions and words of comfort – the mother she no longer knew. Now alone, she lay watching the shadows of dusk crawl across the walls, a chill creeping under her skin.

The house was a three-storey townhouse in the centre of Ingolstadt, near the university. Opposite was the church, and interspersed between similar-looking houses were shops of every description – butchers, grocers, bakeries, haberdasheries and ironmongers. There was a shop that sold only hats and one that made boots. On the corner stood a grand banking house, and many cafés lined the streets. Aunt Heide had bought Lenka new clothing fit for town. Although these things were not to her liking, there was little she could say without sounding ungracious. But the gown was drab, long and grey with a plain shawl, the boots stout. And her hair had been braided into coils that sat atop her ears, a severe style pulled tightly back from the face. It did not make her look attractive; it made her look like a ridiculous schoolgirl.

She lay now with her flame hair fanning out across the pillow, gazing at the poppet given to her by Baba Olga. Strange thing. She'd forgotten about it until arriving here. Completely forgotten about it. In fact, it was only when unpacking her case that it had reappeared – discovered on top of the neatly folded blouses – presumably placed there by her mother. Oddly, though, it was comforting. And thus, she slipped it inside her pillowcase – a possession purely her own, something to hold on to like life itself.

The house here was soulless, a hollow shell that was absolutely silent apart from the ticking grandfather clock in the hall downstairs. Talking was forbidden at mealtimes, which were taken in the formal dining room at the back of the house; the room was bare of all adornments, with any kind of idolatry – as Uncle Guido described ornaments and pictures – banned. All was sparse, from the stone floors to the cold grates, the polished, dark oak furniture to the starched bedsheets.

And each evening, as was his habit, Uncle Guido recited a long prayer of thanks to the Lord, after which she and her aunt must wait until he'd piled his plate with food. Only when he had begun to eat were they then permitted to share what was left. The first time this happened, it was annoying. The second, and each subsequent day, her irritation grew. He chewed noisily, tongue flicking out to lick his lower lip after each mouthful. His lips, red and moist, were as startling as a campfire in the woods, his gingery facial hair tinged yellow around the mouth from smoking a pipe. She noted with distaste the globular particles of unknown substances lurking in the wiry coils of his beard. Of particular repulsiveness were his ears – protruding and large, the lugs full of curly, pubic-looking hairs and yellow wax. Guido was tall and angular, all knock-knees and pointed elbows, in contrast to her father, who was shorter but more muscular. And where her father was tanned with sandy hair and warm eyes, Guido's complexion was the colour of limestone, his eyes as warm as flint.

She would be starting lessons at the university tomorrow, he stated that evening, with Herr Blum. Well respected, Herr Blum specialised in teaching the English language as well as French, and it was a great privilege for her to be taught by him. She should be extremely grateful.

"Thank you, Uncle, I am looking forward to it."

"Your mother insisted on this particular tutor. She must indeed have saved hard; I am sure he is not cheap." He was making a show of cutting up the *Schweineschnitzel*, popping it into his mouth, then dabbing at the corners with a napkin, all the while those flint eyes darting from Aunt Heide to herself. "Hmm? What do you say, Lenka?"

Aunt Heide kept her eyes downcast. It was rare for her to say anything at all, except to sigh or remark on the weather. *Her head is made of ash*, Lenka thought. *She hates him so much she's on the edge of combusting. She cleans and cooks and sews and shops. She washes and scrubs, goes to church and talks to others as much as she can in an effort to avoid him and stay sane. And at night she wears a long nightdress tightly buttoned, keeps her legs firmly pressed together and rolls away from him in a bed that pits in the middle... But no...I see...ah, he does not want her anymore... Sometimes he grabs and squeezes one of her breasts to remind her he can do so, but she hates it, the feel of those bony fingers mauling her. And when she is alone, she cries...*

She made the mistake of looking up in response to his question. Uncle Guido's penetrating stare locked with hers, and for an uncomfortable moment she flailed around before looking down again.

"What is wrong with your eye?" he asked.

All week she had kept her head down, spoken meekly and done what was asked. Waiting. Just waiting. For the true purpose to be revealed. Her parents had said she would go to private tutorials in the evening and during the day was to help Aunt Heide with the chores. Her aunt and uncle, childless, were both busy with the church, and Guido worked at the local orphanage as a Bible master. They would welcome the chance to get to know their niece, her mother had said, and she was sure Heide would be grateful for the domestic help. That was fine, well, this would not be for long…but here Uncle Guido was staring and staring; there was something about him so irksome, so detestable. And what was this about her eye? As far as she was aware, there was nothing wrong with her eyes. She had good eyes, steady and grey, perfect sight.

"I do not know what you refer to, Uncle."

He made a little jabbing motion with his fork, dripping gravy onto the pristine white tablecloth. "There is something wrong with your eye. You are a little blind in one, are you not?"

It had been a mistake to look back at him like that. He was riled. Resentment seemed to rise in this man at the slightest provocation, a surge of temper he could not easily control. He preached about Christ, but he was about as Christian as Baba Olga. And it almost cost her. She should hide her knowledge better because he had seen something in her that made him fearful, something he very much needed to hide.

A good Christian, and yet he thinks nothing of beating his wife and daughter should they make him fearful…

Recovering quickly, she stabbed a piece of pork.

Uncle Guido badly needed to hide that true nature of his. He would not want anyone looking into his soul and seeing what was there. Oh, how right he was to be defensive and fearful. She tried not to flinch at the pictures being shown to her, one after the other in a cinematic reel… There was a small recess inside the church, which was set apart for Bible classes. With the swish of a moss-green curtain, this small room was utterly private, an area for a child to be comforted or to speak in confidence. And it was here that he stroked the parts of them that he should not. Here where he touched the nape of their necks while they read passages from the New Testament, admiring their plump, unblemished skin, cherubic mouths and small stout chests.

The boys were trusting, learning to read and trying to please. While he watched, licking his moist red lips and telling them to come to him with their secrets, their dreams, their fears and their worries. He was their teacher and friend, the one to trust in a world where they had no parents to turn to and the teachers were strict – telling them all this as he began to touch a little more and sit a little closer.

Do not push my hand away. It is a caring thing to do, to stroke a friend, to comfort them.

No, no, I don't like it, please, don't...please...stop...

"Lenka!" Uncle Guido's voice snapped her out of the vision. "I asked you a question." He was chewing methodically, his eyes trained on her face.

Every nerve ending popped as if there was no barrier between them, as if she had no skin, no protection. Her fingers shook. "I am not aware of there being anything wrong with my eye, Uncle."

"Then you should have it looked at. I will make arrangements for you to see a specialist, for spectacles to be fitted."

Spectacles? So she was to be dressed like a nun, hair braided into two ridiculous coils, and now spectacles, too? Not two weeks ago, she had been running free, barefoot in a pretty dress of white cotton, her red hair streaming behind her in the sun. The thought was a kick in the gut. He was deliberately deconstructing her identity. Look at Heide...there was nothing of her true self left...just ash...a head of ash...

"Thank you, Uncle, but I can see perfectly well. There is no need for all this trouble to be taken."

"Do not argue with me, Lenka. It is my responsibility that you are well cared for while you are here. And as such, we will have you examined. Heide, will you make sure to organise this? I do not want to send her back to Wolfsheule blind."

How had she survived the rest of that meal without stabbing him with a fork? Even so, she lay on the bed worrying about it. What could he have meant about her eye? As far as she was aware, there was nothing whatsoever wrong with it.

She wandered over to the dresser. This room overlooked the street, and the dresser mirror faced into the room. With the light behind it, her reflection was shady, but the moon shone over the top, directly into her eyes. She stared hard. No, there was nothing wrong, really nothing.

Puzzled, she picked up a hairbrush and began the nightly routine of one hundred strokes, the silky feeling pleasurable, as was the sight of her own beauty in the mirror. In the high-necked white nightdress and braids, she felt like a child, but now with the buttons undone and her hair shimmering under the moonlight, she was once again a woman. She *was* a woman. Illusion or not, she had known what it felt like to lie with a man and to feel love, had encouraged it, wanted, desired…demanded more…

Leaning into the mirror, she examined her face, the cut of the high cheekbones, the sharp angle of the jaw, the fullness of her lips. Then back to the eyes. Deep grey, there was a ring around the pupils, flecked with gold.

First she focused on the left eye. The pupil dilated a little, but there was no sign of a defect, nothing different at all. Now she focused on the right one, the eye he had intimated had something wrong with it. No, nothing. She stared and stared until it seemed she would go mad...

Then suddenly there *was* something – a tiny flicker in the pupil. Alarmed, she leaned closer and closer towards the mirror, watching intently. There! She had not been wrong. And look there... it came again...a shape shifting inside the pupil. Instead of it dilating or constricting in the normal way, it looked as if there was something inside it. Inside of her! Her heart squeezed, and a fresh wave of sweat broke out.

Reeling back, she stared aghast.

At that moment the moon, which had been shining almost as brightly as the sun, was eclipsed by a mass of cloud, plunging the room into darkness. The candle by the bed flattened as if in a high wind, despite the stillness of the room, and she caught her breath. Swinging round, she stared into the unlit room, determined to face this down, to defy the fear even though her heart was hammering. *Face this, face it!*

Something was coming...

There can be no shadows if there is no light, her mother had said. *Look again...what do you see?*

There were no shadows on the walls now. No light at all.

Then into her mind, clear and sharp, came the face of her bearded uncle chewing the cud. She frowned and banished the thought. Then, whoosh, she was inside his head, experiencing the rush he had cornering a tearful child, as he thrust himself on him, feeding off the terror and the shame, pulling down the young boy's shorts while the child sobbed with shame…

Her mind blacked with hatred. And in that instant, everything in her stomach vaulted up to her mouth. Flying over to the bed, she pulled out the chamber pot and projectile vomited, heaving until there was nothing left but acid before slumping to the floor in a cold sweat. Visions and sickness. This was taking hold exactly as her mother had forecast. Waves of colic gripped her intestines, and bile rose in her throat. Head pounding, she reached for a handkerchief and dabbed at her face, swiping away the tears.

Give us work…give us work…

Moonlight now streamed once more into the room, and this time there were visible movements from within the furniture-shaped shadows. They rose like oil slicks, oozing over the walls and across the floor like giant garden slugs.

Lenka, give us work… Lenka… Lenka…

She sank onto the bed, whimpering as the slithers congealed around her feet in a tar-black pool… Perhaps she was mad after all?

Give us work…give us work…

Wave after wave of sickly colic seized her stomach, and a feverish damp glistened on her skin. Shivering, she slapped her arm as something stung, sharp as a red-hot thumbtack. A fiery pox mark had appeared, followed by another and another. Tears smarted behind her eyes.

Lenka, Lenka, I can take all of this away from you…

"I don't want this. I don't want it."

I am all about you, am part of you already or else how would I know your thoughts – your most intimate thoughts?

Into her mind flashed the explosively passionate moments with Oskar, and despite her fear and her pain, heat rose inside, flaming her cheeks.

We are inseparable, you and I. Do you know how long I have been with you? For a thousand years or more… I can take away all your grief, terror and pain…all you have to do is say yes!

An almighty contraction gripped her intestines; nerve pain screamed down one side of her head. It was getting worse – a dozen more pox marks had broken out all over her arms…

"Yes! I will give you work," she gasped, panicking. "Let Uncle Guido suffer instead of me if that is what you are saying…but please, make this fever stop!"

Immediately the pain siphoned away, the marks vanished and the black shapes receded in a hiss of recoil.

"Show me, then," she whispered. "Show me what to do. I am ready."

***

CHAPTER NINETEEN

Uncle Guido and Aunt Heide were still downstairs. Lenka inched open the bedroom door and peered down the corridor to their bedroom. Every board in this house creaked. How to get there without being heard?

She took a deep breath, deciding to trust that all would be well, and stepped out onto the landing. It was a chilly evening, and the wind gusted around the house, rafters groaning, the sound of Aunt Heide clattering plates in the kitchen below. Where was he, though? Smoking a pipe in the study? Yes, that was where he was.

She took another step. Then another and another. This had to be quick. To be caught in their bedroom, or even outside the door, would without doubt elicit severe punishment. Aunt Heide would do nothing to save her, either. The woman was weak. It was imperative to be cunning, to anticipate every move, every outcome.

Stealthily she pushed open their bedroom door and peered inside. Pearly moonlight streaked across a brass bed covered with starch-white sheets exactly as pictured. A dark oak dresser and chest of drawers stood against the far wall by an inset closet. Her glance flicked to the dressing table. Aunt Heide's hairbrush lay on a silver tray along with a pot of cream and a tortoiseshell hand mirror, but there was nothing of his. What about a robe or coat? Ah, of course – darting over to the bed, she pulled back the top sheet. His nightcap! And inside it were several gingery hairs. At the sound of a voice, she curled them into her palm and exited as swiftly as she'd entered, scooting back across the landing without a single board making a creak.

Back in her own room, she rooted for a piece of writing paper and sat at the small desk with the excuse of writing home should she be disturbed. Conscious now of a dual life, of a silky, cunning presence streaming through her veins, she found herself waiting for a response, pen poised.

Show me! Show me!

Nothing came but a vague and hazy notion that words of intent should be scrawled onto the paper and then burned. But what could she say to make this work?

She frowned, waiting, trying hard to think of the right words. But they would not come. Frowning, she dipped the nib into the inkwell and began to doodle… As before when the floorboards were bound to creak, she had trusted and they had not. She must trust again and let the one inside channel through. Doodle after doodle…until her thoughts began to blur at the edges…and her hand, as if it were no longer her own, picked up a fresh sheet of paper and began to wrap the hairs from Guido's nightcap into its folds.

Then, and only then, did the pen begin to scrawl. And as she inscribed her uncle's name on the packet of hairs, his image burned brightly, searing onto her mind. Every working of his jaw as he chewed and chewed, every flick of his tongue over those wet red lips, and every lascivious gaze falling onto the cherubic body of an innocent child ramped up the loathing.

Words in a tongue not her own fell from her lips: "*Nema Olam a son arebil des menoitatnet ni sacundi son en te. Sirtson subiotibed sumittimid son te tucis, artson atibed sibon ettimid te. Eidoh sibon…*"

Onto the small envelope, under his name she drew a circle, filled it with an inverted pentagram, and painted in the very centre a black sun with rays around it, all the while picturing him in great detail, seeing the demons gathering around him, imagining the shudders as he sat downstairs in the study, smoking his pipe, aware now of a cold breeze on the back of his neck. With the package now complete, she took a hairpin and repeatedly stabbed it, picturing Guido doubling over with pain. Every stick of the pin was dealt with conviction and intent. "As this hair so receives blows and pain, so may its master receive blows and pain."

When the working was done, she held it to the flame. "This is my Will!"

Within seconds of finishing, footsteps creaked rapidly along the floorboards on the landing. A rap came at the door, and Guido walked straight in without asking. He sniffed the air. "Something is burning?"

Smiling inside, Lenka languidly glanced over her shoulder. "Forgive me, Uncle, I was working so hard on a letter to my parents, I had not noticed. I must have scorched my sleeve on the candle."

"You should be more careful, Lenka. How can we trust you if you are careless in such matters? It is time for you to put out your light and go to sleep."

"Yes, goodnight, Uncle."

He closed the door. "Goodnight."

He had been checking on her. He had some inkling she was not as pious and demure as he would like. No, there was something rebellious and dangerous about his niece, and it unsettled him. She smiled more widely now, feeling well – tingling, in fact, with good health.

So now we will see, she thought, *if I really am a sorceress.*

***

CHAPTER TWENTY

The following evening, Aunt Heide walked Lenka to the university, not ten minutes from where they lived. It had gained a reputation of considerable standing, and rumour had it great personages attended. She had heard royalty at one time.

"I do not understand how your mother acquired this place for you," Aunt Heide went on. "It is for the most elite, and here are you – just a village girl."

Lenka shrugged. She did not know either.

"Your parents, they must have put together good money for their only child – money that should have been used for a wedding. I do not know what they are thinking."

"Yes, Aunt Heide. I do not know either, I must say."

On arriving at the gates, Heide kissed her on one cheek in an uncharacteristic display of affection. "Nevertheless, I wish you good luck in your studies. Perhaps your mother wishes you to become a teacher in the village?"

"I think so," Lenka nodded, keeping her eyes averted. "I am sure you are right."

"Well, then. I shall expect you home by nine o'clock. Have someone walk you to the door. You should not be out alone."

Aunt Heide watched until Lenka had walked all the way down the drive to the university building, her footsteps echoing dully on the rain-spattered stones. Ahead, an arched doorway had been left ajar, and seized by a flutter of excitement, she stepped eagerly over the threshold, forgetting to turn and wave.

The corridor, lit by an oil lamp on a small hall table, was oak panelled and lined with portraits of alumni. From a room at the back came a murmur of voices, and tentatively now, she headed in that direction. Expecting it to be full of students, she peered shyly around the door. In fact, there were only two people in there: a tall dark-haired man, slightly stooped, who had his back to her, and a younger man with whom he was engaged in avid conversation. She caught the gist of it in the few seconds before the dark-haired man swung around and saw her.

"Yes, yes, the Kriyasakh has produced external, perceptible, and phenomenal results by its inherent energy—"

"Any idea will manifest itself externally if one's attention and will is deeply concentrated upon it—"

"Ah!"

Their eyes met. And the first thought that struck her, with considerable impact, was how startlingly handsome Herr Blum was. The second, that he was the same man who had infiltrated her mind.

She stood paralysed with shock.

He bowed. "Fräulein Heller? Good evening, I am Herr Blum, your tutor."

His golden-brown eyes danced, the jet hair and pointed fox-like features alive with mischief. He was quite old, she thought, at least thirty. And *experienced*...

Instantly she received a vision of them both with limbs entwined. He was holding back her hair, pushing into her... A rush of heat suffused her cheeks.

"How do you do, Herr Blum? Thank you for accepting me as a pupil."

"My absolute pleasure, Fräulein Heller."

The younger man he'd been talking to was regarding her intently. As her glance fell on him, he began to quickly pack up some papers.

"This is Asp, a senior pupil here at the university."

She nodded politely. The room was astounding, like nothing she had ever seen. Full-length gold brocade curtains hung in luxurious folds, two deep leather sofas were positioned either side of a crackling fire, and atop an ornate wooden sideboard, two cut-glass tumblers had been set out beside a full decanter. A mahogany coffee table between the sofas was strewn with leather-bound books, and a stag's head watched over the scene from above the mantelpiece. Lenka slipped off her satchel. This was not a schoolroom.

Herr Blum observed her, still wearing that curious air of amusement.

A curt nod of dismissal passed from him to the other man.

"This is like a gentleman's club, *ja*?" said the one called Asp. He knocked back the remainder of his drink, turned back to face Herr Blum and bowed, placing his right hand onto his chest with the two middle fingers tucked in and the thumb underneath. "I bid you goodnight, Heinrich."

Then, with a mocking bow in her direction, he smiled. "Fräulein Heller!"

After the younger man departed and the main door had clicked shut behind him, the thought occurred to her that they were completely alone in the building, yet she felt no alarm at the impropriety, only intense curiosity.

"Please, take a seat."

She perched on the edge of one of the leather sofas.

"Drink?"

"No, thank you. Are there no other pupils?"

"No."

"I have one-to-one tuition with you? For English and French?"

He laughed, sinking comfortably onto the opposite sofa, his eyes never leaving hers for a second.

The moment was profound. Flames swirled around the dimly lit walls, and the aroma of whisky and tobacco laced the air, along with something else…musk…herbs…

He crossed a long leg over one knee. "You will need some English and French, of course. Do you have any languages other than German? Czechoslovakian?"

"Yes, both."

He acknowledged this with a small incline of his head, a smile hovering at the edge of his lips. "Serbian? Hungarian?"

"No."

"Latin?"

"A little."

"May I call you Lenka?"

Startled, still uncomfortably hot in the face, she nodded.

"Lenka, you cannot be surprised if I tell you that you are here for a reason and it is not particularly to learn

English and French. You are a peasant girl, a farmer's daughter, are you not, and only just turned sixteen? Yet here you are, unchaperoned, with a private university tutor in Ingolstadt." He waved a well-manicured hand at the opulence of the room. "A university renowned for its excellence and, um…filthy rich splendour. So, tell me why you think you are here?"

I am part of you…I can take away all your grief, loneliness and pain…

"I think I might take that drink after all, Herr Blum."

When he stood, the movement was as gracefully fluid as that of a dancer. And when a moment later he leaned over her shoulder to place a glass of burgundy wine in her hand, the musky smell of him – of sandalwood, cedar and spice – lingered. It was all over him, all over his skin…

Her hand shook a little as she took the proffered glass. Why the hell did she have to be dressed in a schoolgirl pinafore and stout shoes? Indeed, she did look like a peasant from Bohemia, a child peasant with silly coiled braids. She stared at his shoes, at the soft, polished black leather.

"Drink," he said. "It will relax you."

She took a long gulp and then another, the desire to take down her hair and rip off the starched pinafore quite overpowering. She struggled with her sense of self. Until recently in life, she'd always enjoyed the upper hand. "All right, I think I am here because…"

Never speak of who you are or what you know!

"It's all right, you can trust me. Your mother told you there would be someone here who would take you to the next level, yes?"

Her eyes grew wide. She took another deep drink, hoping

her hands weren't visibly trembling. "And this is you?"

"It is."

"And you want me to say what I am and what I can do? Yet people like me, with my abilities, have been imprisoned and put to death – it is more than my life is worth. This could be a trick—"

"Trust me. It is the reason you are here."

"I don't understand. At a university? Who are you?"

He shook his head. "Tell me, have you have had the gift of second sight all your life?"

"Yes."

"Go on, I would like to hear more."

"I…um…" She swirled the plum-coloured liquid around and around, uncomfortably aware of the crackle and rush of the fire, of the heat in her veins, of his intense scrutiny. What was she to do?

She took another gulp, after which the answer came out in a rush, "Well, yes, I've always had it. It could be fun, you know, guessing what was going to happen to people? I knew what they were thinking and how they were feeling. Sometimes I did mischievous things like putting thoughts into their heads or sending them a bad dream. It's hard to explain if you don't—"

He yawned. "Common tricks. Many a gypsy fortune-teller will tell you quite accurately what is on your mind. What I would like to know is what happened when you turned sixteen, after your grandmother passed?"

She downed the rest of the liquor. Her cheeks blazed. "What do you mean? What do you know about that?"

"More than you can imagine. Now tell me what happened at the, um…funeral?"

"It sounds as though you know already, Herr Blum?"

"Do not play games with me, Lenka."

The alteration in tone caught her unaware, and she turned her face away to stare into the fire. "Well, it was not so long ago; it's still very fresh in my mind."

"I am sure it must have been very upsetting." He leaned over and topped up her glass. "Drink, drink… Take your time, but it is very important you tell me exactly what happened. You see, I really do want to know."

The axis of the room shifted, and her words sounded syrupy and slurred to her own ears. "Baba Olga was dying, so my mother and I travelled to Mooswald where she and the family had camped. When we arrived, it was almost too late."

"But she did speak to you?"

"Oh yes. I was told she had a powerful gift of sorcery and that it must be passed on to me. My grandmother had been destroyed by the force of the energy, by the dark spirits attached to her, and died a terrible death. Well, the thing is, Baba Olga thought I was my mother. My mother had pushed me forwards instead of herself – she tricked me, Herr Blum. And so, Baba Olga gave the poppet and the legacy to me."

"You must have been mad as all hell."

"Yes, oh yes, I was."

"Were you initiated that evening?" The manner in which he asked the question was nonchalant, but his eyes burned into hers.

"Yes, but they drugged me, so I don't remember it very well." The terrible night surged into her head as if a door had opened wide and pulled her through it.

"And what was the nature of the ceremony?"

She stared into her empty glass, flinching at the barrage of images. Did he have to ask this? How necessary was it?

"Demonic?"

"Yes."

"The transfer of power was definitely made to you?"

The memory of raw heart being crammed into her mouth, of claw hands holding her down while the horned man raped her triggered an eruption of panic. She nodded, gripping the glass, trying not to cry.

"So, Lenka – now you can do more than just read minds and project dreams, yes?"

"Yes."

"Can you give me an example?"

She shook her head.

"Come, now, try harder."

"Herr Blum, who are you? I do not see why I am here. Is it to study my abilities or something? Are your students going to poke fun or call me a witch?"

His eyebrows shot up. "I have no students. I am not a lecturer, of that you can be certain."

"Then I don't understand—?"

"You have confided in me, so I will now confide in you. My father pays for these rooms in order for us to host meetings here. He is a banker and a good friend of the Dekan, as I am. We make sure the university is lavishly rewarded, of course." He indicated the opulent furnishings. "As you can see."

The urge to walk out was overwhelming, but something about him kept her transfixed.

"Do not look so puzzled and frightened. What we do is work with the best of minds, the most forward thinkers and the most influential people. Not just here in Germany but all over the continent and beyond. Think of the highest families in the world – royalty, those at the top of the military, law, universities, medicine, finance and government – these are the people who belong to our group, the elite within the elite. And this is the core of the movement, right here in Ingolstadt. These are exciting times for those who are enlightened – very exciting."

"And you would like me to be in this group?"

"I am not sure yet. I want you to tell me how things have changed since your grandmother passed."

"And if I do not? If I do not wish to join this group so you can have me tell your fortunes, be the gypsy turn at the circus—"

"How well are you feeling this evening, Lenka? Better than yesterday, I expect?"

Her heart jumped. Immediately she glanced down so he could not see her eyes.

"You have to give your demons work, Lenka, or you will become extremely sick – just like your late grandmother. And I have plenty of that for you. I know you, gypsy, and I know your hidden wishes. We knew your great-grandmother – Baroness Jelinski of Russia. Has your mother told you nothing? You do not know who you are? You do not know how she was chased out of Russia, the family forced to resettle in Romania?"

She shook her head. "I know a little."

"You are quite alone, aren't you, Lenka?"

"My aunt and uncle are here—"

He shook his head with feigned sadness. "Tell me how you have been lately, since the funeral – unwell, yes?"

She sighed in defeat. "Yes, you are correct, although I do not know how you are aware of that. It is true, I have been feeling weak and ill with some kind of fever."

His smile was magnetic. He seemed to read her mind, to have crawled right in. "And now? You look healthy, really rather glowing, if I may say so. How can this be if you are not giving your demons work, I wonder?"

Her tongue loosened, and the truth burst out. "When I first came here, just a few days ago, I could see through to the true self of my aunt and uncle. I saw particularly what he was and what he does. He disgusted me with what I saw—"

"Show me with your mind."

She conjured up the images easily, looking into his eyes as she did so.

"Ouch, that pig makes me sick, too."

"Oh, he's hateful. So I cursed him, just yesterday evening, and I think he will become very ill soon."

Heinrich laughed.

Allowing herself a small smile, she sat a little further back on the sofa. "He was looking a little peaky when I left this evening, but my own illness has completely vanished. I feel very well indeed – as you say, healthy."

He nodded. "Well, please do keep me informed regarding your uncle's health."

She smiled, sipped her drink.

"Tell me, are you at all aware of unrest in the countries around us? Have you heard of Kaiser Wilhelm the Second in Prussia? And the Archduke Franz Ferdinand in Austria?"

"Oh! Um, a little from my father."

"And Serbia?"

She shrugged. "No, I am sorry."

"That's all right, you are just sixteen, how could you? But I can teach you these things, more about history and politics. An example for you – for many hundreds of years, Prussia and the Austro-Hungarian Empire have been the rulers, and the church has steamrollered the people with its hypocrisy and lies, stamping out our origins and beliefs. Thousands of witches were burned or drowned here – more than anywhere else in Europe, eradicating ancient knowledge and customs. What is happening, Lenka? Do you think we should do something about this?"

She nodded.

"Do you have a religion of your own? In your village?"

"I attended Bible classes."

"And do you believe in Christ? In God and Jesus?"

She shrugged. "I'm not sure."

"The Christian Bible is instructed here at the university, did you know? It is all done with force and indoctrination – thou shalt not do this and thou shalt not do that…"

For an hour he talked about religion and questioned her about her friends and schooling, finally coming around once again to the reasons she was here. This time it was much clearer, and it seemed he had confided in her quite a lot, was talking to her as an equal now, not a gypsy fortune-teller.

"Kaiser Wilhelm is suggestible, highly volatile – not adhering to the policies of his advisers. He is what is known as a hothead, Lenka, which is an excellent opportunity for us. There are problems arising in the Baltic countries, and with some manipulation we can bring the entire system crashing down. Within our lifetime, both empires could be brought to their knees...there will be tremendous death and destruction, but then after that—"

Her head became suddenly dizzy with images, of lights dimmed and the haunting sound of sirens echoing across deserted towns. Hordes of people were running along cobbled streets, ushering children along, carrying masks... She clutched her temples. "This will happen!"

He sat straight up as if electrocuted. "What do you see? Tell me what you see!"

She shook her head. "I don't know. People running down the streets, running for their lives...no, nothing more, it has gone, faded."

"You need practice, technique. You have a clarity and precision beyond your years but no teacher. You barely read and know little of politics, yet you see and you know. You transfer thoughts and infiltrate minds, intuit weaknesses and manipulate. You will join our group, our club, of course?"

The man's arrogance was staggering. "What? Just to make you rich—"

His mouth dropped open. And then he smiled the dazzling smile of illusion and foul play. "Please, do not think I and my father are merely greedy bankers with a moneymaking plan. And do not underestimate who is in our club or who we bow down to. Not only will your demons have plenty of work to do, but you will be wealthy beyond all imagination, and that will set you free, Lenka. You will have the key to every material luxury you ever desired and more. How pretty you will look in the new-style dresses! Or of course you can go back to your aunt and uncle's house, scrub their floors and get sick."

"I can have an apartment? Of my own?"

"You can have a house of your own. And servants."

He refilled both their glasses.

"So, you want to join?"

She smiled, already picturing the new-style dresses and hats, the ones ladies who travelled in carriages wore. "Does this club have a name?"

"Of course. We are der Orden der schwarzen Sonne."

***

CHAPTER TWENTY-ONE

Herr Blum, or Heinrich as she was to call him when they were alone, walked Lenka home, the dutiful tutor carrying a pile of books. She would attend the university every weekday evening for one year in order to study European politics, English and French. Intensive study was required before being admitted to the Order, and this included instruction in the occult. The dark arts were practised routinely and openly by the ruling elite, and, as such, there was a great deal to learn.

"In short, acknowledging and channelling powerful energy from the hidden world gives one unimaginable advantages," Heinrich explained. "The trick is to pretend it doesn't exist, that it is the domain of the mad and the bad. You see, while ever the people are kept ignorant of its reality, they have neither the ability nor the inclination to see what is really happening. They simply don't believe in it. Yes, it is important to keep them poor, fully occupied and fearful; then they will do anything."

His politics left her confused, but the look in his admiring eyes did not. Nor did the promise of independence and wealth. *Satan has his ways*, she thought, *of luring us in like fish on a reel – suffer pain and disease or be healthy and strong*. Live like a gypsy in the dirt or enjoy untold riches. He made it easy. What was there to lose? Her soul? Such tales from Faust and Dante even she did not believe.

Reaching the end of the street, he stopped. "I will leave you here."

She nodded, taking the books.

"By the way, Lenka, if you ever discuss the existence of our group or repeat anything you learn, you will be locked away and tried for witchcraft. I will personally make sure you hang, do you understand? You must keep all of this a watertight secret, shared only with the Order or your life will be over. And no, you will not have time or the opportunity to pass on your legacy – that will follow you into the afterlife."

The abrupt switch from friendly and informative to menacingly cold caught her out for the second time that evening.

Had she not already had proof of the hidden world, she'd have thought Heinrich a madman with all the rhetoric about secret clubs and bringing down empires. But she had. And if there was still any room for doubt, then what happened shortly afterwards would throw all further scepticism to the four winds.

***

On arrival at her aunt's house, the doctor was hurrying away down the steps, and all the lamps were on. Aunt Heide let her in, and as she entered the hallway, the most wretched howls emanated from upstairs.

"Is that Uncle Guido?" she asked, wide-eyed.

"Hurry – take off your coat and fetch some hot water.

We must bathe him. He has a stomach poisoning."

She hurried to the kitchen and set some water on the stove to boil. A stomach poisoning? Perhaps he had been careless with his hygiene? Smiling, she made herself some tea while waiting for the larger pot to boil, enjoying the warmth of the fire. Overhead, Uncle Guido, she knew, was lying in a pool of his own sweat, the contents of his gut and bowels long since emptied from the chamber pot. The stench of his excretions permeated the fabric of the house, and she pitied Aunt Heide the task of cleaning it all up. She took a sip of tea. Still, Aunt Heide had said not a word when she knew what kind of man he was and what he did to small children, had she? Of course she knew! The knowledge plagued her mind day after day after day. How? Had she caught him in the act? Heard a rumour? Had a child tearfully confided in her, only to be clipped around the ear? Ah yes, that was it…the latter.

She took another sip of tea. The large pot of water had been boiling for a while now, but he could wait for his wash and change of nightclothes. He could wait until she had finished her tea and reflected on what had happened this evening.

When, for instance, would her house be ready? She had failed to ask. That must be clarified or she would not do as he asked.

Oh, you will, Lenka…

She smiled wider, her insides tingling with merriment. Heinrich Blum was not his real name, of course. The man was a liar and a magician of the highest order. *We will see who you are in time, though*, she thought. At times he seemed ardent, serious about overthrowing established order and infiltrating the church, at others mischievous and cleverly malevolent, as if throwing influential people into conflict amused him. Perhaps he simply liked the notion of chaos and destruction?

A prolonged groan emanated from upstairs, and her aunt called down.

"Lenka! Is the water ready yet?"

She finished her tea and slowly rinsed out the cup. "Yes, ready now."

Upstairs, the front bedroom was dimly lit by an oil lamp, an acrid stench trailing all the way across the landing and down the stairs. She tapped on the door.

"Yes, come in, Lenka. Hurry with the water. He needs to bathe and change his clothes!"

Uncle Guido's face was slick with oil and grey of hue. Reddened eyes squinted as she set down the jug of water and a pile of fresh towels. His scraggy neck and sparse hair, gaunt face and soiled bedding was repellent. How quickly he had withered from man of the house, master of the Bible class, abuser of helpless orphaned boys, to this sickly, stinking specimen.

"Help me take off his nightshirt. We must wash him and change the sheets."

Guido, so severely weakened by the rapid and violent purging of his system, could do nothing but sag against the bosom of his wife as she yanked off his shirt and dipped a flannel into the warm water.

"Did Uncle Guido eat something that disagreed with him?"

Guido's stomach caved inwards visibly as if it had been punched. He panted through another violent spasm as it drained his remaining strength. Terrible, embarrassing noises emitted from his body, a tide of greenish fluid spreading across the bedsheet.

"We don't know what it is," Heide said. "I cooked the same meal as usual; he has eaten it a hundred times. The doctor said—"

"I am sorry, but I'm going to be sick—" Lenka said, running from the room.

She made sure to make noisy retching noises in the corridor outside. Like hell she would mop up his foul and putrid emissions. Darting into her room, she shut the door and sank onto the floor behind it, laughing so hard it hurt.

Whatever Satan had to offer, it had to be better than this. Hell was here already, she thought. On God's earth.

***

CHAPTER TWENTY-TWO

True to his word, Heinrich Blum did provide Lenka with a house. On the leafy outskirts of Ingolstadt, it would be shared with a mature lady companion, who, for the sake of outward appearances, must be referred to as Aunt Sophia.

Sophia, an adept in the occult, would provide instruction on the dark arts – how to invoke and banish demons, practise astral travel and projection, communicate with entities, and, most of all, how to protect herself from psychic attack. It was extremely important to remain in control.

The move to her new life happened swiftly, within hours of relating to Heinrich just how ill Uncle Guido had become. They'd been sitting in the opulent lounge at the university the following evening, Heinrich leaning forwards, fingertips pressed together while she talked.

"A most impressive result, Lenka. Indeed, it is a fine demonstration of what is to come. Will you lift the hex?"

She shrugged. "Well, here is the thing, Heinrich. I do not know how to."

Neither could contain their mirth, bursting into fits of giggles like children.

He dabbed at his eyes. "Your aunt will have quite the problem explaining to your mother how her husband contracted a fatal stomach disease within days of you being here, and then she lost you as well. She lost her daughter! So very careless!"

Lenka nearly fell from her chair, laughing so hard. "It is so careless of her, yes, to lose two people so quickly."

"What will she do, your poor Aunt Heide?"

"I think she will have to go looking for a spine," said Lenka.

"You have contempt, then? No feelings for either?"

"No, none for anyone anymore."

"What about me? Do you have any feelings for me?"

His eyes were glinting, the stare unflinching. Was he mocking her? The rapid unpinning of her life so far had left her scrabbling around for an identity, but here was a possible solution. A replacement life. But so personal, so very personal… She tried to form her thoughts. He'd had everything already planned, hadn't he?

He smiled, reading her mind. "Correct, yes. All down to the finest detail, long before you arrived in Ingolstadt."

She nodded. But he was implying a relationship. "I don't know about any feelings. I only met you yesterday. And you are my tutor, a man twice my age!"

He swirled his glass of burgundy for a moment before lifting his gaze to hers. "I could visit your house tonight. Imagine!"

A stirring of deep excitement tingled inside her, but…she bit her lip… "Heinrich, who are you really? You say a banker, but—"

"Ah! Now, that I cannot say to someone outside of the Order. No member of der Orden der Schwarzen Sonne shall be revealed one to the other until they are sworn in."

"And when will I be sworn in?"

"Patience, Lenka. I told you one year. Preparation is essential – this is not a commitment to be taken lightly. For one whole year every initiate must serve an apprenticeship, and that includes you. In your case, it is to learn languages and history in addition to perfecting your particular craft. This is so you can mix with the highest echelons of society, do you understand?"

She nodded.

"How can you expect to be of use to us if you have the wits of a peasant girl and the occult expertise of a fortune-teller?"

She dipped her head.

"Normally, this process is much shorter. We recruit from the most highly educated, the most skilful adepts, and those climbing into positions of enormous power and influence. Yet here we are taking the time to educate one of the lower orders such as yourself."

A hot rush of blood shot up her neck, suffusing her face, and tears smarted in her eyes.

"So it will be one year of hard work before the final initiation process. This is not a school club or a child's game – our ultimate aim is to disrupt the order of the entire civilised world as it stands. You can presently have no concept of how gravely serious this is. It could take ten years to effect the smallest changes, but that is okay because we have a hundred. Or more. A thousand, even."

"A thousand? How can that be?"

She caught a glimpse then, a slip of words that revealed the startling splinter of illumination, another reality to this one. But just as quickly as the door had opened, it banged shut again, and the fog of confusion descended.

"A figure of speech," he said, immediately lightening the tone. "We have decades if necessary, and decades are what it may take."

"Yes, I see. Well, I hope I shall have fun before then – before I am enclosed in this terrible club of yours, with all its graveness."

He held her gaze, and the strangest feeling of falling came over her.

"I think you will like the house I have chosen for you," he said. "And the bedroom, it is…most restful. Come, let us drink to this – to Lenka and the start of her new life!"

"Thank you. To my new life!"

They clinked glasses in the university room neither would return to. By the following evening, the suite of rooms would be transformed into more conventional classrooms, and the visiting young lecturer known as Herr Blum would cease to exist.

***

CHAPTER TWENTY-THREE

One Year Later. Autumn 1891
THE INITIATION CEREMONY

The Lodge was situated on the outskirts of Ingolstadt, on a salubrious tree-lined avenue. Devoid of windows with the grand front door permanently locked and chained, the building incited little interest, and most people walked by without a second glance. Shrubs obscured its lower half, and in the autumn of 1891, coppery leaves shimmered and danced in the sun on the pavement outside. A sparsely populated area predominantly used for offices and banks, it was particularly quiet in the evenings. As such, there was no one around to notice the elegant young woman dressed all in black, who alighted from a carriage on the drive at the side of the building, blindfolded with her hands tied.

Lenka, flanked by Aunt Sophia on one side and Heinrich on the other, was being guided towards the back door, shielded from unwanted curiosity by the body of the carriage. Heinrich knocked three times with a cane, and at the sound of bolts sliding back from inside, Sophia nodded curtly, retreating to the carriage. For now, her work was done.

Once inside with the door shut and bolted behind her,

Lenka's blindfold was removed. The room was small – an unlit vestibule or high-ceilinged porch with no windows. She indicated the binding around her wrists. "You can untie me? I will not run away. I do not see why—"

"Hush now. You must trust and obey. We have discussed how important this is, Lenka. Everyone entering der Orden der schwarzen Sonne must commit fully to the process. No more questions. Always questions."

Indeed, she had been meticulously prepared for today's initiation ceremony. Fully versed in Prussian and Hapsburg politics, royal dynasties and Serbian rebels, she now had the same vision as Heinrich, that of a whole new world. This was monumental – nothing would ever be the same again, and she fully accepted her role, aware of the vital secrecy at this delicate stage. These were the seeds being planted, seeds that would grow into something overwhelmingly and unstoppably powerful. Moreover, the identities of those involved were shortly to be revealed. Never had she been more excited or grateful. It had been a wonderful time and would now culminate in full membership.

Belonging to the Order had become increasingly important to her as the months passed – the desire to be one of them and move in the highest circles ever more attractive, necessary even, to her future self. It transpired that her great-grandmother had been a baroness and much revered at the Russian court before being ejected on catcalls of witchcraft. It was Lenka's birthright to be among nobility, and no churchman was going to have her thrown out or he'd be sorry. This now was her place, her destiny, and it was right at the top – on the world stage.

Olga had been stupid not to comply with the Order's wishes – look how she had ended her days! But today, as for all initiates no matter how high their rank, humility and submission were necessary in order to bind with the others. Allied by the initiation, they stood strong and loyal, and there were no, not ever, not one, dissenters.

Today her courage, loyalty and trust were to be tested to the limit of endurance. She took a deep breath. Of course, she would fly through. It was just one day. One day. And afterwards, the best the world had to offer would be hers. Like marrying into royalty, she told herself…yes, exactly like that.

Her eyes adjusted quickly to the gloomy stone-walled chamber as the bolts to the outside world were shot home and a wooden bar slotted into place.

"We have been riding for hours," she said to the masked man who had bent to remove her shoes. "This must be another city, not Ingolstadt?"

Beside her, Heinrich laughed. "My dear, we have simply been travelling in circles."

On the right-hand wall was a large painting of an owl, on the left the same sigil that had been burned onto her wrist – a circle enclosing a pentagram, in the centre a black sun with black rays around it. But on this one, inscribed over the top in an arch, was the name 'Der Orden der schwarzen Sonne' underneath 'Courage, Loyalty and Obedience'.

Obedience?

The man tending to her shoes stood up, and recognition flashed in her eyes.

He bowed slightly, this time with no conceit, amusement or contempt. "Fräulein Heller."

"Asp?"

"*Kommen Sie.*"

Despite her ability to tap into the thoughts of others, Asp's mind was unreadable. Thanks to Sophia's tuition, she now knew why, understanding the shroud of invisibility he protected himself with. He was hiding something, a complex web of emotions – chiefly, she realised, that of fear. Why fear? Yet the fear trapped in this building was palpable…maybe because all initiates would be afraid? *No matter how well prepared we are*, she thought, *it's the unknown that grips even the most intrepid of hearts.* Swallowing a sudden lurch of unease, she followed Asp to a small door leading off from the side, and down an unlit flight of steps.

It looked like the entrance to a wine cellar. Peering down, she shot one last glance over her shoulder at Heinrich, who nodded encouragingly, then took one careful step inside. Immediately the door slammed shut behind, a key turned in the lock, and they were plunged into total darkness. Alone now with Asp, there was no choice but to walk down. Forty-four steps in all, each one felt for cautiously, each deeper than the last, the walls narrowing on the descent so that by the time they reached the bottom, it was claustrophobically difficult to squeeze through.

It was as black as a pit. Stepping inside, she stood perfectly still.

"Asp?"

His footsteps echoed and trailed away. A door then opened and shut somewhere along a far wall, followed by a shot of yet another set of bolts. A cold shiver ran up and down her back, upper arms, and into her hair. Fear crawled all over her. Was she alone? What was going to happen?

"Hello?"

Sophia had taught her a method of self-control, how to keep both mind and body alert and receptive while in a state of terror. If adrenalin flooded the brain, she said, the finer senses and perceptions will not come through – you will only feel the fear. Recalling what she had learned, Lenka took several long, deep breaths to stem the adrenalin rush, then tuned in. There was no one else here in this chamber. Nothing human. But there was *something* in here.

Something that slithered.

With a stab of panic, it came to her what it was. The floor was alive with snakes. Despite all her training, panic and anger blasted through her in equal measure. Damn, damn and damn! That had been a lesson and one she'd missed. Hell, oh no, hell, hell… Anything but snakes.

She had told Heinrich her one fear. And what had she been taught? That no matter what the relationship or circumstances, you never ever told anyone your greatest fear or what you prized the most. But they were on the same side, were they not? Not just on the same side but in love and to be married? She'd told him on a night of intense lovemaking, too, wrapped in satin sheets, he tracing a finger gently down her spine, kissing her shoulders with champagne lips. He had idly confided his own worst nightmares, asking for hers…

Stupid, stupid, stupid!

She had been five years old and lying in the sun when an adder had crawled across her legs. It had happened before she'd realised – at first, still sleepy in daydreams, she had shaken her leg. But the crawling sensation had grown heavier, moving upwards. She'd sat up to see a long, scaly snake with its forked tongue flicking in and out of a bulbous head, slithering up her thigh towards her chest. Jumping up, she'd run screaming down the field, convinced it was in her hair, climbing up her back, still on her! And night after night since, she woke with a violent lurch, expecting to see it wriggling across the floor in the moonlight, climbing up the bedclothes... Nothing frightened her as much as snakes. And she had told him!

She stood now, shocked and quaking, with a heart rate speeding up by the second. One of the snakes was winding its way over, its muscular contractions raspy on the stone floor, closer and closer. Her father always said they wouldn't harm you if you didn't invade their space, but that was not true. People could be swallowed whole by huge ones longer than a whale – there were pictures of them in books – of anacondas and reticulated pythons thirty feet long. How big was the one now slinking over on its belly? And how the hell could Heinrich do this to her? He must have known what was in this pit! Must have known as her shoes were removed...and when she'd turned to look at him before descending into the snake pit...

Barefoot, trembling from head to foot, she stood listening as more and more reptilian bodies slithered out of the walls and began to move around the room. A terrible thought occurred to her – what if they were above her head as well? In the rafters? And dropped down?

Her legs began to shake uncontrollably. *Think...think...this is a test...you must think...* There had to be a way out. Adrenalin had blocked rational thought exactly as warned – but there had been preparation for this, and it was crucial not to fail, to fall at the first hurdle. Sophia's words replayed: 'Your first test is courage – you must override terror and not panic. This is called the Gate of Men, and it is imperative. You can never give into personal fears, not even in the gravest of situations – not ever – or you jeopardise the Order, and we cannot risk weakness in our ranks.'

Prior to this, for three days she had been starved of food. Nothing except water had passed her lips. Nausea, dizziness and headache also threatened to cloud her judgement. Repeating the technique learned, she spoke out loud, "I will endure. I will endure. I will endure!"

Carefully, she backed to the wall, reaching out for the stones behind while suppressing with every breath the need to scream and run. *Imagine if this was enemy territory…this is the lesson…you cannot cry out and be rescued…* But it was not, so there had to be a door, there must be! Focusing more clearly now, she inched around the edge, shuddering as a heavy snake passed over her bare foot. "I will endure…I will endure…"

At last! The stones gave way to a wooden doorframe. Whirling around, she felt for a handle and, fully expecting it to be locked, was stunned to find that it gave way. Instantly she flew through it and fell onto a cobbled floor on the other side. Whipping back round, she kicked the door shut so none of the snakes could escape, then brushed herself down all over several times, checking her hair, visibly shuddering and shivering. How many had crawled over her feet or dropped onto her shoulders, she had lost count of, knowing only there would be nightmares about this for the rest of her life.

Panic, however, soon gave way to confusion. Was this supposed to happen? What was this? It looked like a jail. Dimly lit, there was nothing in it but a cage, and next to that a masked man standing with his arms folded.

"Asp?"

He nodded. "Turn around. I will untie you."

Had she passed the first test, then? There would be two more, but surely that was the worst? Anything was better than the snakes.

"Into the cage, please."

Approximately six feet by six, the cell was furnished with one small wooden stool and a table on which there was a jug of water and a glass. She gulped it down.

"Slow down. You will be here for two days, and there is no more."

In the corner was a chamber pot. Yes, a prison cell, then…but no bed. As she took in the new surroundings along with the fact this would last for two days and nights – so not a day of initiation, then, but far longer – the cage door was chained shut behind her, the candles were snuffed out and the door to the room bolted.

She sat down on the stool in the dark, occasionally leaping up, convinced a snake had got in from under the door. Without any light at all, it was not possible to see even her hand in front of her face. Nothing. Except the sound of dripping damp.

After a while time ceased to exist, and a deep chill permeated her skin, sinking into her lungs, muscles and organs. Once or twice, she toppled from the stool with fatigue and lay curled in a tight ball on the freezing cobbles. And it was during this fitful, uncomfortable sleep that the lessons learned over the past twelve months began to replay. In a cinematic reel some were shown more than once, others slowed and then repeated with increasing lucidity – a theatrical show of moments missed and clues overlooked. It was as if someone or something was pinching her awake, determined to point out hurtful yet significant moments. *Look…look…did you not see? You have been blinded, look, look again!*

She moaned in her semi-consciousness. How her stomach cramped and her head ached. Nausea swelled and rose, and once the visions came, they piled in, one after the other. This had not happened in such a long time…why…why now…?

What was that? What did the whispers say?

She squeezed her eyes shut and tried to blank out the images. No, it could not be true. Had she been sleepwalking? Blind? Certain interchanges, glances and references not previously noticed, much less acknowledged, were now quite clear. Painfully so.

Suddenly, any notion of sleep became impossible. In fact, never in all her life had she been so awake. Why had she been sleepwalking all these months and not seen this? Dutiful, she had been a model pupil and enjoyed every minute. The house was luxurious, the clothes beautiful, the reading surprisingly interesting. It was vital to be healthy, Sophia had told her, and, as such, she had eaten everything provided and happily downed the healthy drinks Sophia made each evening. Every lesson had been absorbed, every test passed. Always she applied herself fully, longing, yearning to be admitted to the Order and begin travelling the world. Indeed, she had hardly left the house or seen another soul!

Sitting upright now, on the small stool in the

underground prison, her mind sparked alive with information. All of this had been on show, all of it…yet she had seen nothing. Why?

Show me…show me…

The spirits that had been kept at bay with tricks taught by Sophia…

Show me!

Memories crowded in – Heinrich and Sophia laughing together, an exchanged conspiratorial glance, his hand on the small of Sophia's back, distant chatter as Lenka drifted into sleep…a drugged sleep?

Had they lain together? Were they man and wife?

A gold ring on her dressing table, one which Sophia had quickly slid out of sight…

My God, they were man and wife!

And the house, it was theirs, yes?

A document flashed before her.

Image after image, truth after truth, was shown to her. Those milk drinks Sophia had brought in after studies in the evening… Yes, how quickly Lenka had fallen asleep, how dreamy the mornings… And now, here without the sedation, without the hypnosis he'd exerted and the diversion of intense studies, the situation was clear! Her powers of clairvoyance were back. He'd been right on that night he'd walked her home this time last year – keep people distracted and they noticed nothing. No wonder the house had been ready so quickly. There had not even been time to pack. Instead, she'd been taken straight there to a fully furnished home.

The pain when it came, delayed by denial and shock, was immense, the wound searing, all dreams for the future and realities of the past a lie. Her heart squeezed into a fist, her throat constricted, and tears streamed down her face. Sophia and he were lovers, husband and wife. But she'd thought… Oh no, oh God no, the pain was terrible, terrible, like nothing ever in her life, not even Oskar. Heinrich and herself had been together so intimately, night after night after night!

Like a wild animal she howled, tilting back her head and roaring, screaming with soul pain.

He had not felt the same, had not even cared. All illusions lifted now, veils obscuring truth after truth removed. For him she had been nothing more than a job, a recruitment. It seemed odd, though. If she was nothing more than a task, that meant he was a puppet. So who, then, was the puppet master?

All tears dried. So what was really happening, then? If all she had been told was a lie and everything was an illusion, what the hell was going to happen now? Had nothing been true, including what would take place at the initiation? It was supposed to be one day, yet already it was two more… A cold wind blew against her face as if a door had opened somewhere. Yet the air was still, damp dripped, and silence hissed.

Who were der Orden der schwarzen Sonne? How had he found her and been in touch with her mother, a man like that?

We knew your great-grandmother, the baroness…

Why had she never even thought of this before, so blinded by desire and the wonderful thoughts he had projected for her future? Panic now gripped her. She'd been cornered.

While all concept of time had dissipated, it was at the precise moment she realised her clairvoyance had been suppressed while they'd indoctrinated her that day two in the prison became day three.

I could turn this around, I am more powerful, he's lured me here for…

Footsteps clicked in the corridor outside, cutting off all further thoughts. And on the strike of one minute past midnight, a visitor arrived.

***

CHAPTER TWENTY-FOUR

#

The man sat on the opposite side of the cage, observing Lenka through the bars. She screwed up her eyes in the glare of his oil lamp. He had on a black woollen suit, a fedora pulled low over his eyes, was clean shaven and very old, with an ashen, deeply etched complexion. As ancient as one of her grandmother's crones, there was an odour of decay about him that seemed oddly familiar, although she couldn't place it.

Evidently, the man did not want her to see his eyes, but there was no disguising the wide set of his nose or the jagged teeth when he spoke.

"Good day, Lenka."

Her jaw had become rigid with cold, and it felt strange to speak. "Sir."

"May I say what a pleasure it is to meet you? I knew Baroness Jelinski personally. It was too bad she frightened the priests. But now, look, you are here!"

His voice had an edge of malice, an undertone of amusement.

"I did not know her, sir."

"Of course not, she died before you were born. However, we are immensely pleased to have tracked you down. Your grandmother, Olga, was a bitter disappointment and unfortunately not of the same calibre as the baroness. She would not comply – not a worthy successor at all. But thanks to your mother, we now have you!"

Lenka frowned. Ah, so it had not been Heinrich alone, had never been a chance connection or a lead followed – her mother had been in league with der Orden der schwarzen Sonne all along.

"I do not wish to continue with this. I want to go."

The bottom row of spiky teeth, his smile that of a catfish, faded. "Ah, I understand you are nervous, but there is no need. No need at all."

Shivering, she regarded him more closely now her eyes had adjusted. There was something so strange about this man, the bridge of his nose unusually wide and only the lower teeth showing, the outer ones larger and spikier than the others. The backs of his hands, too, were not simply veined and crinkly but scaly like a lizard. He really was extremely old.

"The transfer ritual was excellent, by the way. I enjoyed participating immensely!" The chuckle arising from his throat was caught in phlegm, and as his mouth cracked open to cough, the spiky lower teeth appeared now to be missing altogether, the mouth an empty cavern.

"Enjoyed participating? Who are you?"

Tell me who he is…show me…work for me!

"You can call me Uncle Toby."

"Uncle Toby? We are related?"

He laughed, this time the lower teeth reappearing. "No, but you can consider me your uncle, someone to turn to for help and advice. Look at it this way – you can unburden yourself, tell me everything, use me in a similar way to a Catholic confessing to a priest." Another throaty chuckle bobbed up and down in his throat. "So that is how we will proceed, Lenka. We will have no secrets from each other, and you will come to regard me as your most trusted friend."

While he talked, the light from the oil lamp dimmed, the yellow flame fading incrementally until there was little more than a wisp of grey emanating from it. He doused all light, the darkness of his aura seeping across the floor, crawling up the walls, spreading like a contagious disease.

"You can pour it all out, my dear – how the people you cared for deceived, disappointed and upset you. And we will write everything down in order to analyse things, help you understand matters better. You can keep a diary, write all you can remember from your home life, going all the way back to your very first memory. You will explain your weaknesses, desires, and the responses of those around you. After that we will move to your experience here in Ingolstadt. In time I will know everything about you and your mind and what your reactions are likely to be in any given situation. In this way we can assign to you the most suitable work. So, you see, it is very important not to deceive us, Lenka. I will know if you hold anything back."

Tell me who he is…show me!

"And if you do hold back or attempt deceit, be assured the punishment will be of a kind you cannot even conceive. We excel in this particular field."

She felt the cold trickle of understanding. And recognition. The smell of him…

The goats head, the fire, the rape!

"And most of all, Lenka, you will tell Uncle Toby,

who is your friend – the best friend and only friend you will ever have – all that you foresee, receive from Spirit, and discover through mind reading. I understand you have excellent abilities, so nothing less than excellence will be accepted. In return for such loyalty, you will of course be rich beyond your wildest imagination. We look after our people. You will enjoy the fruits of a most privileged and exalted life to be envied the world over. Every success will be yours. You, my beauty, will live in abject luxury with no cap on material wealth. Most of all, you will belong to the most important movement in history and be right at the heart of der Orden der schwarzen Sonne."

She nodded.

"You must thank me. Say, 'Thank you, Uncle Toby.'"

"Yes, thank you, Uncle Toby."

"I will ensure every need is met for the rest of your life. All you have to do is be a loyal member of der Orden der schwarzen Sonne. Loyalty, Lenka. Total, unquestionable loyalty. You understand?"

"Yes, Uncle Toby. Thank you."

He nodded, stood up, then left without another word, his footsteps echoing dully on the cobbles. He had not revealed his eyes, keeping the hat pulled down at all times. And no wonder, she thought, because if anyone were to look into them, they would know he had no soul, no spirit, not even the tiniest spark of human life.

The chill of his presence lingered.

The next part, what was it? Trust or obedience? Which was true? What about failing it? If she failed, would they cast her onto the street and refuse to let her join? Because that would be preferable. This whole thing had been an illusion, a gilded trap she'd fallen right into. Already, the heartache of Heinrich's duplicity had faded, knowing now that he was nothing more than a seductive conjuror with a black heart.

You knew…you knew…

She quashed the voice. Yes, she had known, deep down. Yet the longing for pretty dresses and the admiration of a handsome man had won out. Stupid, stupid… She gazed into the blackness. What would happen next? Was it possible to escape? Once out of this dungeon, up the steps to the light…yes…

Her stomach growled. And it was freezing. When Asp came back, she'd ask if it was possible to leave and not complete the process. Yes, that's what she'd do. Take her chances with the demons – after all, at least she now had more knowledge of the occult and how to manage the dark ones.

Shivering violently, she talked herself through it. The essence of Uncle Toby still crawled all over her skin, the memory of his violation repellent and despicable. It had definitely been him – the stink of that scaly skin was unforgettable.

Fortunately, it wasn't long before Asp's footsteps sounded in the corridor outside and the bolts shot back.

She stood up, hands gripping the bars.

The door was opened, the cage unlocked, and he yanked her upright. For a second or two, she wobbled and held on to his arm. "Asp, I need to ask—"

He shook her off as if she were a leper. This wasn't Asp. He was thinner, wiry, the voice a snap. "Stand up straight! Come with me. Hurry up."

"Where are we going?"

"Third gate – Gate of Death."

Confused, she stumbled along. They were not going to kill her or that would defeat the object of the process.

"I don't want to do this, to carry on."

The man's thoughts were impenetrable. There would be no help forthcoming.

Show me what's happening, demons. I'm giving you work – inform me!

All she had wanted was to be young and pretty and flirtatious, to have fun, to have a better life. She had to get out of here. Her feet dragged.

"I have changed my mind. I don't want to continue."

"Hurry up!"

Look where her ego had brought her – being rushed headlong to a fate from which there was no escape. They had all seen her weaknesses, from her mother to Heinrich. Stupid, stupid, stupid…and now it was too late. What had she done?

The final door loomed ahead.

The Gate of Death, he'd said. Death? No one had mentioned death. This did not make sense, not at all.

"No! Listen to me, please—"

"Quiet!"

After three knocks, the door was opened to reveal a vast tank of water. At which point a sheet was thrown over her head, her arms were bound with rope, and she was thrown in.

There had been no warning and no time to hold her breath. Flailing around wildly, she gulped down water, kicked and bucked, but to no avail. She sank to the bottom in seconds.

Pain ripped through her chest, and her mind blacked.

And when she came to, it was to find someone untying the sheet and another banging hard on her back. Gasping, coughing and ejecting water all at the same time, she only vaguely heard the command "Get her ready now. Take her to the hall."

A masked woman stepped forward with an armful of towels and a white robe for her to wear. "Now you are dead from your old life. You have passed successfully through the Gate of Death and, like a serpent shedding its skin, can begin anew. With us. You will have a new name, a new identity and a new code of conduct. Congratulations, Lenka. Follow me and we will take you to the hall. I am very excited for you. Are you not excited?"

Numb, shivering, she could only stare back at the woman and shake her head.

"Ah, don't be afraid. The final part of the initiation is always the worst, but once you have crossed that line, it will become easier."

Crossed that line?

A vague notion she could still leave floated in her mind, even as they were hurrying up the staircase, this one well-lit and wide, to the hall. At the top was a large, ornate arched door. At least the end was here. It was nearly over... Then she would go back to the house and collect her things. Whatever the Order wanted her to do, she would not do it but instead flee and take her chances. They would never find her. She would cross oceans.

After three knocks, a door a foot thick and studded with iron was opened from within. A waft of air escaped from the great hall, and even before she stepped inside, she knew it would have a high vaulted ceiling, that there would be tiers like a theatre gallery for onlookers to survey the scene below, and that she would be the only one on stage.

She stepped inside.

Entirely unexpected was the sheer number of silent observers – at least a hundred, maybe more – filling every candlelit tier along the galleries. All were dressed in white robes like herself, except they wore animal heads, the scene disturbingly macabre as they stared down into the pit where she stood alone in the dark.

Behind, the door to the staircase clunked heavily shut.

Swallowing hard, a light sweat broke onto the surface of her skin.

"Stand in the circle, in the centre, Fräulein Heller."

Still damp and shivering, she jumped at the sound of the disembodied voice from behind, or was it to the left or the right? Disorientated, she looked down at her bare feet. A large circle had been marked on the floor, two large *X*'s inscribed inside.

The Order has been at the root of everything, right from the start; it was them at the satanic ritual, everything...all pre-planned...

Frantically she looked around the hall, at the circular opera house–style building with its walls of mirrors. Not a single door. No way out.

"Fräulein Heller! Into the circle, please."

Within the circle was an inverted pentagram, and outside of it four triangles had been drawn. At each of the four 'watchtowers', a large black pillar candle burned, and every segment of the pentagram contained a different symbol.

She stepped into the eye of the circle onto a symbol of

the black sun at the very centre. Immediately a power-wave of alarm bolted through her.

This came from the depths of hell.

The disembodied voice, one from behind a mask, one she recognised, spoke into the silent hall.

"Listen to the instructions. You will now take the life of another human being."

The words slowly filtered through.

"Immediately afterwards, you will drink the adrenalin-filled blood from the chalice given to you. After you have completed this, the ultimate test of obedience, you will become a member of der Orden der schwarzen Sonne. Hand her the sword."

So it was obedience after all, not trust…blind, forced obedience! She had lost her will, her autocracy, her freedom as a human spirit. Sold, in other words.

Are you rich now, Mutter? Were you paid for this?
And you, Heinrich, you lying, cheating bastard pig!

A thrashing, screaming innocent was dragged across the floor in a sackcloth, the odour of stale alcohol and street filth assailing Lenka's nostrils.

Rage blinded her, and her hands shook as she took the gleaming sword. Only, however, for a second. As soon as she had hold of it, every scar, every infliction of pain, every lie, betrayal, trick and violation replayed. Hate surged through her veins. And as if it were someone else's hand, not her own, she watched as it rose in the air, then plunged with a passion over and over and over into the living, breathing flesh of another human being.

That was for Heinrich.

And that was for Sophia.

And that was for Uncle Toby the rapist.

And that was for her mother.

After a dozen or more stabs, someone came forward to retrieve the sword, but the grip of fury had not left her yet. Repeatedly she stabbed the now silent, inert victim until a pool of ruby-red froth ebbed across the floor.

"Enough now!"

A chalice was thrust into her hands. Blood-spattered, she finally dropped the sword, took the cup and drank from it before raising the chalice to the galleries.

Removing their masks one by one, they began to clap.

Now she understood why none of them had a soul or a heart or a readable mind. They had all crossed the line, and there was no way back. Every single one of them was bound to the Order, and in time she would know them all, their faces made infamous in newspapers across the globe.

"Hail the Dark Lord!"
"Hail the Dark Lord!"
"Hail the Dark Lord!"

***

PART THREE

EVA HART

'The real voyage of discovery consists not in seeking new lands, but seeing with new eyes.'
   Widely attributed to Marcel Proust.

'If you know the truth, the truth will make you free. Ignorance is a slave, knowledge is freedom.'
   The Gospel of Philip. The Nag Hammadi Scriptures.

CHAPTER TWENTY-FIVE
1978

Lenka's story cut off as abruptly as a power cut two days before my sixteenth birthday. I woke up with a hammering heart, shocked and breathing hard, having known the enormity of extinguishing someone else's life.

For eight years I had lived every detail of her existence as if it were my own – felt the passion, crushing disappointments, horror and betrayals. But after the murder and initiation into the Order, there was nothing more. A lifeline severed. What happened to Heinrich? Had he really been married to Sophia all along? Believe me, Lenka had shown me everything – and that man had loved her, had held her in his arms so tenderly and desired her so intensely, it was unbelievably difficult to believe it hadn't been real. I endured the heartbreak every bit as much as she did, the pain of illusion stripped away, and the desolation of abandonment. There were so many questions.

Perhaps the most pressing of those questions was - how come I hadn't fallen ill on receipt of the poppet eight years ago?

But of course, at that point I hadn't known we must turn sixteen.

From beyond the grave, Baba Lenka waited, I believe,

until I was no longer a child before she lifted the veil of protection and handed over the full force of the demonic alliance. Until then her presence had been a constant in my dreams and thoughts, as if we were one and the same person. But on the day I turned sixteen she cut the cord, leaving only sporadic memories. I was, it seemed, now on my own.

She had been a thorough teacher, though, illuminating the path ahead with a depth of emotions and experience now deeply enmeshed. It was not a fairy tale. It had happened. And she had been right about hiding from the world who we really are. Psychiatrists, it seemed, were not in the main to be trusted, nor doctors, church officials, anyone paid by the government, or members of the aristocracy. They would, and did, have people like us locked inside institutions, labelled as nuts and consigned to history. Snapshots of German and Austrian psychiatric hospitals, where barbaric punishments awaited should she not comply with what the Order wanted, were frequently flashed into my mind lest I forgot – a Belisha beacon of warning whenever I came close to revealing the level of dark knowledge a girl my age shouldn't have.

My path was mirroring hers, although I was almost to lose sight of that. And just as it had for Lenka, my family betrayed me, too. Heartachingly so.

For eight years I'd continued living with Gran and Grandad Hart. Not a few weeks but eight long years! After arriving back in Eldersgate at the tail end of 1970, I'd been expecting to return home in the New Year. The nightmares had ceased, and the wardrobe door and haunted house no longer seemed daunting, because I had Lenka with me. In fact, the prospect of going home was so exciting I couldn't wait for Christmas Day.

Mum and Dad were due to come for the big day, and a fizz of anticipation built up inside. At four in the morning, I lay wide awake listening to the sleet spatter against the windowpane, wondering if Father Christmas had filled the old darned sock at the bottom of my bed, if there would be chocolates that day, and, most of all, if Mum and Dad would take me home with them. The ordeal was nearly over.

Later on that morning, while the Greenway Moor brass band played 'Silent Night' and 'O Come, All Ye Faithful' on the gramophone, Grandma Hart asked me to help with dinner preparations in the scullery. Grandad had opened a bottle of sherry in the front room and was tapping the chair arm in time to the music. The more he drank, the harder he beat time.

We set to peeling and chopping, chatting, rinsing and stirring.

I was beginning to think about packing, and if Dad had painted my bedroom purple yet, when Grandad started shouting. Neither of us paid much attention. He seemed to be ranting to himself, but Grandma Hart had tensed up, chopping and peeling faster now, the conversation dying on her lips.

"Bloody bastards! Did you hear me? I said bloody bastards!"

I took in a bowl of crisps and set it down next to his glass. As I did so, he looked up and glared. Did he want something else? I didn't know what to do. His eyes were bloodshot, and the lower part of his face had set to grim.

"If it weren't for our lads, Eva, they'd 'ave marched all over us. You kids don't know you're born!"

He poured out another glass of sherry, slopping it over the rim.

From the scullery, which was full of steam, Grandma's voice warbled over the top of 'Hark! The Herald Angels Sing'.

"Me dad were just a lad, seventeen when he went to t' trenches. Most of 'em lied about their age – thought they were going to fight for king and country and back 'ome in no time. Bloody tragic it were, and all because them at t' top decided it were a good idea to wade in. Millions were killed in them trenches, just kids, sent to their deaths like they were nothing—"

I slipped up. "That was the First World War. Weren't you in the Second?"

Half a bottle of sherry he may have had, but he was quick on the draw. "And what do you know about it? Were you there?"

"No, of course not—"

"Well, shut the bleedin' 'ell up, then!"

He stared me down, red-veined eyes burning a hole in the side of my face. I had the feeling, as Lenka had done with Uncle Guido, that he saw something in me he didn't like.

Fortunately, Gran came to the rescue. "Eva, love?"

"Yes?"

"Set the table in the parlour, will you? I'm almost ready."

I shot back to the scullery, rooting in the cutlery drawer. "Mum and Dad aren't here yet, though."

She gave me a tiny pat on the shoulder. "No, love. They're not coming. Just set it for three."

It was a bullet to the gut. "What? Why not? Why?"

"Don't take on, love. We had a telephone call last night to say they couldn't come. So we'll just have to make the best of it, eh? Now be a good girl and set the table."

The effort it took not to burst into tears was immense, Christmas dinner interminable. Every time I caught her eye, she shook her head and turned away – pandering to Grandad Hart, trying to make him laugh, to cajole and divert him in order to avoid an explosion of rage.

So it was not until he'd lolled into a snoring stupor by the fire that the truth came out.

We were washing up. Would they be coming over tomorrow, I wanted to know? Why not? Was I still going home after Christmas? When could I see my mother?

"It's like this, Eva, love. Your mum and dad have gone what's called bankrupt. The house has got to be taken back by the bank, and your mum's not well. They've got to go into a Bed and Breakfast, you know – a lodging house – but your mum's got a bad chest, a nasty bit of flu, so it's best you stay with us a while longer."

I blinked back the tears. "How much longer?"

"Don't make a fuss, Eva, and for goodness' sake, keep your voice down. Don't wake 'im up. They'll get themselves sorted, you'll see. It'd help, mind, if your mother pulled her weight – our Pete's 'aving to work night and day."

"Can I see her?"

"Not just yet. When she's better, p'rhaps."

"What about Sooty? Is Sooty all right?"

No one told me what had really happened, though. That didn't come out for years. The truth covered up, further questions went unanswered, and in the end I stopped asking. Maybe that's why Lenka's story became so important over the years, and why it was such a blow when the dreams stopped and she too, it seemed, had cut all ties.

When I woke up on my sixteenth birthday, my first thought was to wonder why there had been another dreamless night. My second was that I could now leave if I wanted! Why not, except there was nowhere to run to? Besides, it was sunny and there was a party to look forward to. Being sixteen, I honestly thought it would be a brilliant day and even held out hope that the whole nightmare had ended. Looking back, there was a nagging feeling that something cataclysmic was brewing…but maybe that was because of what happened to Lenka when she turned sixteen? It didn't have to be that way for me though, did it? I shoved it to the back of my mind, anyway.

Nicky's mum had organised a huge celebration, and most of the street was invited on that heady blue-sky day in May. Even Eldersgate looked pretty with cherry blossom in full bloom and green grass dotted with daisies instead of litter-strewn mud. People had hung up baskets of geraniums, and the ever-present smell of petrol and soot was now laced with the early fragrance of lilac and honeysuckle. I wore a pair of navy culottes and a white halter-neck top. Nicky had a red halter dress. I'd have killed for something like that, but Grandma Hart had taken me to C&A and bought 'something serviceable'.

Mrs Dixon went to a lot of trouble. There were sandwiches and sausage rolls and birthday cake, all set out on a trestle table in the backyard, and after everyone sang, 'Happy Birthday', we played games and danced.

'Everybody Dance' was Nicky's favourite. 'Night Fever' by the Bee Gees was mine. She had better taste, but the thing that united us more than anything was dancing. We danced ourselves into a trance until the velvet of dusk descended and a few of the neighbours shouted, "Turn that bloody racket off, it's fucking ten o'clock!"

It was a good day, though. The best. I'll never forget it. Some things you just hold on to, don't you?

Because exactly as Lenka's world had eclipsed the day she turned sixteen, mine did, too. Although it happened somewhat differently, the outcome was pretty much the same.

I was walking home, still smiling because Mark Curry had come to the party and he'd looked at me. A lot. He'd worn brown baggy trousers with big pockets stitched onto the sides, and a denim jacket. His hair was black and straight, his grin mischievous, which was to be expected – I'd experimented a little, popping thoughts into people's heads, and the images I'd popped into his would definitely make him smirk. We had a slow dance to Yvonne Elliman's 'If I Can't Have You', and he held me. It felt so nice, his hands circling my waist like that, kind of warm and safe…but when the dance finished, neither of us knew what to do, and his mates were jeering. So he sauntered off and lit a cigarette and stood there staring at me until the sun went down, and Mrs Dixon told all the boys to scoot off home.

He liked me, though, I know he did. Those feelings were so new, so raw, and I recalled how Lenka had yearned for Oskar – how her heart had snagged at the sight of his eyelashes glittering with water droplets.

I was in such a dreamy state as I ambled home, sighing

at the sight of the terrace in the shadows by the pit wheel. Did I really have to go back inside, into the shadows again? Just then, a familiar Elvis Presley song played inside my head, an earworm, as loudly as if it were on Nicky's mum's record player.

I stopped dead.

Everyone knew the song. But until that moment it had never registered that it was the same one Lenka heard in the farmhouse kitchen the day she'd returned from Mooswald. She'd been drinking a glass of water, upset and angry, when the voice of a child had sung the old folk song so clearly she'd thought her in the same room.

Elvis's beautiful melodic voice sang:

Treat me nice,
Treat me good,
Treat me like you really should…

He stopped. There was a lull.

Replaced now by a deep, distorted demonic one, as if the turntable speed had slowed to 78 rpm instead of 33.

Muss i' denn,
Muss i' denn,
Zum Städtele hinaus,
Städtele hinaus,
Und du, mein Schatz, bleibst hier.

Stunned, and a little drunk from cider, I stumbled against the garden wall. The sound of children's tinkling laughter was all around, echoing from every direction.

The fun and games were over, weren't they? There had been no Oskar for Lenka. And there would be no Mark for me. The deserted street darkened rapidly, and despite the balmy evening, an icy wind blew against my face. To think I'd believed the nightmare could be over…

Oh God, what was coming? That was all I could think…what the hell was coming?

***

CHAPTER TWENTY-SIX

The previously ethereal dusk turned thickly brooding. Menace hung in the air. Shadows now followed me, standing when I stood, walking when I walked, looming over the hollow click of my footsteps like a giant winged bird. This wasn't coming from Lenka anymore, was it? The moment she was initiated into the Order she crossed over to the dark side, and the demonic took hold. The memories transferred to me had been exactly that – memories from before that time, which meant this was now the same direct channel of darkness she had fought against. And a very real terror gripped my heart. What had possessed her wished to possess me – it was my turn.

There was nowhere to run. I really was alone with this – abandoned by both parents, trapped with Earl Hart and his drunken rages on a poor housing estate where most people were struggling just to get by. What was I supposed to do? Would someone show themselves as they had to Lenka? Was there a person waiting to take me to the next level? Where was my instructor? The tears were blinding, even as shivers of fear crawled up and down my back.

If only I could talk to my mother. Where was she? Since that desolate Christmas eight years ago, all attempts to find her had drawn a blank. She was poorly and not of sound mind, the place she was kept in not suitable for a child. When she came out, I could see her then and not before. Yet years had passed. Stranger still was Dad's behaviour. His visits, always brief, had quickly dwindled to rare. First he said he was working away somewhere, then, shockingly, that he was considering remarrying. I sat in a daze when he said that, speechless while he patted me on the back of my head and said I could go and stay with them sometime, with this woman I had never met and her three children. I could tell he didn't really want me to do that, though. When he looked at me, he saw my mother, was reminded of the issues I'd had as a child and the ones he must have had with my mum. A mad wife and a mad daughter. He wanted to step away from all that, you could see. There were deep lines around his eyes, and his sandy hair had turned peppery, his zest for life all fizzed out.

Oh, he came over on birthdays, and of course he'd visited that morning and left a present – a small green plastic radio that was undoubtedly the cheapest in Dixons. It didn't even pick up Radio One properly, let alone Radio Luxembourg for the charts. So I couldn't go to Dad with this. Not in a million Sundays, as Grandma Hart would say. He had another family now.

I walked down the gennel to the backyard and let myself into the scullery, feeling oddly watched. Grandad Hart's snores were reverberating through the walls, and the double bed upstairs creaked and groaned with their combined weight. A mixture of odours lingered in the stale air of yesteryear – soot, oxtail soup and Vim. All was as it usually was, yet something undefinable had changed, as if the long shadows from the street had accompanied me indoors. After a brief wash at the sink, I brushed my teeth and used the toilet at the back, then tiptoed across the linoleum and upstairs.

Everything looked grainy like a television with a poor reception, my ears crackled with static, and the moon seemed unnaturally bright. Fleeting movements caught on the edge of my vision, only to dissipate when I swung around. By then the sense that someone was standing right next to me, fusing into my skin, was prickling all over.

And now it was nighttime, everyone asleep, the bedroom door shut, just as it had been all those years ago. No Lenka to pick up the story of her daily life. Nothing but this direct channel of evil. And this time, there would be no parents to race up the stairs, no doctor and no priest.

In the front bedroom my grandparents would long since have removed their dentures and put them in a jar by the side of the bed. In deep slumber they rumbled through the night, oblivious to anything other than the turn of each day and the grinding of the mundane wheel. How I longed to be a Mundane. How blissful that must be.

Lying back on the single bed, with the curtains wide open, I racked my brain for the lessons Sophia had taught Lenka – the ones for keeping the legion of demonic servants at bay while she'd learned and prepared for the main role to come. It was all about mastery, about building a fortress of steel around the mind, a strong barrier to prevent total possession. All those in the Order used this technique, as Lenka had discovered when she'd tried to read their minds. Because all of them knew those demons were real, and it terrified them.

From inside my pillowcase I pulled out the poppet and clutched it. This was our talisman, our identity, all of us – from Baroness Jelinski to Baba Olga to Lenka to me.

Muss i' denn,
Muss i' denn,
Zum Städtele hinaus,
Städtele hinaus,
Und du, mein Schatz, bleibst hier...

The song echoed around the dark bowl of my head, repeating and repeating, the jaunty yet lamenting tune heralding a loss? Of what? Of the prospect of love? Or of our souls?

My heart was hammering, eyes boring into the empty space between the end of the bed and the door. Who was here? Would something materialise? If that happened, if eyes flashed from out of empty air, I would die of shock, I would die...

A low, distorted voice broke into my chain of thoughts, continuing the old German folk song:

Wenn i' komm,
Wenn i' komm,
Wenn i' wieder, wieder komm,
Wieder, wieder komm...

"Who are you?" I whispered into the ether. "What do you want?"

And please don't answer...please don't. This is all fantasy, all dreams, not real.

The silence buzzed, and nothing appeared. Eventually, perhaps from the cider earlier, together with the effort of being vigilant hour upon hour, my eyes began to close. I must have drifted, perhaps only momentarily. If only dawn would come and the light would lift…just to get through the night was all…

What transpired, therefore, took a little while to register. Already in the first stage of sleep and wanting to sink deeper, at first I dismissed it. But gradually awareness filtered through that a strong breeze was blowing in my face and the air was freezing. On some level my conscious mind accepted this, only surfacing fully when the breeze became a whistling wind that billowed the curtains and rattled the windows. Hunkering down to keep warm, I tried to pull up the covers, only to have them snatched away by an invisible hand.

Now I woke up!

By then the bed was shaking, rocking like there was an earthquake. The picture of my parents swung on its hook before clattering to the floor; books wobbled on the shelves and tumbled off. Sitting up in a bolt of panic, I glanced at the clock. It was three in the morning.

And then I looked up at the man staring down at me. A man dressed in a black suit, wearing a fedora pulled down low over his eyes.

He smiled, revealing a lower set of jagged, spiky teeth. "Hello, Eva."

***

CHAPTER TWENTY-SEVEN

When I next woke up, it was to a cacophony of bird chatter and my grandma shouting.

"What the bloody 'ell are you doin' on the floor, our Eva? Earl! Eva's fallen in the night - come an' 'elp me."

Between them, they lumped me onto the bed. Sick was stuck to the carpet and the bedsheets, everywhere, even matted in my hair.

"Her arms and legs were all crooked. I don't know what's up with 'er; she might have had a fit. Pass me that blanket."

"Bloody drunk, that's what," said Grandad. "Sixteen years old and drunk as a street tart."

"Now then, Earl—"

"Don't you 'now then' me! That Mrs Dixon wants a word 'aving wi' 'er."

They started to row. Gran was wiping my face with a towel and trying to chivvy life back into limbs that were rigid. "Come on, love. Wake up, Eva. You've 'ad a fall, love."

But Earl's words and the tone in which they were spoken now filtered through the haze of semi-consciousness. "No..." Struggling to surface, a mumbling croak came out. I tried again. "No, Grandad, it weren't 'er. Me and Nicky took some cider from a lad, that were all – it were nowt to do with Mrs Dixon."

"What the 'ell were she doing letting lads in?"

"No, she didn't. It were my fault, not—"

"Earl, no!"

The punch in my face was such a shock, it scattered all further thoughts into splinters of light.

Oh, so you really do see stars…

"Now get up, get washed and get yourself to school," he said. "You're a bloody disgrace."

I didn't go. Made up my mind the second he said it. Instead, I sat at the breakfast table eating toast while he munched through his Full English like a warthog snaffling through garbage.

I'd be going to the canal.

Loathing consumed me. My head was throbbing and my cheekbone was swelling up rapidly. Bloody hell, I couldn't even see properly now. He seemed to have become nastier overnight. Call it intuition, but it felt as though there'd been a shift in the way he regarded me as I lay in bed – a dangerous upping of gears. Lenka had been convinced Uncle Guido had seen something in her he found threatening, sensing perhaps that she despised him. And as I walked along the canal path, it came to me that Earl felt the same way. Oh, he'd always been a ranting drunk who took it out on his wife and granddaughter, but now he'd been triggered on a whole new level. And it was highly personal.

Although the spring day was heady with cherry blossom and birdsong, a sense of doom hung over me. The normally grim canal sparkled, and the grass was bright, studded with thousands of daisies and starbursts of yellow dandelions, yet still it was impossible to shake the shadow of darkness. Who was my visitor last night? He seemed familiar, uncannily similar to the man who appeared to Lenka as Uncle Toby. Yet I couldn't recall anything further...

Reaching the bridge, I stopped to lift my face to the warmth of the sun in an attempt to dispel it. But as I did so, a strange thing happened. The air chilled, and in a repeat of that day long ago in Rabenwald, the sun became the moon, the vibrant colours of the day ebbed to black and white, and day switched to night. Traffic noise ceased. There was not a sound. Except a distant whistle of wind whipping off mountains and chasing through the trees...

It lasted less than a second, before the spring day catapulted back into focus, the brilliance of it surreal and the noise too loud. I fell back against the stones of the bridge and sank to my haunches, dizzy and badly disorientated.

The whispers should not have been a surprise. I knew with near certainty what was going to happen. But they were. Seeming, as they did, to come out of nowhere. Out of the ether. Or my head.

Give us work, Eva. Give us work...give us work...

The stark parallel between the surreal dreams of Lenka's life and my own reality punched me in the gut. Would I now get ill? How ill? How fast? It couldn't really be true...could it? Really?

Once again, the sound of children's laughter resounded from every direction, tinkling on the soft summer breeze in a ghostly game of hide-and-seek.

Give us work...give us work...

How long did I sit there, huddled on the ground with

my head in my hands? Probably all afternoon, until the temperature cooled, school was over, and the bullies who hung around the chip shop would have gone home. What choice was there but to traipse back? There had to be a way out of this, that's what I was thinking. Maybe if I just packed a bag and left – one more runaway teen on a bus to the metropolis?

Anyway, by the time I unlatched the gate into the backyard it had turned five. And Earl Hart was waiting.

He stood at the door to the scullery with a woodbine dangling from his lower lip. If he'd once had a shining human spirit in there, it was sure as hell snuffed out now. A cloud of sooty blackness clouded his aura. So, too, on the breath he exhaled - plumes of it like I'd once seen on a documentary of Hitler dictating to the crowds. It had come out of his mouth in billows that the people below were breathing in. It hung over the hordes like a thunderstorm waiting to burst. They were lifting their heads to hail him while sucking in all that blackness.

Something really bad was going to happen, something that had been brewing for days now, maybe weeks. It was in the way he looked at me, in the curl of his lip. I hesitated, fingers lingering on the latch. Where was Gran?

He inclined his head. "Get indoors!"

Like wading through deep water, my limbs felt heavy and my feet dragged as I crossed that yard. Ducking under the washing line, I hung back a little.

"Where's—"

But his iron hand reached out to cuff the back of my neck, and sent me sprawling inside. Immediately he clicked the door shut behind us and locked it.

Grabbing my arm, he said, "Yer making me a bloody

laughing stock, yer fuckin' little bitch!"

"What?"

His eyes were barely recognisable – hard black bullets. Beer fumes blasted into my face. "Know what they're calling yer on t' estate? Well then, do yer?"

"No."

"A slut, that's what."

"Why? I don't—"

His great spade of a hand struck me across the skull, and for a second I thought he'd knocked it clean off my neck. Then it came again, stinging like fire, then again and again and again, so hard my body was thrown across the room. I fell badly, cracking my head on the corner of the sink, reeling and desperately struggling to my feet when, to my horror, he began to unzip himself.

"What? Oh, hell no! No, no!"

Fuck, no!

There was not enough time to stand up or get out of the way. One hand had already pinned me to the wall, the other yanking up my skirt and wrenching down my knickers. His knee was pressing into one thigh, and the struggle was futile.

It's not happening, can't be, can't be. It isn't me...not me here...not true...

The familiar scullery with its yellow Formica cupboards and chequered linoleum thumped in and out of my vision, in and out, in and out, along with the pain, the excruciating, burning pain of rape.

He crushed my spine into the cupboards, banged my head against the corner of the kitchen unit and slammed a hand over my mouth to stop me from screaming.

And after it was over, he shoved me off, instructed me

to get washed and not to breathe a word or I'd be homeless by tomorrow.

Then and there I vowed I would take Uncle Toby and Satan any time – any day of the week – over this

***

CHAPTER TWENTY-EIGHT

Like all those with something to hide, Earl Hart lied. Within hours he set about a smear campaign, expertly manipulating my grandma's weaknesses. I lay on the bed upstairs while he told her I was no better than I ought to be, and she was not to take up any tea. I could 'stew in it'. *Fancy lying on the bedroom floor in her own sick, so hungover she couldn't even find the bed – a slut just like her mother. Hadn't she been a bit of a tramp before she'd met our Pete?*

Well, that played into Grandma Hart's dislike of my mother, who had never been good enough for her son. I pictured her nodding.

"You were right about 'er all along," Earl went on, pressing home the advantage. "And this one's just as bad. Right little tart. I wouldn't be surprised if she doesn't get knocked up. There's talk she's been going with lads, and that'll be another mouth to feed then – more work for you to do wi' a screaming babby! What a bloody disgrace, after all we've done for 'er an' all."

"It's that red hair," Gran said. "Red-haired and far too pretty for her own good."

I turned onto my side, so desolate even the tears wouldn't come. No more, no more… It was true I'd never been happy here, but it had at least been a safe haven. How could your own flesh and blood turn on you like this? And so brutally? Where did you go when you had no family? I stayed curled in a foetus ball for hours, rigid, trapped in time, until eventually they went to bed. The bedsprings squeaked as they climbed in, quickly followed by snoring vibrating through the walls.

Then, and only then, did I dare creep downstairs for a glass of water. Every step on the stairs creaked loudly. My whole body hurt, stinging with cuts and bruises on the outside, throbbing with an unfamiliar ache inside. Weight-bearing sent shockwaves of pain up my leg as slowly I limped down the hall towards the scullery.

Moonlight streamed in. Carefully, so the pipes wouldn't crank, I turned on the cold water tap and had just started to fill a glass, when a mass of shadows appeared on the far wall. It floated like a cloud of dust, spreading now across the floor and cloaking my figure in darkness.

Give us work…give us work…

I finished filling the glass, drank it down and refilled, trying to keep calm.

Give us work…give us work…or we will make you sick…

A memory of Lenka tiptoeing into Guido and Heide's bedroom flashed into my head. But I was not ill yet. No, I couldn't do to Earl what Lenka had done to Guido. My grandad was, after all, simply a product of his time - a hard-drinking, fist-fighting misogynist with little education. And he had fought for his country and provided for his family. No, I couldn't do what Lenka had done. Besides, I did not know how to. So I stood at the scullery sink, looking out at the full moon, drinking water. Thinking.

Come on, Eva, give us work…you must…or you know what will happen.

Use of the dark arts was a slippery slope. Cross the line and you could not then cross back again. And Lenka had become extremely unwell, desperately sick, so what choice did she have? Whereas I…I was fine.

The lovely cool water trickled down my throat, soothing and fresh.

Draining the glass, however, I was just about to pour another to take upstairs when the most almighty spasm of colic gripped my intestines. The intensity had me doubled me over, panting, gasping, until it passed. It must have been the cold water hitting an empty stomach?

Muss i' denn,
Muss i' denn,
Zum Städtele hinaus…

That was right, an empty stomach…

Carefully, with only a slight sigh from the seal as I opened the fridge door, I did what was forbidden and took something out of it without asking – just one slice of bread and a small piece of cheddar. That was all, a tiny sandwich.

At first it felt good to eat, the peristalsis of solid food working its way down to line the stomach, comforting. God, that was good. So much better. Finishing it off, I picked up the glass of water and turned towards the door. Which was when a near tidal wave of colic washed over my whole body. Whoa! Then it came again. My stomach clenched into an angry fist. It took my breath, and a cold sweat broke out all over, the bread and cheese weighing inside like lead balls.

Holding on to the side of the sink, I stood shaking, waiting for it to pass. Bloody hell, that was horrible. But it was just a reaction to the cold water and food. It wasn't what happened to Lenka. It wasn't the onset of something sinister.

Was it?

Back in bed, though, I could get neither warm nor comfortable, and a dull ache cramped down the right side of my head. None of this was surprising after such a physical assault, especially on top of the night before. I told myself repeatedly this was only to be expected. And tomorrow would be better. Tomorrow I'd make plans to get out of here. He'd never get to do that to me again. Not ever.

What about finding Dad? Couldn't I go and stay with him for a while? Didn't he say he and this new woman were in Leeds, that he was buying a house? Thing was, last time I'd mentioned it, Gran said they were in the process of moving and not to keep pestering. If I wanted to see him, she'd ring and he'd come here. Okay, well, I'd ring him, then…

Mind chatter together with a sore head and stomach prevented sleep, but eventually I did drift off, on some level aware the pain was increasing. Surfacing periodically, I told myself it would pass…to just sleep and then tomorrow, tomorrow…

In the end though, a series of violent convulsions forced me to wake up. A terrific roll of colic broke out, crunching my intestines into contortions. By then I was shivering violently, coated in sweat and short of breath. I tried to hold out until first light, but at five when Grandma Hart got up, there really was no option but to shout for help.

She took one look and said she'd fetch the doctor. Downstairs, the call was made on the phone in the hallway, but it turned out he was busy with a childbirth and couldn't come.

"It'll wear off," she said, bustling back upstairs. "These things do. It'll be the gastric flu or summat. You'd best stay in bed today, love."

By evening, though, even sips of water came hurling back up. A sickly cluster of migraine worked its way from the back of my skull to the nerves in one eye, and all I could do was lie there in a fever of exhaustion, praying for relief. But that relief never came, and the racking pain continued through the night into the next day.

The following morning, on day two, a sore appeared on my upper arm – a large, oozing blister that pulsed and throbbed as if something live was pushing up from underneath.

Gran brushed the matted hair back from my forehead. "Well, I'm flummoxed – I don't know what's up with you, love. It looks like food poisoning. Summat foreign you ate at that party. Mrs Dixon, well, she's not like us, is she?"

This was the Mrs Dixon who had fed and looked after me like a daughter all these years? The Mrs Dixon who cared, who laughed and danced and bought me treats and clothes the same as she did for Nicky, her own daughter?

"What do you mean, 'not like us'?"

"Black."

The shock of what she'd said dropped like a lump of dirty rock into a clear lagoon.

"Anyhow, I've to go and put your grandad's tea on or

– well, you know what he's like?"

"I'm glad she's not like you," I said.

She patted my hand. "I know you're a good lass, really, underneath, but your grandad's right: once you're better, you'll probably need to think about getting a job and leaving school. He says you're to stand on your own two feet from now on. I don't think you can stay here much longer, love."

I told myself it was their upbringing and a lack of education. I told myself that for a full minute after she'd left the room and plodded downstairs to grill his pork chops. But it didn't work. I found I was gripping the sheets in both hands, screwing handfuls of them into balls, the pain of her ugly words beyond comprehension. I don't think I could have ground my teeth together any harder.

I loved Mrs Dixon almost as much as I loved Nicky.

Give us work…Eva, give us work…

The demons were gleeful, laughing…triumphant…dancing…

Another sore appeared on my arm, followed by another and then a whole rash of them rose up in a plague, blistering and seeping. What the hell was I going to do? Was there anyone I could turn to? Who? Please God, there had to be someone.

***

CHAPTER TWENTY-NINE

There was only one person, wasn't there? I didn't want to burden her with my darkness. But she really was the only one.

We sat on her sofa, Mrs Dixon and I. She took my hand in hers. "Oh, Lordy. Child, look at the state of you!"

I was bone thin, shivering and doubling up with colic every few minutes. Each seizure wrung me out. I couldn't even sip water.

"Why hasn't Maud called the doctor?"

"He were busy. She thought it were food poisoning and it'd get better. I dunno." I squeezed her hand. "Mrs Dixon, I can't stay there any longer. I don't know what to do. I need some 'elp."

Her eyes grew huge as full moons. "Can't stay there? Why, whatever's happened to make you say that? He been hitting you again? I know he's handy with his fists, everyone knows—"

"Worse than that—"

I held her gaze until comprehension registered and a cloud of revulsion passed across her features. And then she took me into her arms and bear-hugged me while I cried.

"You'll have to go to the doctor's, and you'll need a story."

"No, I'll wait and see first if, to find out if, you know?"

She nodded.

Nineteen seventy-eight and the police barely considered domestic abuse a crime. Besides, people like us would never consider legal action. Not only did we not have the money, but no one brought family business into the open like that. You didn't wash your dirty laundry in public so that other people got to know and looked at you funny! Incestuous secrets were buried, and those it happened to thought they were the only ones, that they'd got what they deserved just like the abuser said.

Mrs Dixon, though. Well, the expression on her face was the first indication this perspective might be wrong, and the effect on me was that of fog rising off a murky pond.

After a while she said, "I don't know how much to tell you, Eva, but it's probably best you know a bit more about your grandad. And your dad, come to that. It might help you decide what to do."

She worked in a care home for the elderly. And those old folk liked to talk – some of them about 'Earl the Hammer'.

"The *Hammer*?"

She nodded. A few years ago after overhearing a heated discussion between some of the residents, she'd asked one of them, an elderly lady called Maureen, who they were talking about and what they meant.

"I was thinking about you, child, and so I asked her, 'Didn't he fight in the War? Are you talking about Earl Hart, the union leader?'

"'Aye, 'im! And he were kicked out o' t' army an' all, so don't let him tell you no different. Dismissed for extreme violence, he were – bare-knuckled fights and an out-of-control temper that saw him slam a hammer in the back of a man's head.'"

My hands flew to my face.

"Eva, I knew then I had to watch over you. And there's more to it. Maureen said, 'Aye, and I knew his missus an' all. Miscarriage after miscarriage she 'ad because of how he knocked her about. And little Pete were never a day without a black eye. No wonder he left home at sixteen, poor little bugger.'"

I looked up sharply when she said that. "My dad? But he put me back here! With Earl. I was only eight."

Mrs Dixon shook her head, confounded. "Maybe your mum and dad had worse troubles? Maybe they didn't know what else to do and hoped it wouldn't be for long? They must have had good reason, they must have."

My heartbeat rocketed, the impact of this new revelation blurring all rational thought. My own father had abandoned me, dumped me with his violent father, and then left Mum for another woman. What had he done with her? Was she still alive? Had he killed her? Was he just as bad as his own father? Why couldn't my mother even be visited? They'd lied and lied and lied. All of them. All lies.

I looked down at my hands. They were shaking. Sores had broken out all over my legs now, too. I couldn't eat, my hair was falling out in clumps, and black fungus was growing under my fingernails. Gastric flu had me clutching at my stomach as it racked and twisted. The fatigue was overwhelming. I really couldn't carry on like this for much longer.

"You're not at all well, child."

I shook my head as another wave of colic took hold. I gasped for breath, tears running down my face. "I don't know what it is. Food poisoning or summat. I don't know."

She frowned. "Food poisoning don't make your hair fall out, don't give you sores, and it don't turn your nails black—"

"What's going to happen to me? What shall I do? And where's my mum? I don't understand."

"All right, I'll tell you what I think. I think you should go right now and tell your nanna you're coming to stay with me for a while, and tell her why. Then come straight back here, and I will get you to a doctor."

My tears dried. "With you?"

"You can tell her I've agreed and it's so you and Nicky can study together for a year before college."

"College?"

"Yes, college. You got to get some qualifications in this life. So, you can stay here until you're educated – you're a child and you have a right to be safe, do you hear me? So this is what we do – if your nanna objects, although she did say you had to go and get a job and live somewhere else, but if she does, then you tell her straight about your grandad and that you don't feel safe in that house no more. If she refuses to believe you and threatens to tell Earl, then you tell her in no uncertain terms that you will go to the police unless she persuades him this is for the best. We're calling her bluff with that one, but you focus on what you got to do and it will turn out just fine."

"Do you mean it? That I can come and stay here? Really, really, really?"

She smiled a warm-honey smile. "You're here most of the

time anyway. And it will make my Nicky very happy."

I saw the wisdom of her words, saw myself repeating them to my grandma, and then I saw Earl's face when he found out. He would rage and curse and deny it all, probably smash her in the mouth for telling lies. Would he come around here, too? Would he hurt Mrs Dixon? And Nicky?

That could not happen. Would not happen.

Dark shadows crept across Mrs Dixon's bookcase then, eclipsing the television, crawling over the carpet...

Give us work, Eva, give us work.

"Mrs Dixon, can I ask you one more thing?"

We both glanced at the clock. There wasn't much time before Earl would be back for his tea and notice my absence.

"Nicky once told me you did voodoo, and—"

"Say what?"

I loved the way she shrieked like that, and I almost laughed. "It's just, I wondered, you see, I have this poppet. I got it in Bavaria when I was seven, and—"

With her eyebrows almost in her hairline, she listened for all of thirty seconds while I tried to explain, before holding up her hand. "That Nicky Dixon's got some answering to do. I most certainly do *not* practice voodoo."

"Oh!"

"My sister and I once stuck pins in a doll we made at school because some girl was causing mischief, but we got badly scared after what we did. And I mean, real scared. You don't ever mess with things you don't understand, not ever. That girl got sick, see? She nearly died. And then we had some bad things happen to us, too – things I can't ever talk about. Whatever it was we connected with was real, and, believe me – you don't ever want to meddle with the black arts. Not ever, Eva. You got to burn that poppet, and you don't bring it into this house, either, do you hear?"

Shame filled me, and my eyes prickled.

"Now don't take on. But if you're thinking of sticking pins into a poppet of your grandad and asking me if that's okay, then all I'm saying is, tempting as that might be, don't!" She ruffled my hair. "Now, go and speak to your nanna, child. Go tell her what he's done to you and that you're leaving."

"Mrs Dixon, do you know where my mother is?"

"No, I don't. But why don't you ask your daddy?"

"I can't."

"Why?"

"Because when he comes to the house, Gran and Grandad are always there, and they've told me not to upset him and pester him. That she's a sore subject."

"Go to his house and see him there. Ask him in private."

"I can't. He's in Leeds with another family now. I think they're moving into a new house there."

Her voice shot up another octave. "Leeds? Leeds? Who told you that?"

"Er…"

"Eva, I see that man all the time. If he's in Leeds, how come he uses the same paper shop I do? The nursing home is at the end of the main road, and he lives round the corner. Ten minutes from here!"

"No…yes…of course, yeah, I knew that…"

When I stood up, the room was spinning. My face in the mirror over the mantelpiece was as tiny and pinched as a grey, deflated balloon, the eyes hollow. The whole fabric of my life was fraying at the edges. Soon there wouldn't be a single fragment of reality left.

Outside, someone was bouncing a ball up the pavement, getting closer.

"That'll be Nicky," said Mrs Dixon, standing up and smoothing down her skirt.

Nicky played netball for the school team. I was useless at sports, but she was quick and agile, strong too. I imagined her sunshine smile when I told her I was going to be her sister for the next year... We could have so much fun. I could live again...

But the whole room was shrouded in gloom, as if there'd been an eclipse. Couldn't Mrs Dixon see it? Why wasn't she shivering like me? Goose pimples rose and spread across my back, my skin like ice.

Give us work...come on, Eva. Say yes...

A good life could still be mine. It could happen. But not like this, not weak and ill, with my hair falling out, sores all over my body, poleaxing headaches and permanent stomach pain.

"Okay, I'm going to go and tell Gran now, Mrs Dixon. I'll be back in about an hour with my things, is that all right?"

"Is what all right?" said Nicky, bursting in.

"Eva's going to come and live with us for a while. I've asked her and she's agreed."

Nicky stared at us, from one to the other. Then, throwing her arms around me, she hugged me and jumped up and down all at the same time. "Oh, that's ace. Brilliant! We're going to have such a—"

Abruptly she broke away, frowning. "Eva, what is it?

You're shaking and you look awful. Are you okay? Has something happened?"

"Well, yeah—"

She peered at one of my eyes, then zoomed in close. "What's happened to your eye?"

I touched the one she was looking at. "Nothing, why? Is it bruised?"

"Yeah, but I don't mean around it. I mean in it. Like there's something growing inside the pupil – a big black smudge. Go look in the mirror – it's really weird."

***

CHAPTER THIRTY

Gran was in the scullery, elbow deep in suds, when I broke the news. She listened, continuing to wash out smalls while I told her what her husband had done and that there was no choice but to leave.

What could she say? What more could I say in response? You can't allow the same pattern to play out again and again, can you? When it's over, it's over. So I left her there, staring out of the window into the backyard. To think.

Besides, I felt too ill to stand there any longer. And despite what Mrs Dixon had said just minutes before, Uncle Guido's nightcap was on my mind.

Earl – I could no longer refer to him as Grandad – had a habit of cutting his toenails while he watched television, leaving them to fester. As soon as I remembered that, I went straight into the front room and knelt in front of the hearth to ferret around. Yes, there were quite a few dry, crusty yellow crescents stuck in the cracks of the tiles. They would serve the purpose. Quickly retrieving half a dozen or so, I wrapped them inside a tissue and sped upstairs to pack.

Today was the day this ended, and he was going to pay and pay and pay. Why should I suffer this horrific pain while he laughed and joked in the working men's club, drinking beer and playing snooker? I'd seen all those pornographic newspaper cuttings on the walls, heard the way they talked about women, knew they had strippers perform while they sat there in a nicotine fog, jeering and swearing.

Deep inside, though, a nagging voice conflicted with my shadow self. What about my grandma? She'd done her best with a troubled young girl not her own. Guilt snagged at my resolve for a moment, and I slumped onto the bed. To make it all so much worse, every kindness she had ever meted out now flashed before my eyes – from the soldiers of toast with treacle, to the games of whist and the freshly pressed school uniform.

Yet she'd done nothing when his fist cracked across my eight-year-old skull. And she'd been lying all this time about Dad and probably about my mother, too. She knew Dad lived just down the road and never said! She wouldn't even tell me what had happened to Sooty, despite my crying and pleading. I put my head in my hands. Everything ached, every single part of me – from the sprained ankle to the swollen cheek to the oppressive, pounding headache. Why had everyone lied? Why?

Her mouth had worked like a fish in a bowl, bewilderment in her eyes. She was who she was, beaten down, utterly reliant on a violent man for basic survival. Really, I knew nothing about Maud. Only that her parents had both been killed in the First World War.

I was fluctuating wildly, picking at one of the sores on my arm, all the fire of moments ago now doused with guilt.

This illness really could be food poisoning, and all the other symptoms due to stress and malnourishment. And maybe Dad's house purchase had fallen through or something? Or he and this woman had separated? My mother was probably ill in some mental hospital…and my crazy dreams were because I was…well…crazy! I'd been crazy since I was eight years old, and it was all because of what I'd seen at that funeral. That was it. It's what any adult would say by way of explanation. Well, maybe they wouldn't use the word *crazy* – but whatever they said, it would amount to the same thing.

What was real and what was not? That was the difficult bit.

The sore oozed with blood when the scab broke off, and the release of that felt good. But even as that one popped, a fresh batch itched and rose on my back, spreading like the pox.

These sores were real enough. Being raped was real, as were the bruises to prove it. Being slapped hard across the head by an iron-fisted man twice my size was real. My dad living around the corner when he'd said otherwise was real. That he'd left home at sixteen because of his father's violence was also real, and the fact he'd abandoned his daughter to the same fate, knowingly, and never come back as promised. All real. Mrs Dixon had said it – this wasn't food poisoning.

What about the voices, then? The whispers and shadows, the nightly visions of a life not my own, the people, cities, towns and languages all foreign in every way yet implicitly understood? Total madness?

Ah, the poppet! Of course, yes. The poppet was proof. From under the bed, I pulled out the rucksack used for a school trip and tipped out the crow doll. Still here. Solid. Real. My mother had seen it, confiscating it to burn. So, yes, the Bavarian funeral had happened – I had been there and flown over that mountain with the hut clinging precariously to the jutting rock at the top. In addition to that, I'd done well in school and had a true friend who loved all the same things I did. I was no crazier than anyone else. The difference, the only one, between me and most other people was the legacy. The magic.

The poppet seemed to purr and throb when stroked, like a warm, sated cat. The tiny amethyst glittering on its chest glinted in the light, the feathers silky, fluttering gently as if caught in a breeze.

I wondered, though… Could this theory be taken a step further, if only to satisfy my own mind that I was not insane but truly in the possession of a spiritual gift?

In my rattan sewing box were hair ribbons. One tied around the poppet's neck would turn it into a pendulum. Well then, here was a surefire way to see if an external force really did exist – a test to decide once and for all. Was this illness due to demons, or had I inherited nothing more than a legacy of madness?

The use of a pendulum had been brought to my attention by a gang of girls at school, way back when we were about thirteen. This gang, they would huddle together, plotting the downfall of other girls as a way of life. Nicknamed 'The Coven', they'd succeeded in frightening the entire third form. Each could fix an evil stare, and mutter under her breath about how your card was marked, thus instilling both terror and control. One girl in my class wet herself just from one look! They had not one jot of supernatural power, I can vouch for that, but their rule was unquestionable.

The trick was to stay off radar. But one day, in the

cloakrooms, my eyes met those of the coven's leader.

"What the fuck you looking at?"

A bitch.

She stared back for the longest time. The other two flanked her, and the three of them manoeuvred me against wall.

Around that time Lenka had been telling Heinrich about projecting thoughts into someone else's head, so while the coven leader glared and jabbed at my shoulder, saying my card was marked, I sent her an image to think about – really just to see if it worked. Next day she was subdued, not quite herself. And shortly after that, when I walked into the girls' toilets and the three of them were in there, intimidating whomever was inside the cubicle, well, it was clear the little high priestess wasn't well.

It was kind of hard not to smile. Bloody hell, it had worked! I'd sent her a black mamba. Had it slither under her bedroom door just as she was dropping off to sleep, muscling over the floor towards her bed, where she lay paralysed with fear as it climbed up the pale pink sheets, forked tongue flicking in and out towards her face and her hair…

She wasn't sleeping, had terrible nightmares. So we eyed each other that day. My lips twitched ever so slightly; I couldn't help it. And she paled. Somehow she just knew. They didn't pick on me again, anyway, and Nicky never had her blazer ripped again either. But I couldn't be sure I had the power – it could just be I'd had the nerve to eyeball her back – and there was this thing, a caution, if you like, about how black magic rebounded. Threefold. Or was it tenfold?

But to get back to the pendulum. I was walking home

through the woods one afternoon when I caught them using one. All three looked up and glared.

"Fuck off, Ginger Spaz!" That little high priestess – God, she was terrified. The pounding of her heart was nearly audible.

They'd been asking it yes or no. If the answer was affirmative, the pendulum would swing side to side, back and forwards if negative, and if not known, it was to spin around in a circle. The question had been whether Gary Nicholl from the fourth form fancied the little high priestess or not.

It did nothing. The one with the Suzi Quatro haircut made it swing, but anyone could see she was forcing it.

All three glowered at me. "Piss off! You deaf?"

"Okay, I'm going. Although the answer, if you want it, is yes – he does!"

Oh, how they'd wanted to know more, but pride forbade it. Three kids from neglectful homes, two of them with violent fathers. How badly they'd wanted to find some kind of power in a world in which they had none. But they were dangerous, too, because they were damaged, merciless and just as cruel as the bullies who'd taught them the rules.

"How did you even know the question?" Suzy Look-alike shouted.

I glanced over my shoulder. "Dunno."

"She's a witch," the little priestess said. "Don't pick a fight; she's a fuckin' witch, I'm telling yer."

Would the pendulum work for me now, though?

Whatever it was we connected with was real, and, believe me – you don't ever want to meddle with the black arts. Not ever, Eva. You got to burn that poppet, and you don't bring it into this house, either, do you hear?

I closed my eyes and held the poppet in the warmth of my hand until our spirits merged, my life force pulsing into the inanimate object. Then, keeping my hand steady, I dangled it on the ribbon until it settled.

My heart rate picked up a little. The room was still, the house silent. Had Grandma Hart rushed out to find Earl? Or was she sitting downstairs rigid with shock? It seemed a little too quiet.

"Okay – side to side for yes, back and forwards for no, circles if you don't know… Spirit please tell me – shall I curse my grandfather for what he has done?"

The poppet did nothing. It hung inert, exactly the same as for the girl with the Suzi Quatro hair.

Ask it an easier question!

The advice came as a thought insertion, nothing more. But I was learning to act on those. "Is my name Eva?"

The poppet twitched but not enough for affirmation. Look, if nothing happened, I was a lunatic, pure and simple – a badly disturbed teenager who needed to get well and get a grip. I had a future planned – it was just a case of getting healthy. Mrs Dixon was going to sort out a doctor and… But even as my thoughts raced, the blisters rose and spread like plague buboes, and my whole back began to prickle.

Offer it drink – liquor!

Now that was a crazy thought but an insistent one, so in the absence of a better idea, I crept downstairs. No one was in, after all. So she had gone to find him, then! Right, well, time was now of the essence. His whisky was in the Welsh dresser along with some miniature glasses for liqueurs. Quickly I poured out a small measure, then ran back upstairs.

"The drink is yours. It's on the desk!" The poppet dangled, swinging lightly before stilling. "Okay, now here's an easy one – is my mother's name Alexandra?"

This time, the poppet twitched more definitively. No, I had to be making it happen. I mean – how the fuck?

It moved, you felt it, it jumped with life…you did…you felt it!

Stilling it once more, this time resting my elbow on the desk so there was no room for error, I asked again. "If I curse my grandfather, will I get well again?"

The pendulum swung from side to side without any doubt whatsoever, cutting, in fact, a ninety-degree angle. Nor would it stop. It was like a live thing in my hand. My heart jittered wildly. Was this telekinesis? Uri Geller did it like a parlour trick, causing objects to move or bend with the force of his mind. They said it was energy, something like that. Yes, that was all. I bet a scientist could explain this away.

But what if I asked something I didn't know the answer to?

I steadied it once more. "Right, is my mother alive?"

Immediately it swung from side to side. No question. Its motion was far stronger, the poppet quivering before eventually calming on its own.

"Is she in a mental institution?"

Affirmative. My eyes must have popped like organ stops. It was swinging widely, and so strongly it felt as if it might fly from my fingers! *Oh, freak!* The room was empty, I swear – there was no one and nothing there. And not a breath of air.

"So she is alive and in a mental hospital?"

Side to side.

The air was electric, crackling, daylight flickering as if a storm was coming. I think my heart rate must have shot up to a hundred and ten. Who was making this happen? Was someone standing beside me? Someone I couldn't see?

"Is someone here?"

As if in answer, a cold breeze wafted against my face as softly as if a bird had flown too close.

Muss i' denn...

Muss i' denn...

A terrible fear got a hold of me then. It shivered up and down my back. I had to get out of there, out of that room.

What had I done? Holy Christ, what had I invited in?

I could barely breathe. My head pounded, and my heart felt like it was about to give out, sweat pouring off me. It was like the worst case of flu and food poisoning all mixed in. Frantically, I stuffed all the possessions I had into the rucksack. I had to get to Mrs Dixon's. A new life beckoned. Medical help. A fresh start... I wished I hadn't done this, really wished I hadn't.

Eva, Eva...give us work...!

It was at the last moment, just as I was scanning the room for anything left behind, that I saw it and remembered. On top of the sewing box lay the screwed up tissue containing Earl Hart's toe clippings. For a second I hesitated. Was there time?

Gran had gone to fetch him.

I could see his face while she was telling him at this very moment what he was accused of...saw his eyes dilate to black, his teeth visible through the beer glass as he drained his pint before slamming it onto the bar.

"Right, I'm ready for you, you bastard!" Rage, that perfect channel for evil of the most powerful kind, came riding in like a devil on horseback. And not a damn thing could stop it.

Knocking back the poppet's whisky and glad for the burn of it, without further thought, I took one of the candles kept in the desk drawer for blackouts. Memories replayed in quick succession as I worked – every hard slam against the kitchen cupboards, every single painful thrust over and over and over, the lies, the betrayal, the deceit, the interminable self-righteous rants, temper, punches and slaps…

Uttering words not known to me, my mouth worked as if pulled by the strings of a puppeteer: "*Nema Olam a son arebil des menoitatnet ni sacundi son en te. Sirtson subiotibed sumittimid son te tucis, artson atibed sibon ettimid te. Eidoh sibon…*"

Tipping the toe clippings inside a piece of notepaper, I folded it into a small envelope, drawing onto the front an inverted pentagram filled with a black sun surrounded by rays. The only photo there was of him was in their bedroom. I darted in, grabbed it and cut out his body to fix to the front. And when the little package was ready, I took a pin from the sewing box and repeatedly stabbed him in the groin with it.

Every thrust of the excruciatingly painful rape correlated with every stab of the pin. And with every stab came the satisfying image of his cock shrivelling to black necrotic tissue, wizening with disease as rip-roaring ball pain consumed his every waking breath. He couldn't walk, couldn't pee, his red-veined eyes as terrified as a bull realising too late it was lined up for slaughter.

And when the hexing was done, I held the paper over the candle flame and burned it. "This is my Will!"

Would it work?

Blowing out the candle, I speedily cleared away the remnants of the evil deed. The whole thing had taken less than two minutes, but it was two minutes too long. He'd be back soon. All hell, as they said, was about to break loose, and it hit me now what he'd do when he found me gone.

Shit, I can't do that to Mrs Dixon and Nicky, can I? Think...think!

Flying into the front bedroom, I flung open the top drawer of his bedside table. That's where he kept his winnings from the horses. Gran had a tin on the mantelpiece containing a meagre amount of housekeeping for the Co-op and a once-a-month visit to the hairdresser. I would never take that. But this was Earl's betting money – cash he really ought to have given to her – and my eyes bulged at the amount he'd stashed. Lousy git! He could have replaced her threadbare overcoat, taken her to Blackpool for a weekend, something she said she'd love to do. But no, it was hoarded. And there was at least seven hundred pounds.

His footsteps pounded in my head along with my heart.

They were halfway down the street...

Separating the wad, some went into my jeans pocket, some inside my shoe and the rest in my underwear. Then, thundering downstairs as Earl Hart was still stomping down the road from the working men's club, several feet in front of his bustling, hand-wringing wife, I slipped out the back door into the yard – trusting that within hours he would be unable to even think about revenge.

Or anything at all. Except the searing pain of his rapidly decomposing cock!

***

CHAPTER THIRTY-ONE

It was only later I realised just how fast my recovery actually was. Barely had I reached the end of the street before the banging headache cleared and the stomach cramps stopped. Funny how you can live with pain day in, day out, praying for it to end, but the precise moment it goes can pass unnoticed.

Besides, escape had been fully occupying my mind. That and protecting Nicky and Mrs Dixon. No way could they be subjected to violent recriminations because of me. Eldersgate was an estate where laws were enforced by a few individuals, and Earl Hart was the boss of that mob. Escape to where, though? There was only one obvious option, and that was to track down my dad – seeing as how he lived so close.

The loaded rucksack banged into my spine as I hurried down the gennel linking our street to the main road. The priority was to put as much distance between me and Earl as fast as possible. By the time he worked out I'd packed and gone, hopefully the agonising pain would have kicked in, an ache somewhere deep inside his scrotum – a sickening thump that would consume him to distraction. He'd have to sit down for a moment while his eyes watered.

On the main road, level with the bus stop, the street

opposite led to the nursing home where Mrs Dixon worked. On the left, about halfway along was a row of shops that included a newsagent, and it must be that one Mrs Dixon had referred to. It was still impossible to comprehend – that all these years Dad had been living just around the corner. I mean, why say he lived in Leeds? He must seriously have wanted to avoid me.

My stomach clenched into a fist that wanted to punch someone. It just hurt. I can't tell you how much it hurt. I was going to ambush him next morning, anyway. And he was going to explain this and also disclose where my mother was. God, what had happened that was so bad she'd ended up insane and their only child had to be dumped with a violent man?

I'd find out. Damn right I would!

Careful, the hyenas are out – a young girl alone, with money…and a bag of belongings…

Once again I thanked that silent voice. To the rear of the newsagent was a locked yard containing rubbish bins and a rickety shed, presumably for the newspapers? Well then, that would provide a few hours of undisturbed protection. Not comfortable, not by any means, but I had a couple of sweaters in the rucksack to sit on, and it wasn't cold.

Strange what happens on the streets at night. Sleep was impossible amid drunken shouts from those falling out of the Greyhound pub and cans being kicked down the road. This estate was rougher than ours and scrawled with hate-filled graffitti. It pulsed with anger, fear and resentment, many houses boarded up, and the thin-walled maisonettes of the elderly quiet and dark.

At one point a crash jarred the padlocked gate to the

yard, a fight or scuffle broke out, followed by a nasty laugh. And then it was quiet, as silent as death, the drugged and the drunk finally falling into slumber before dawn filtered in.

I was out of the shed well before the papers arrived, rubbing my hands, standing in a single ray of light opposite the shop. Waiting.

He showed up exactly as Mrs Dixon had said, at the same time she would be passing on the bus for her morning shift – ten to eight. As he came out of the shop, scanning the headlines of a tabloid, he shook out a Silk Cut and fished in his denim jacket for a light.

"Hi, Dad!"

The cigarette on his lower lip wobbled precariously. It seemed a lifetime ago that he'd popped round on my sixteenth with that cheap radio. He had of course been a different man two days ago – a busy, successful one preparing for a new life with a new family. A man sorted after a difficult relationship with a mad woman. Only that was a lie. *Wasn't it, Dad?*

"It's not what you think," he said, removing the unlit cigarette and wedging it back into the packet. "Come on, we can't talk here."

We walked back to his house in silence, both of us trying to cohese our thoughts. Eventually we rounded a corner into a cul-de-sac of pebble-dashed semis. His was at the end – the one with a rusting gate, an overgrown front lawn and dingy curtains. This was not my dad. He wasn't like this, he wasn't!

"Come on in; don't mind the mess. I'll put the kettle on."

The front room was drear, with an Artexed ceiling and

a swirly orange carpet. The tea he made sat cooling on the coffee table while we sat there wondering where to start, the only sounds those of screaming, shouting children from the nearby primary school. He was poor and broken, that much was obvious. How on earth he'd managed to put on such an act for me and his parents, I couldn't guess. It explained the cheap radio, anyway, that image of three other children having everything I did not, now dissipating as quickly as the illusion itself. There was no new family, was there?

He glanced at the rucksack. "Going somewhere?"

"Yeah, I was coming to you."

He stared at me for a long time before speaking, before deciding how best to phrase this. He had no need to explain how it was for him here, with the cardboard-thin walls, empty beer cans, overflowing ashtrays and well-thumbed tabloids. But he told me anyway. How they'd taken a bank loan for the trip to Bavaria, not wanting anyone in the family to know about it on account of Earl's aversion to all things German. He couldn't ask his dad, he said, for the flight money, so he'd taken out a bank loan. At the time they'd both been in work and I was healthy.

"Of course, when we came back, you were ill and then your mother lost her job."

"And you bought an expensive house."

This he acknowledged. But my mother had been unable to find another job, he said, with the hours she'd had before – the ones enabling her to babysit me while he worked shifts. And as my health deteriorated, there had been no other option but for her to stay home pretty much all the time. The mortgage, bank loan, and building jobs on the house had sunk them, he explained, and as a result, they'd had to leave me with his parents so Alex could work full-time. At least until I got better and they'd paid off some bills.

"For a short time, you said. Not eight years!"

He looked at his hands, examining the nails. "Aye, well—"

"Eight years with Earl Hart, Dad. When you knew, didn't you, that he was violent?"

He looked up sharply. "He's handy with a slap, but—"

"You left your eight-year-old daughter there, when in your own words he was 'handy with a slap'? I get that my mother needed a job, but you didn't have to dump me there for the rest of my childhood when you knew! You knew he hit Gran and that he'd hit me, too. Did you know he was a rapist, as well?"

He looked as if he'd been punched, and at the sight of his shock, all the bitter recriminations of rage, pain, fear and bewilderment fired out in a volley of despair. It consumed the whole of me, and even when the look on his face told me all I needed to know, that he was saddened beyond words, I still couldn't stop. I kept on going until I was shaking and crying.

He hung his head, staring at the swirls on the carpet.

I was past needing to be hugged and consoled – that never happened – and far too upset to just sit there. Pacing back and forth, I railed at him through blinding tears. "I need to know why you lied and continued to lie. Why tell me you were in Leeds when you were here all along? And how come I never got to see my mother ever again? No one would tell where she was. They wouldn't even say what happened to my cat! Nothing, bloody nothing."

"She went to the neighbour," he said quietly. "The lady next door took Sooty, love."

"So why couldn't I be told that?"

"In case you wanted Sooty and made a fuss. I couldn't leave the cat in his house, could I? The man shot his own dog when I was a kid."

The view through that front room window was depressing: gardens piled with discarded furniture and rubbish, bedroom curtains still drawn, gates hanging off.

"It doesn't exist, this perfect second family, does it? It's been one lie after another and all because you didn't want to look after me anymore. Was I honestly that bad?"

I would have got my bag and left there and then; such was my anger. I could barely look at him just sitting there staring at the bloody carpet like a sodding victim. But if I left, the chance to find out where my mother was would be lost.

Eventually, when he realised I wasn't going to slam out of the front door and really did expect answers, he raised his bloodshot eyes to mine. *So he drinks to numb the pain...smokes for something to do with his nervousness...hides from something worse...*

"I had to protect you, Eva."

"From what? My own mother? Why couldn't I even see her? People visit relatives in psychiatric units all the time."

"From the truth. Sit down, love. Listen, you don't understand – your mum was in a terrible state, and I couldn't let you see her like that."

"What terrible state?"

He kept his eyes on the swirls, mumbling the almost unsayable. "It was when she was left alone in that house, after we took you to Eldersgate. She had some books from her great-grandmother – the old lady who gave you nightmares, remember?"

I looked away. For fuck's sake…as if I'd forget!

"I didn't know she'd brought them back from Rabenwald, but one day I came home early and found her reading them in the attic. She was on the floor up there, rocking back and forwards while she read, and when she looked up and saw me, there was this horrible malicious grin on her face. It made her look like a totally different person. I barely recognised her. It took a good few minutes for her to compose her features and become Alex again, and it stayed with me, you know? That image, I'm telling you it left me shocked, really badly disturbed. Anyhow, I asked her what the books were, and she told me – said they were the diaries Baba Lenka kept during the World Wars."

"Diaries? Really?" So they contained the rest of the story, and that information had sent my mother mad? I tried to keep the astonishment off my face. "What happened then?"

"Well, I had more pressing issues, I suppose – put it to the back of my mind. Anyhow, she managed to get a part-time job and for a while it looked like we were back on track. But she'd changed, Eva – become a different person. I can't put it any other way. She started to go up to the attic at night to read those bloody books instead of coming to bed. I asked her why she didn't bring them down so we could read them together, but she said no, they couldn't be brought into the house itself, into our living space. She became very furtive, sneaking up there with a torch, devouring the things. One night I heard her laughing in this horrible way, maniacal and nasty, and talking in a language I don't think she even understood. It got worse and worse."

"How so?" *And where are the books?*

"About a week or so later, I came home to find her in the corner of the kitchen on the floor, talking to herself in gobbledygook. Her eyes were wide and excited, she was biting at her fingernails, and she kept swinging round to stare at invisible things. And talk to them! But her voice, Eva…I don't know that I've got the words, but it were low and masculine – not hers anymore. And she were sniggering and whispering to people that just *were not there.*

"Oh, Eva, I'm sorry, love, but I was scared. She wasn't my Alex anymore – more like some sort of demon. I called the doctor, and he gave her a sedative. But she continued to deteriorate. She wet the bed, she messed the bed, she smashed up the room… We had to have her sectioned in the end. Only I couldn't tell you because you were just a child and I wanted you to get better and have as normal an upbringing as possible."

"Did she ever recover? I mean, ever?"

He shook his head. A single tear dribbled down his cheek, dripping from the end of his chin. He wiped his eyes with the back of his hand. "It was terrible to see. I've used every last penny to pay for private treatments and assessments, paid for her to stay in top clinics and see leading psychiatrists. But whenever they try to wean her off the drugs, it starts again. Eva, I've seen her every single day for the past eight years, and there isn't any improvement at all."

"And the books?"

His face darkened. "What do you want to know about them for? Burned the bloody things, didn't I?"

"Oh."

"I did have a quick glance before they hit the incinerator. It looked like they were full of curses and spells, mostly in Latin and Russian and another language, too – maybe Arabic or Egyptian, but I'm no expert, and, to be honest, the whole thing gave me a really bad feeling. Those books were evil. And not only had your mother been reading them, she'd been actively learning from them, too – underlining certain words and circling these diabolical pictures, things you wouldn't want to see."

"Give me an example."

"What? Why? No, Eva."

"Were there inverted pentagrams filled with symbols, and lists of demonic names attached to distorted half-human figures with lizard tails and animal heads?"

He nodded.

"Dad, you asked if I remembered the old woman who gave me bad dreams? I've not just had vivid nightmares ever since that trip to Bavaria, I've had a whole eight years of nightly visits – of living Baba Lenka's life. But you wouldn't know what I've been through because I've had to go through it alone, to believe I was insane. So what I'd like to know, and deserve to know, is if this book contains what I've seen in these nightmares, because that would make it more real. And don't water it down, because what I've seen so far would make grown men wet themselves. So tell me – what else?"

He stared at me for several long seconds. "Castration!

Men having their genitals hacked off. That was one of them."

"Okay, yes - that matches. See? You should have known I was affected like this – I told you when I was eight, and I wasn't making it up." I tried to keep my voice level, realising he couldn't possibly understand. He was a Mundane, as Lenka's mother had explained.

The fire suddenly went out of me. At least he'd tried to help my mother.

"I'm sorry for shouting, Dad. Sorry. But if only we could have confided in each other, it would have been so much easier."

"No, you've nowt to be sorry for. I'm the one who's sorry – and there are no excuses except every waking moment has been about your mother's treatments, therapies and private clinics. I even took her to the Vatican!"

It could have been my imagination, but I'm sure someone snickered when he mentioned the Vatican. A laugh, quickly smothered, had come from out of the ether.

"Why did she read those books, I wonder? I mean, she always seemed terrified of the supernatural."

"I don't know. Maybe she was curious and it got the better of her."

"Or she was looking for a spell to attract luck and money?"

He nodded. "Possibly."

"Dad, I understand, or at least I'm trying to. But why did you make up that stuff about a new family and moving on?"

"I couldn't have you with me and continue going to

see your mother every day, could I? I had to work full time, and on top of that you would have pestered to come with me. I didn't want you asking about her. Full stop. It was easier to just say, look, I've moved on—"

"Throw away the key, good riddance? Then make yourself scarce?"

"Yeah."

"And my grandparents were in on this?"

"No. Kind of. Well, Mum knew Alex was very ill and I'd all on dealing with that, so she agreed it'd be best to make something up to keep you at arm's length. We thought that, in the end, it would be for the best. Like me, she just wanted you to have as normal an upbringing as possible. She said she'd keep you out of Earl's way and encourage him to join the union and the darts team and get an allotment – anything just so we could get you through."

Inwardly I cringed at how often I'd raged at Maud, how ungrateful I'd been and, most of all…the look on her face when I'd told her what her husband had done.

"Eva, I lied and lied, tying myself into knots. Maybe it was the wrong thing to do, but anything was better than you seeing your mother like that, like she still is. Or worse…"

He fell silent abruptly, caught himself from saying something he'd regret.

"Dad?"

"I loved her, you know that? Still do."

"You should have told me. I think we'd have been all right. Better than you leaving me with him, anyway. And those nightmares, the terrors, they never went away. I had no one to talk to, no one to help me. No one."

He shook his head. "I'm sorry. I've handled the whole thing badly. But—"

"I could have coped. You have no idea what I already cope with, what visions I have and have had ever since that funeral. Lenka comes into my dreams and relates her life in explicit detail."

Now I had his full attention.

"Notice I didn't even flinch when you mentioned castration? That I knew all about satanic rituals and demon summoning? How do you think I know all this? The only way I could possibly know is because I've been drip-fed a legacy of occult information for the last eight years. It's in the family, and there's no escaping it."

He frowned. "It's all mind-bending rubbish, Eva. I can only think that somehow you saw those books and that's how you know all this stuff. Listen, you were a highly disturbed little girl. I had to separate you from your mother, who was absolutely out of her tree, and I don't want you going the same way. It stops here and now, do you hear me? It stops."

"No. I never saw those books. Anyway, I'm sixteen now and I need to see her, to talk—"

"No!"

"Nothing will frighten me, if that's what you're worried about."

"This will," he said quietly.

"No, it won't. I can probably even take her madness from her. I can tell her what I know and that it is real not crazy. I can make her better, I know I can – explain the whole thing. At least let me try."

"Eva, no. I've said no, and I meant it. Your mother's in a very bad way. She has lucid moments, but you really cannot see her."

I jumped up and yelled, "You're blocking me. I need to see her – she's my mother, for God's sake!"

He grabbed my wrist and held it fast. "Eva, I know what my dad's done is bad, really bad. It makes me want to go and kill him. I'd give my right arm not to have left you longer than the few weeks we planned, but you have to believe me now, on this one thing, there really are worse things—"

"Worse than rape, incest, abuse—?"

"Yes, far, far worse."

I shook my head, pulling free of his grip. "You have no idea who I am or what I come from—"

"Eva ..." He wiped his hand up and down his face as if washing himself of the filth. "There are no words. You must never know what her family, your family, did. No one can. Believe me, the knowledge would send you insane. You'd never be the same again."

***

CHAPTER THIRTY-TWO

In the end, we struck a deal, and I stayed over for a couple of nights while he found me alternative accommodation. Dad was convinced Earl would be on the rampage, and it wouldn't be a great idea if he found me. And like he said, he couldn't be there all the time to act as a bodyguard; he had to go to work. I could hardly tell him there wasn't much chance of Earl Hart even being able to walk let alone throw his weight around, so I sat back and let him make the calls.

Through a friend of a friend, it wasn't long before he got wind of a room in a house with a family who needed extra income, so off we went to look. It was a bedroom on the top floor of a large Victorian house in north Leeds. Most of those large stone-built mansions with long, shrub-lined driveways had been converted into flats and offices long ago, many acquired by the National Health Service for nurses' homes or outpatient facilities. But one or two were private.

The couple was professional, he a dentist and she a social worker, but clearly they were working all hours and the house needed renovating. She looked harassed, kept pushing her hair back off her face – bit of a drama queen, I thought, but nice. A good person. Dad settled on a monthly rent and paid the deposit, unaware I had a hell of a lot more cash than he did. I could hardly tell him that one either, but every time I thought about it, a smile twitched into a grin – Earl had to have discovered his missing stash!

"She's looking for a job," he told the woman, Helen, "so if you hear of anything?"

She nodded straight away. They were desperate for care assistants at one of the nursing homes she frequented. I started work there less than a week later. Lying came easily to me, and I now realised where that came from.

"Aye, she's eighteen," Dad told Helen, without even pausing for breath. If you looked carefully, you could see the heightened defensiveness in the tightening of his facial muscles, but you'd have to know to see them. Anyway, what was so wrong with a white lie that helped people? Helen was glad of both the rent money and the young female lodger who would double up as a babysitter, and the nursing home sister practically dragged me inside. Nothing was checked in the way of references. All she did was ask a few questions and take my dad's word on date of birth. That was it.

After he'd helped me settle into the flat – which was, thankfully, fully furnished – we went out for a bite to eat. He seemed pleased, the downtrodden air about him lifting a little.

"Love, can you not let this drop about visiting your mother? You need to have a life, forget about all this, it will only upset you and—"

"I'm not kidding, Dad. I've told you what I'll do if you won't let me see her!"

He sighed, gazing out of the café at passersby. The

afternoon was bright with sunshine. It was days like those when it was hard to believe in darkness, cruelty, violence and madness. Radios blared out of open-top cars, and cherry blossom fluttered in warm confetti breezes.

He was weighing up the options, you could see. Was it worth the risk? Would his daughter really report his father to the police? What about the repercussions and, of course, his own part in this? What would come out about his wife? The whole hideous family secret would spread across the estate in a sweep of rapacious gossip. It had happened to others – houses daubed in paint, bricks through windows, catcalls of 'Sickos!' and 'Perverts!' He had a part-time job as a security guard with a small family firm that wouldn't want trouble. It wasn't much, but it paid the bills and meant he could see Mum every day.

"If I take you, you've got to promise you won't try to go again on your own. You only visit her with me, okay?"

I could see her; the rest was detail! "I promise."

So he took me. Not that day, he had to work a night shift, but he'd come back the following week.

"If you don't, I'll track her down myself. Now I'm here in Leeds, I can go through the care homes one by one."

"Don't do that, Eva. Tell you what, I'll ring them tonight to let them know we're coming together, that you're only sixteen and I'm bringing you for the first time next week."

He was going to make sure Mum was sedated, wasn't he? Tip them off so she wouldn't make a scene or say anything. But it was a start.

I'm going to see my mum!

"But don't think you're going to grill her and find out

what Baba Lenka did. You won't find that out, Eva. Not over my dead body. That dies with me and your mother."

I stared deep into his eyes. *Like fuck it did…*

***

I was so excited. At long last the mystery would unravel. And that first night, opening up the rucksack to pull out all those things packed in fear and haste just two days before was a joy. Smiling, I took out the crow poppet, holding for a moment the only connection to those who had travelled this path before me. The tiny amethyst on its chest glinted, the ebony feathers lustrous. As ever, it felt comforting, protective, and part of who I was.

In addition to being able to see Mum, I would have a job, had money, and was no longer forced to sit watching Earl Hart chew the cud and pick his nose night after night. Free…free…and so very, very happy. For two whole days I was on a high, playing the radio and dancing round my room. Two blissful days of hope and light, plans and dreams.

But on day three that all came to an end. I woke up to the sting of a hungry mosquito, and there on my upper arm was a single sore as bright and shiny as a red jelly bean.

Give us work…more work…more work…

Already? I sat up in bed staring at it. And tears filled my eyes.

The previous night I'd rung Nicky from the call box on the corner, to tell her I'd found Dad, and also had a job and a nice place to live – better than overlooking the pit wheel, anyway - this one faced a huge green park.

"I miss you," she said.

"I miss you, too."

"I 'eard Mark Curry were looking for you an' all."

My heart had skipped. Mark's dimpled smile and mischievous brown eyes twinkled before me. "Was he?"

"Yeah, he said he liked you. He came right up to me and asked where you went after the party."

That night seemed so long ago, a tiny starlit moment in time.

"Why did you disappear, anyway? Mum said you could stay with us, and I were dead excited. You could've gone out wi' Mark, and we could've both got jobs together. I'm gutted, Eva. I don't mind saying."

"I'm sorry, Nicky. Please, will you tell your mum I'm sorry as well? But I had to run like hell. It were me grandad… Something bad happened, and—"

"Oh yeah, that reminds me – Mum said there were an ambulance outside your grandparents' house yesterday. They took Mr Hart out on a stretcher."

Fuck – it had worked! I slammed a hand to my mouth. "Oh?"

"We didn't know how to contact you. I'm right glad you rang. I think they took him to Wakefield General if you want to go and visit?"

"Oh, right, thanks."

"It might be a heart attack or summat. I can meet you there if you want?"

"No, you're all right. Nicky, listen, the pips are going to go in a minute, and I haven't got any more ten-pence pieces. I'll ring back soon, okay? We could go out? We'll easily pass for eighteen!"

"Oh, that'd be brill—"

There were ten pips, and the call was over. I missed her badly and Mark, too, but hopefully Nicky and I would have our night out. That would be exciting, the first time in a pub, and here in this upmarket part of Leeds the pubs had outdoor areas with patios and parasols. It buzzed with promise, the smell of beer and cigarette smoke intoxicating on the sultry, warm air. I had the feeling I might meet someone, too…In fact, I was convinced of it.

Looking back now, it breaks my heart, that my young spirit had soared with such hope even then, even after all that had happened and all I knew. Yet still I'd hoped, like any other normal young girl.

Helen was cooking for her three kids when I got back from phoning Nicky. Already I felt part of their life, of life in general with all its possibilities. And smiling, I sprinted up the three flights of stairs to my room on the top floor. Mark Curry was pining for me, and Nicky and I were going to go out to a pub…

But that night, as I drifted into sleep, a cool wind blew against my face, and quite unexpectedly the dreams with Baba Lenka resumed. The darkness was back. I should have known I'd wake up ill again.

However, these dreams were nothing like the ones before. They were not coming from an emotional, vibrant young girl. Rather, they were a series of images shot in black and white, like a scratchy old film. Instead of being in her skin and living her life as if it were my own, this was more akin to watching an impartial documentary through a long lens, as if the person presenting was simply projecting tape reels from an archive. I was inside her head but disconnected from feelings. Whoever this was, looked and talked like Lenka, but it wasn't her…I can't explain it…except it wasn't her anymore.

The first dream sequence showed a middle-aged man who was vaguely recognisable. The most distinguishable characteristic was a huge upturned moustache in the shape of a joker smile. The second notable aspect was a Nehru-collared uniform ablaze with medals. He wore long boots and was stomping around a palatial room, behind him full-length windows that opened onto expansive lawns that glistened with snow.

He wore an expression of enormous petulance, pale blue eyes darting with madness. He would make a speech to the nation and damn this or that adviser! I had the impression of lying on a bed, watching him with the kind of disdain reserved for fools. Reflected in a long, gilt-edged mirror opposite, a woman turned to stare directly at me and our eyes locked. Yes, it was Lenka, definitely… Smoking from a slim cigarette holder, she was wearing a long silk chemise, her red hair wavy and bobbed. A ripple of pleasure at her appearance flickered inside of me, and for a moment we regarded each other with interest. Unable to stop myself, I felt drawn, looking deep into eyes that were my own. Yet at the same time, they weren't mine at all, but solid black.

Solid black?

My heart lurched. And at the very moment that hit me, her image zoomed with lightning speed towards my third eye.

Wake up…wake up…wake yourself up!

Still half awake, half asleep, my heart was kicking so

hard in my chest it set the pulse points burning to a deep ache. Those eyes had reflected my face. My face as it is now, in the mirror, in photographs. And that reflection had been upside down.

Wake up, wake up...

Oh, I wanted to wake, to come out of the nightmare, but could not. The scene pulled me back in and resumed, weighting me down and forcing me to watch. I think a fragment of the real Lenka remained. She needed me to see this, to witness as much as possible, and as such she turned her focus back to the wildly gesticulating, ranting man with the moustache. A channel of energy was being sent into his brain, which required a magnitude of concentration. He was being shown a picture of himself on a balcony, beneath which thousands of people were waving flags, chanting his name and cheering. The rush of power was so great it elevated him to the status of a god. No one was above him. The gratitude of the peasants was overwhelming, how they loved him for his immense greatness, leadership and wisdom. Yes, he would and could stamp all over opposition.

He regarded the woman sending him this marvellous vision, and his glacial expression melted. Smiling, he began to walk towards the bed, already undoing his belt.

Thankfully she spared me the grunting loveless sex, and at that point I woke up. Stars glittered through the skylight, and it took a moment to think where I was. My stomach was aching a little. And despite the unnaturally cold air, sweat coated my face and chest.

I'm going to get ill again...

I popped a paracetamol to numb the worst of the headache, and immediately drifted back into the same dream. The man with the comical moustache was now lying naked and breathless beside her.

"Fucking English," he said, ringing the bell for a servant. "They side with France and Russia. We will fight and we will win – we have two entire empires against Russia and France."

She was smiling a false, bright smile that did not reach her heart. "And you will win, my love."

Snatching the bottle of champagne brought in by a servant, he popped the cork. "To Prussia!"

"To Prussia!"

The image then shot to black, and a deep bass voice resounded in my head, repeating the words 'All roads lead to the Black Sun' over and over and over. *All roads lead to the Black Sun, all roads lead to the Black Sun, all roads...*

Those two days and nights of bliss were over. And after the first thumbtack sting of that new sore when I woke up, a host of others rapidly followed. It looked like smallpox. I lay back and closed my eyes. Opened them again, and there were more. This time on my hands.

Fuck! It was impossible to cover these. I had to go to work. Oh my God... Running over to the small sink in the corner of my room, I stared into the mirror. Shit – there was even one on my face! A huge fuchsia spot shaped like a spider was spreading across one cheek.

Fortunately, the uniform covered my arms, and I got to the nursing home without anything awry being noticed. What the hell was I going to do? I mean, what? What? The sister would notice for sure.

Give us work, give us work...

I had done. So hexing my grandad was not enough?

Give us work...more, more...always more...this will

never stop… never!

I was scared, okay? Scared and desperate. And that fear triggered a primeval reaction that suppressed all rational thoughts, exactly as it had the day when at just seven years old, I'd stabbed another child with a compass. Only this time, it would be far more horrific than a compass stab.

Once you've crossed that line, it will become easier.

In the side ward at the very end of the corridor lay an elderly lady who weighed less than a small child. Of bird-fragile bones, with a mouth that gaped open in a toothless cavern, she was rasping her last.

That morning, I stood at the door.

There was no one else around.

Static buzzed in my ears, my footsteps hollow, heartbeat rapid as I walked into that room stealthy as a cat.

Immediately her eyes, half blind with cataracts, flicked open.

An icy wind blew in, and a shadow loomed over the far wall above her bed, larger than me, wing-shaped and raven black

Her tiny claw hands began to scrabble out from underneath the bedclothes, scratching helplessly in the air.

Oh, she's looking for the buzzer.

A hand that looked like mine but seemed far away, picked it up and placed it out of reach, on top of the bedside cabinet.

My conscience then disconnected. And the deed happened fast.

From the nearby armchair by the window, Eva Hart took a discarded pillow, turned, then slammed it over her face and held it down hard, snuffing out the light of her life.

After a minute, maybe less, the tiny hands stopped flapping frantically. The temperature climbed back to normal. And the dark shadow on the far wall slipped away.

***

CHAPTER THIRTY-THREE

Every single symptom vanished. Immediately. And it wasn't only the illness that had gone, but good health was now in abundance – I mean, I was practically bouncing! And despite the enormity of what I'd done, a filament of excitement fizzed inside, a sense that crossing the line had been a test passed, and would now be rewarded. I was a step closer. But to what? Because someone was definitely coming; they were on their way. The air practically sparked.

As promised, I met Nicky the following evening. I had this feeling, an overwhelming conviction, that with every passing hour the person who would take me to the next level drew closer. My hands shook while applying mascara, the intensity of anticipation so great I had to break off, turn up the radio and dance away the surplus energy. It wasn't until sweat was pouring off that the overload abated, slightly, enough to resume getting ready.

We'd decided to go to a pub nearby. It had a beer garden out the back, and that summer night it was packed out. We didn't know what to order, but Nicky said she'd heard lager and black was good, so we got a pint each of that, and before we knew it, we were laughing at things that weren't funny and the multicoloured lanterns were zooming in and out of focus. She had on a white crochet top with shorts, and I was in a sleeveless denim dress. Both of us had makeup on, and while Nicky's hair was in tight braids, mine was cut in layers that flicked out in flames around my face.

"Don't look now, but there's a lad staring at you," she said.

I looked. Of course I looked. And she was right. Nor did he shy away when our eyes met. Instead, he held my gaze with laser intensity.

It didn't register fully who he was until later because his frame was silhouetted against the lights of the pub, but I felt riding shockwaves of attraction, and my insides flipped. Why me? There were grown women in low-cut evening dresses, and tiny hot pants. And there I was in a Chelsea Girl denim dress and espadrilles – a kid, really, with Farrah Fawcett hair and black-cherry nail varnish.

Nicky was spluttering with giggles. Luckily, Ma Dixon had agreed she could stay with me that night, seeing as how Helen was a social worker and had set a ten o'clock curfew. It was such a happy night, my last one.

"Well, I'm glad you're all right, anyhow," she said. "I was so worried about you, especially when I heard about your grandad. I know he wasn't nice to you, but even so…what a way to go!"

Go? So he died? Fuck me!

I'm not joking, this terrible thing happened then. A volcanic eruption of laughter nearly shrieked out. I had to keep my eyes down, focusing hard on blades of grass while desperately trying to think of something other than Earl Hart's withered black cock, of how he had passed away from gangrene of the cock and balls… I wondered what they'd put on the death certificate. In the end, I couldn't contain it any longer, and the mirth came spurting up in a fountain. It sprayed from my eyes, spluttered from the corners of my mouth and contorted my face.

Nicky shot around the table, thinking it was grief. She put her arms around me and muttered soothing things while my entire body shook with uncontrollable hilarity. By the time she pulled away, I was dabbing at my eyes and asking if my mascara had smudged.

"No, you look fine." She went back to her seat, leaned across and squeezed my hand. "Are you okay?"

I nodded. God, yes. I was on fire. I felt as if I could conquer the world, like I'd overdosed on fly agaric or LSD. Not only that, but it was as if a channel of secret knowledge had opened up. I could have gone around that pub garden and told each person exactly who they were and what they were thinking. Their thoughts transmitted directly into my head, the collective chatter suddenly chaotic and massively overwhelming. Some had towering shadows around them, dark energy that sapped their light and inserted malicious thoughts… *Put a shot in her drink…Say she was brave to wear a dress like that…*

What had Sophia taught Lenka? What was it? I struggled to remember until the answer appeared. Yes, it was to imagine a cord that switched those channels on and off, and to pull it.

Because the only one of interest was the man behind me, the one whose eyes were still boring into my back.

Nicky stood up to fetch the next round of lagers and black.

"Do you believe in the supernatural?" I blurted out.

She sat down again and frowned. "We 'ad this

conversation before, a long time ago, didn't we? Wasn't it about you 'aving nightmares when you were little?"

"Yes, and you said your mum did voodoo?"

Nicky looked sheepish. "She told me off about that, said the conversation had come up and you went and snitched. I told you not to say owt!"

"Sorry, I didn't think you meant your mum."

"Yeah, well, I don't know what she admitted to, but she did this thing once with her sister. They stuck pins in a doll. Did she tell you that the girl, the victim, got sick?"

"Yes."

"It were my auntie who told me originally. She said it was important to stay with Jesus, and if you did then you wouldn't go far wrong. It scared me. I mean, we don't know what's out there, do we? We have no idea what we're messing with. Everyone thinks that when we die we're dust, so Ouija boards and stuff like that are just a laugh! Anyway, for what it's worth, I think spirits exist. Some people go mad, you know – when summat bad 'appens?"

My mum came to mind then.

"Are the nightmares still happening, Eva – those with your great-grandmother coming to you? I know you used to be right scared."

"Sometimes."

"You have to pray to Jesus and ask him to save you. I'm not kidding. My auntie said after they'd asked the spirits of the dead to help them and stuck pins into this doll, that a shoe went flying across the room and hit the wall. And the lights flicked on and off…all sorts…then they found out what happened to the girl. So, it is real. You're not doing stuff, are you? Practising black magic?"

"Erm, no–"

She reached across the table and squeezed my arm. "I worry about you."

"Don't, I'm fine, honest." My smile was frozen, though. If she had even the slightest inkling about what I'd done, she would cut the cord between us, and the only friend I had in the world would be forced to turn her back on me. What else could she do?

The conversation put a bit of a downer on the evening, and for another hour or so we just chatted and discussed the other kids in school, boys in particular, and made plans to go and see 'Stardust' at the Odeon. Then at ten to ten, we stood up to leave. It'd be a sprint to get back by ten.

By that time most people were rowdy and drunk, and I was following Nicky as she pushed through the throng of bodies towards the exit when it happened. It felt as if an invisible thread was pulling my attention, forcing me to look over my shoulder. I crashed into several people all at once, drinks spilled and someone called me a stupid bitch.

But all I could do was stare.

It was him. The man whose eyes had been boring into my back all evening. This time though, seen through the smoky haze of the lit bar, his face was clearly visible. So, too, the long legs, expensive jacket and the slight stoop due to his height.

My heart fair stopped. No, it couldn't be. How was this even possible?

He lifted his glass in salute.

It was Heinrich Blum!

***

CHAPTER THIRTY-FOUR

In the end, it was longer than a week before we went to visit Mum. Another month, in fact, on a drowsy midsummer afternoon, when the curtains in the nursing home where I worked were drawn against the glare of the sun, and fans had been placed next to the old people's beds. It blew their fine white hair into ice-cream wisps, many of them staring glassy-eyed into the distant past. Occasionally a gnarled hand would snatch at my arm as I walked past, forcing me to bend down and lock eyes with their lonely bewilderment. I bet they wished they hadn't, though. Despite their earthly existences now rapidly fading, I swear some flinched, seeing something there that frightened them. They knew. Even those who could no longer recognise their family and could not recall their own names, knew what dwelt within me. Yet the nursing staff did not. Intelligent people often refused to see unpalatable truths, it seemed – their busy, tutored minds suppressing a deeper wisdom.

After the pillow incident, the nurse who'd responded to the buzzer that day told me I'd been standing by the bed ashen-faced and mute. In shock, I'd let her lead me to the staff room amid murmurs of "It's her first death. She's only eighteen – never seen a dead body before."

Hot, sweet tea was made as I sat there shaking. "I just

found her like that," I said "All limp with these staring dead eyes…"

I drank the tea, and they murmured reassurance, but the rest is a blur. The murder had been about as real as Lenka's satanic initiation – a dream, an illusion, a memory not mine…until about a week after that night out with Nicky, when reality struck hard, and I was forced to wake up.

My God, I was ill. This time, I was to find my hair falling out in handfuls. I'd been having an explicit and highly disturbing dream. In a large bath of blood, there'd been dozens of us rubbing it into each other's bodies, smearing it into the skin, writhing and chanting, 'Hail the Dark Lord! Hail Satan!'

On waking up, not only was my hair coming out, but there were patches of vomit on the sheets, and the bed was soaked with urine. In a panic I shot over to the sink and splashed my face with cold water. This wasn't happening…couldn't be… But the girl reflected in the mirror was ugly beyond all comprehension. Cracks had opened up around the mouth, the scalp shiny and pink where it was balding, the eye whites jaundice yellow. And the skin….what the hell was happening to it? Backing away, my hands flew to my face. Boils were pulsing underneath it, rising in hot, red lumps.

The room stank. In panic, I ran around stripping off the sheets, opened the skylight, grabbed towels and soap. This could not happen. It was not real. It was not. Please no, and especially not now, when I'd found someone who liked me and who I liked back. I wanted life. I was just sixteen! And what about Luke? That was all I could think. Tears poured down my face. What was I going to do about him? We were supposed to meet again that night!

The man from the pub was not Heinrich at all, he just bore an uncanny resemblance. After the initial shock of that wore off a little, I'd returned his smile and he'd inclined his head, indicating I should go over and speak with him. I couldn't. Nicky and I were already late and Helen, my new landlady, would give us hell if we didn't get back for ten. So he followed us out to the car park and walked with us. His name was Luke, he said, and he worked in Leeds, rode a motorbike and liked Punk - particularly the Sex Pistols. All three of us chatted about music for a bit, then when we levelled with Helen's house, Nicky hurried to the door, while he and I hung back.

"Look, do you want to go out some time?" he said.

Hell, yes!

I told Helen I was going to the pictures, but the following night I met Luke and we just walked to the park and held hands and talked. I had to be back for ten, as before, but the time zipped past too quickly and by the time he was kissing me up against the wall outside the house, I thought it might be love.

That night was to be our second date.

But there really was no way I could go. The only option was to stand him up. I couldn't let him see me like that. What if he turned up, though? I mean, knocked on the door? That's what I was thinking. And what about Helen and the kids? They'd all see me, too!

Give us work...give us work...Eva!

What to do? What to do?

My rational mind then blanked completely and an automaton took over, exactly like before. Vaguely aware of my actions, I had a hot shower, shoved the dirty linen into the washing machine, then dressed and hurried over to the nursing home early.

Instinctively knowing who to pick out, I took the back stairs two at a time, heading straight for the top floor. One of the ladies had developed a nasty chest infection following a fall a couple of weeks ago. No one expected her to last more than another day. So what difference would it make? She'd had her life, and I wanted mine – that was it.

Bedridden, her lungs were rattling with fluid, the oxygen mask hissing when I walked in and softly shut the door behind me. She lay prone, having toppled sideways off a mound of pillows, deep in an opiate-induced dream.

Yet the second my shadow crossed the far wall, her eyes snapped open and her hands gripped hold of the sheets. The whites of her eyes grew large, fingers scrabbling for the buzzer.

Calmly I moved it from her reach and turned off the oxygen supply. Then, pulling off her mask, tugged loose one of the pillows from behind her. Once more, it was like watching someone else commit the act, only this time there was a significant pause, an extra moment taken in which to witness the build-up of terror in the victim's face. It was curiosity, nothing more, noting how her horrified stare flicked to the all-enveloping shadow reflected on the wall in front. The shape had spread into one of giant wings that towered over the bed, and the rush of an Alpine breeze whistled over the sheets. The room that had been bright with the dawn sun a moment ago, now darkened to night, and the fluorescent light buzzed and flickered overhead.

"Get away from me, demon," she whispered.

My head cocked to one side as, poised with the pillow, a transfer of information began to take place. Knowledge channeled into me, relaying in full every indiscretion she had ever committed – from the baby angrily shaken but declared a cot death, the letter concealed from a close friend because she wanted the man for herself, to money stolen from petty cash. And just before her wrinkled mouth could work itself into a scream, I snuffed her out.

Later that day when I walked out of the nursing home, commended this time 'for taking it well', my hair had already returned to its previous state of glossy and full, the sores had disappeared, and my eyes were as bright as a squirrel's. I would be keeping my date!

The automaton feeling, however, persisted, with only the dim realisation this could not continue. I couldn't murder people every other week for the rest of my life! Besides, sooner or later it would be noticed. But how, then, did I stay well?

The only person who might have the answer would be my mother. I'd let the pressure on my dad slide because of Luke and because of work, but now the urgency was back. What had she read in those books, and was there some other way to control this horrible legacy? Because if there wasn't, then what hellish path lay ahead? Die but take the demons with me into eternity? Or murder my way through to the bitter end? I wanted a normal life – that of a teenaged girl who enjoyed music and dance, boys and fun – what was wrong with that? Instead, I was going to go down as a mass murderer – one of those vacant-eyed people led away from court after the gruesome truth came out – a tabloid sensation, a mystery, a monster.

As it transpired, the delay in seeing Mum was because of Earl Hart's funeral. Dad had been obliged to spend time with Gran, consoling her and making arrangements not only for the funeral but also for her future. She wasn't coping well. Maud told him the details of Earl's gruesome death, about the gangrene that had spread through his genitals into major organs, how his private parts had turned ebony before being amputated. He'd died in agony and terror, screaming for mercy. She would never get over it. Never.

"I wouldn't have wished that on anyone, not even him," Dad said as we sat on the bus on the way to visit my mother. "Not even after all he said about my wife – your mother – or what he did to me and then to you. I wouldn't want that for my worst enemy. It were evil. Pure evil."

Indeed.

We fell silent, and for a moment I felt bad. For my grandma, anyway.

"At least I'll have a bit more money to spare now," he said.

"How come?"

A flush spread up his neck. Oh, he'd made a mistake! Wanted to backtrack. But the thought had surfaced, and I caught it. "Oh, I see. You were paying them for my keep?"

The moment of guilt and shame I'd briefly felt, now dissipated.

"Well, it were only right. But now I can afford private psychotherapy for your mum. It's expensive, but she can 'ave it. I'd do anything."

All that time and they were paid…

"Anyhow, it got me thinking," he said. We were on the top deck, heading towards an old Victorian asylum on the outskirts of Leeds. "You should be allowed to speak to your mother. She's your family, and no matter what her grandmother did, you have a right to know. I still say it's going to shock you, though. You'll not be the same again, so don't say I didn't warn you."

"So she's not sedated?"

"No. I thought I were protecting you, Eva. But you're right – you're older now, and you've worked in that nursing home and settled in really well. The decision I made to leave you with Earl and Maud is something I've got to live with. At the time I really did think I were doing me best; I were at the end of me tether, I suppose."

I nodded, gazing out of the window as the tree-lined roads gave way to roundabouts and a dual carriageway.

"I've taken this bus journey every single day for years, sometimes just to hold her hand for half an hour. Some days she's all there, if you know what I mean? Others she's away with the fairies. But there were never anyone else. I just didn't want to be asked about her every time we met. I didn't think you'd be able to move on… Ah, shit…"

"What?"

"Seeing as it's confession time, I admit I found it hard to look at you sometimes, too. It weren't your fault, I know that, love, but what happened after that funeral – well, you were ill, really ill for a long time, and I couldn't help thinking it all went back to that. We'd 'ave been all right if it weren't for—"

"Me?"

His turn to look out of the window.

After a minute I patted his arm. We weren't demonstrative as a family, never had been. "It's okay. I understand."

He nodded. Clouds of sadness exuded from him. There he sat, so alone, so hopeless. Now was not the time to tell him about Luke, so the opportunity came and went. Besides, he probably wouldn't approve. We'd been seeing each other almost every night. How quickly he'd become my world. He lifted my heart. Gave me hope.

Although his remarkable resemblance to Heinrich Blum had been a jolt - perhaps Lenka and I simply shared a physical type - there the similarity really did end. Luke was not a clever manipulator, from a wealthy family, or sent to recruit me into a satanic sect. He was just a guy in his late twenties who Dad would consider far too old for his sixteen-year-old daughter. So I didn't tell him. Or anyone. It was easy to lie to Helen, to make up late shifts, extra shifts, fabricated meetings with my dad…She just smiled and told me to make sure I was back by ten.

Aware suddenly of the dopy look on my face as my thoughts drifted back to Luke, I brought myself up sharp. He must be kept a secret. At least for now.

The journey turned out to be far longer than expected, the bus trundling along the dual carriageway, then onto an A road leading to Harrogate. The psychiatric hospital had been built well away from the city, a mansion that stood alone, its stone walls weathered black. Set in lawned grounds at the end of a drive lined with rhododendrons, the surrounding fields, which blew flat with sleet and northerly winds for six months of the year, were today studded with daisies and dandelions open to the sun.

"Hot day," said Dad as we jumped off the bus.

"Yeah."

My mother's room would be stuffy. As we walked up the drive in the full blaze of the heat, I slipped inside her skin, inhabiting her mind. She didn't want to feel the fan of a cool breeze on her face despite the sheen of perspiration glistening on her face and chest – nothing Alpine, nothing wintry. She sensed our footsteps echoing on the stone steps to the front door, clicking now along the tiled corridor towards her room at the end, facing the back of the house in the shade. *The sheets are cream, and she's sitting up, wearing a pale pink nightdress. She's been sickly, the crown of her head still pounding with the weight of sedatives, and her wrists are sore from restraints. But her feeble heart is jittery now, anticipation shooting through her arteries, tingling in her fingertips, sparking hotly in her cheeks. Someone is coming. Someone she must speak to.*

Dad knocked on the door, and in we went.

My eyes locked with hers.

"Eva, thank God!"

***

CHAPTER THIRTY-FIVE

"I'll leave you to chat, then," said Dad, plonking down the chocolates he'd brought. He kissed Mum's cheek. "Glad you're feeling a bit better, love. I hate seeing you like that, you know, like—"

She never took her eyes off mine. "It's all right, Pete, you go for a walk. The lake's pretty at the moment."

"If you're sure?"

"Yes, positive. Go – Eva and I need to talk."

After he'd shut the door, she said, "Bloody 'ell, you've grown!"

"Course I 'ave."

She laughed. "Come 'ere, love. I've missed you something chronic."

I rushed over to the bed and hugged her, snuffling into the warmth of her hair and neck, inhaling the scent of her skin – a hint of rose talc mixed with the sourness of a heavily medicated body. "I've missed you, too." It was hard not to cry, and my throat was constricting with the effort of not doing so. I could feel the pent-up sobs in her, too.

After a few minutes I pulled away a little to look at her, to take in the reality of her presence, swallowing repeatedly until my voice was steady enough to speak. "Have you been here in this room all these years? No one would tell me anything."

"Eva, listen, we haven't got much time. Your dad agreed to an hour at the most, and that was only because I said I'd scream the place down if he didn't. He doesn't want that, he's worn out, and I'm weak and getting weaker with every episode, you know, with every relapse. To tell you the truth, love, I'm usually sedated. If I'm not sedated I get ill very quickly. So this visit is an exception."

I nodded.

"Okay, well I'll get straight to the point because we've got so much to say and not nearly enough time. Nor do I know when I'll be well enough to see you again. Anyway, as soon as you turned sixteen I knew that no matter what - we had to talk."

"Yes, me too."

"I'm frightened for you. Eva." She stroked my arm, up and down, her eyes glistening with tears.

I nodded. "Because of the legacy?"

"You know about it, then?"

"Mum, I need help. I've been having vivid dreams about Baba Lenka for eight years now – visions—"

She nodded. "Yes, your dad told me. Okay, right, well there are things you need to know and fast. Your dad 'asn't got a cat in 'ell's chance of ever understanding this – he still thinks you can lead a normal life, but I can see just from looking at you that's not the case."

"It started when we got home from Rabenwald. Every night I've lived her life like I was her, in explicit detail, right up to when she was initiated into der Orden der schwarzen Sonne—"

My mother's eyes flashed. "Oh, my giddy aunt."

"The dreams stopped dead on my sixteenth, when she became a member of the Order. Since then, there've only been brief flashes of scenes, kind of like a bad signal on TV – of journeys through forests, always at night, sometimes in carriages, other times in the back of luxury cars, various men, castles and underground tunnels with rooms underneath–"

"Rituals?"

"Yes, blood rites and people wearing animal masks, all chanting and humming. Usually it starts with a bell being rung, a call to the underworld, I think?"

She nodded, bit her lip.

"I lie there paralysed and forced to watch. It's like she's trying to show me what was going on, but since her initiation it's all taking place from a distance. It's so hard to explain, but it's as if the real Lenka fell backwards down a tunnel – like she was taken over and became a robot...I know, it sounds mad but–"

"She was possessed."

"How do you mean?"

She shook her head. "So you understand what Baba Lenka was? You know our family was embroiled in the black arts?"

"Yes, and Mum, I get ill, really badly sick and—"

She narrowed her eyes. "Yet here you are, all glossy and healthy?"

She was focusing on my eye, the one Nicky had commented on, and I looked away.

"I heard your grandad came to a sticky end? Painful way to go, that, wasn't it, love?"

I nodded, staring at the floor.

"There's nothing wrong with you, is there, Mum? I mean you're not mad at all. You're possessed, aren't you? Is that what happened?"

She glanced at the clock. "Ten minutes have gone already. You have to listen now because this could be our last chance."

"Why, what do you mean by 'last chance'? And what is possession? Who possessed Lenka and who possesses you? Is that why you're sedated all the time and look so poorly? I mean, look at you, Mum! You can't weigh more than six stone and you're covered in bruises."

Gently, I pushed up the sleeve of her bed jacket, and gasped at the extent of the dark purple marks on her arms.

"I'm not always myself, that's what I'm trying to say. I can only think straight when I'm not sedated, but when I'm not sedated the attacks happen. Like I said at the start, I get weaker with each relapse, so this is dangerous for me, Eva. It's when they get in."

I felt the cold breeze then, and I know she did, too.

"Who gets in? The demons?"

She nodded. "Just listen now. First of all, when we went to Rabenwald for Baba Lenka's funeral I wasn't happy about it, not one bit. I did not want us to go, and we couldn't afford to go either, but we were tricked."

"Tricked? By—?"

She shook her head impatiently at the interruption. "When I was about six years old, my mother, Marika, committed suicide, and I was brought up in a children's home, as you know. I had few memories of her apart from tales of the forest where she grew up in Bohemia. Now, do you remember those old folk at the funeral?"

"Yes."

"Right, well, they're called the Watchers, and they raised her like themselves, pretty much as a gypsy. She never stayed with her mother - with Lenka - but the older she got, the more was revealed to her. There was no mother and daughter bond, I can promise you that – Baba Lenka terrified my mother. She called her a satanic witch. Anyway, as soon as she got the chance she fled, and escaped to England just before the war, which was where she met my father - your maternal grandfather. Unfortunately he was killed in action shortly after I was born. But this is what you need to know, Eva – the Order tracked my mother down."

My heart lurched.

"She knew about them, you see, and of course she also carried the family legacy. They traced her and tried to make her return to Rabenwald, which was where Baba Lenka was living by that time. After the Second World War ended, Lenka crossed over the border to Bavaria along with thousands of other Sudetens and took up residence in that farmhouse – the one we went to and I wish to God we hadn't, especially after what I found out later. So anyway, my mother had to pack up and run again. She took a train up to the north of England, where she left me in a children's home before taking her own life soon after. Maybe she hoped I'd disappear into obscurity and be spared. Maybe she thought it would end there; I don't know."

"Took her own life?"

"Yes."

"How did you know? Was it in the books?"

"In Lenka's diary, yes."

"You said you didn't want us to go to the funeral but we were tricked? What happened?"

She was beginning to get tired, her eyelids were fluttering, and I reached for her hand and held it firmly, as if I could squeeze strength into her.

"Yes, I used to get a birthday card every year from distant cousins Jakub and Vanda in Munich. You may remember me mentioning them from time to time? Well, I'd always assumed my mother told them which children's home I lived in before she died, so there would be someone to watch out for her child. Anyway, those cards came every year. They even sent a wedding card and one when you were born, too. So, when Baba Lenka was on her deathbed, they wrote to say she'd probably be gone before I got there, but a solicitor had informed them that the farmhouse had been left to me if I could be found. And I'm afraid your dad and I took the bait. We weren't as well-informed as my mother had been, and we were stony broke. We thought if we took a loan for the flights and put the farmhouse on the market, it would make us some money. It looked like a godsend, to be honest."

"Why didn't it? What do you mean by 'bait'?"

She took a long, deep breath. "Jakub and Vanda are Watchers, Eva – the ancients. They were never in Munich—"

"Watchers? The same ones who brought up my grandmother, Marika?"

"Yes. I pretended I didn't know who they were at the funeral, but I did. They are the ones who guard and transfer the legacy. As soon as I realised what the old crone was telling me that day at the farmhouse, on the morning of the funeral, I knew we'd been tricked into taking this diabolical blood heritage."

"And now they're looking for me?"

"Yes."

"Are the Watchers one and the same as der Order der

schwarzen Sonne?"

"Not exactly. The Watchers are demonic guardians, sent to keep an eye on their gatekeepers – Lenka, and now you. The Order uses us because we have a direct channel from the Dark Lord to the human realm. Now this is where it's your turn to take a deep breath. Try to accept what I'm telling you. I know it's hard. But the people in the Order do not have a conscience or a moral compass. They bow down to the one they call Sakla, or Satan, and nothing is off-limits – in fact, the more abominable the act carried out in his name, the better.

I'm not sure if you understand the full magnitude of this. The thing is, Eva, you don't just have one or two demonic entities attached to you, you have a direct route to Satan and access to his entire legion The goal is to extinguish the human spirit, to provoke war and chaos, hatred and division, to keep us all suppressed in ignorance, poverty and fear. Lenka did a sterling job for them during the World Wars. Look how much death and terror there was, and how much money the Order made as a result!"

"And we brought this into the world – with dark arts?"

"Essentially, yes—"

Even as the enormity and horror of what she was saying sank in, I still clung to one last vestige of hope. "But I haven't been contacted by the Watchers or the Order–"

"You will be now you're sixteen. They will know where you are. Eva, have you—?"

A horrible thought suddenly crossed my mind… *No, my mum would not do to me what Clara did to Lenka!* Nevertheless, the question flew out. "Is this legacy really mine? Or yours? Because I don't understand – I mean, you're so ill!"

Her eyes were closed now and she struggled to open them again. The hand holding mine felt as feather light and feeble as a dying bird. "Yours, love. And I'm sorry about that, So, so sorry. But once you showed me the poppet, I knew everything had been about getting you to Rabenwald. The farmhouse was, is, worthless. Not only is it falling down, but it was also built on a mass grave. No one would touch it. Lenka was involved with some terrible people, officers who committed mass exterminations. Her house was built over the top of thousands of corpses in order to help cover up the extent of the massacre. You were meant to be there that day, and you were meant to receive the poppet. I realised too late. I told your dad I didn't understand what those old women were saying and what was going on, but I did. There was nothing I could do by then, though, except instil in you not to take anything or pick anything up, to scare you into doing as I said so we could get away as fast as possible."

I struggled to digest it all, but the clock was ticking, and here was my mother, after all these years. "But what happened to you? I need to understand...Dad said you read the books."

"Yes, it was after I burned the poppet..." Her voice trailed away and her eyes began to close again.

I squeezed her hand to wake her up. "Mum, I have to know. I'm sorry but I have to know about the books."

"Yes, yes you do. There was a grimoire. It was written in Sumerian thousands of years ago. Some of these ancient grimoires were smuggled out to Turkey and later filtered into Europe. This one had been translated into various languages with Russian and German scribbled over the top. The other books were line-by-line instructions to Lenka from the Order, along with a diary she kept."

"Did the grimoire explain the initiation rite – the rape of the dead sorceress and the cannibalism?"

"You learned this from dreams?"

"Yes."

She blanched, two tiny spots of fuchsia high on her cheeks. Her eyes seemed sunken, the bones of her face angular, her fingers pinching through my sleeve. "Oh, love, I am so sorry – you see, this is what we carry!"

I squeezed her hand and blinked back another wash of tears.

"Baroness Jelinski experimented with what she called the darker half of creation – the shadow force, the nonhuman or demonic, as I was trying to explain – and she brought them in. I read the parts translated into German—"

"How come you know German?"

She held up her hand. "I was taught it as my first language up to the age of six, but, Eva, I made sure I learned my mother tongue. It felt natural, and, like you, my dreams were informed dreams."

I nodded. "Okay."

"Anyway, you asked about the books. I became interested, that's all. But the more I read, the more the world as it had been, spiraled away and became lost to me. The grimoire described how Sakla – or Satan, who is titled in different ways depending on which texts you read – rules a shadow force. These shadows hail from a realm of absolute blackness, yet they walk among us, feeding off ignorance, anger, hostility and jealousy, to name a few. Their energy is fed just as much by ignorance as violence - all that is grey, dark and without light, in fact. Some call them demons, some call them archons, and others will say evil spirits. And it is these who possess the people who bow down to Satan." She paused, and then added, "Never call a demon forth by name, Eva. And never call on Satan, because whatever riches you are given in this world, will be paid for in eternity. And that's a long, long time."

"But if they feed off us, how come they want us to be killed in wars?"

"Not just killed, not all of us. What they want is to stop humans knowing who they are and where they came from. They want us to be obsessed with sex and money, envy and hatred. They want us kept in the dark but yes, war and chaos is an absolute feast!"

"And Lenka helped bring about wars?"

"Yes."

"Mum!" The truth hit me. "I think she was tricked. I mean, I know she was…and then it was too late—"

She nodded. "Which is why you must have the knowledge. Your dad was adamant you shouldn't know what she did, but the thing is, Eva – the truth sets us free. And you have to understand that once you make the connection with them, your life will no longer be your own. They will make it unbearable."

"A Shadow force, you said?"

She nodded.

"Black winged shadows brought in on a cold wind? Is that what you see?"

"Yes."

It seemed to me that as we spoke, the room darkened a shade. My mother shivered.

"And you read those rituals, didn't you? You spoke the words, and you—"

"I learned exactly how to commune with them, yes."

"Talking to them? Getting answers?"

"Yes, and now they're attached to me, and I can't get rid of them. Unlike you, though, I cannot give commands but only be tormented. The gift and title of sorceress was passed to you. You are their mistress in this world, and they expect you to use their energy."

"Mum." I glanced at the clock. Fifteen minutes and Dad would be back. "What did Baba Lenka do, exactly? I have to know what lies ahead. Dad said if I knew, it would send me insane, but I have to, don't I?"

"Your dad read through the other two books when he burned the grimoire. There were two large tomes, thousands upon thousands of pages of instructions and photographs from the Order. Baba Lenka spent a lifetime working for occult sects and satanic lodges at the highest level – with the world's most prestigious and powerful elite, people you would never imagine in your wildest nightmares could be involved in things like that. There were names in those books, along with photographs – remember she had to recognise them – of royalty, government ministers, military commanders, aristocrats, artists and film stars, top psychiatrists, university professors, judges and police chiefs – people it would shock you to know were involved and whose descendants still are. Killing and even consuming children, Eva. They torture them until their eyes bleed, and drink their blood."

Tears dripped down her tissue cheeks. "I'm getting cold again, oh so cold."

From a nearby chair I grabbed a blanket, and on a hot day in a hot room, wrapped it around her shoulders.

"What a trick it is, what illusion, yet humans have such a weakness, such greed and such egos that they are prepared to do such things…"

I felt myself spiralling downwards. "Hell on earth and few people even know about it?"

She nodded. "Oh, it's hushed up good and proper. Anyone speaking out will either be committed or quietly removed. These people bond together on pain of death. It isn't a secret that the SS used the dark arts. There were even counter-occult groups sending incorrect information back to them. So more ordinary people than you think know about it, but most have been programmed to believe it's not real. If they did, they could fight back you see - spiritually."

We had less than five minutes left. By then, the midsummer afternoon had darkened considerably, the air hot and still. But despite the insufferable heat, goosebumps rose on my mother's skin and her teeth chattered.

I rubbed her arms in a vain attempt to keep her warm.

"Mum, I get badly ill. What am I to do?"

She gripped my hand. Three small squeezes one after the other. "Most important. Listen. You have to know. It is all in your mind, Eva. It is an illusion, a trick, and nothing is solid. How do you think you get well again so quickly?"

"What? I don't understand. But others can see I am

ill."

"Step outside of your rational mind for a minute. It is illusion, Eva. Other people see how you don't eat, that you are thin; they see you tormented and anxious, reacting to pain. But believe me, the power over you is all illusion because they want you to facilitate their agenda. But it only works if you let it! Do you see? This is not real but a spiritual battle between the light and the shadow force – between human creation and the dark, inhuman one. Use light, they hate that. Remember, darkness can only dim the light, but light can obliterate the darkness. Fill yourself with love and hope and all you have been given as a human spirit. Remember there is always a human weakness or flaw that makes it possible for them to ride in. It can be greed or hate, rage or jealousy, take your pick—"

I hung my head, remembering the rage. "Lenka's was vanity, wasn't it? She wanted to be admired!"

My mum smiled wanly. "Always there is a weakness or they wouldn't get in. Everyone calls them demons, their demons…you see…deep down, people *do* know—"

My dad's footsteps were in the corridor below, about to come up the stairs.

"How do you know so much, Mum?"

She sighed. "I made it my business. When I'm not out for the count, I try to read and so should you."

The fire door to the main corridor creaked on its hinges. Suddenly she reached forwards and pulled me close.

"Understand one thing, Eva. Do not, under any circumstances, work for the Order. They are the scum of the earth. Do not fall for what they offer or you will be lost… If it looks too good to be true, it probably is."

I pulled back so I could look into her eyes, realising on a deep, unspoken level that it would be for the last time. She was gripping my hand like she never wanted to let go.

"I'll be all right, Mum. Now I understand more. Thank you. I'm going to try and do what you say."

Her grip tightened, and I kissed her forehead.

"I've got a job in a nursing home, did you know? And a few weeks ago I met a really nice lad. Don't worry, he's definitely not wealthy, he's just ordinary and kind and—"

She started to pant, the hair matting to her forehead. "Met someone? Who?"

"His name's Luke. He's—"

"He didn't seek you out, did he?"

"Well, sort of, but—"

"Is he very good looking, charming and funny?"

"Yes, but honestly he's not—"

"No! No! No! Eva, no—"

Her screams ricocheted round the whole hospital. Dad flew in along with two male nurses.

"Sorry, love, we're going to have to ask you to leave."

She was still gripping my hand, but her eyes had rolled back in her head, and her body was contorting violently.

Dad glared at me as I stood up and backed away.

"I knew this would happen. Eva, I told you not to upset her. She might not recover this time—"

"Mr Hart, we need you and your daughter to leave now, please."

***

CHAPTER THIRTY-SIX

There was nothing about Luke to cause alarm. I worried about what Mum had said the whole way home, but he was about as mundane as they came, with a job in an office somewhere in Leeds. Definitely not a member of the ruling classes, he had a local accent, rode a motorbike and wore jeans and t-shirts. It was true the attraction was strong, but he definitely wasn't pressing me to learn politics or offering a house!

My heart, so heavy in my chest on the journey back to the flat that midsummer evening, soared at the sight of him leaning on the wall by the bus stop when I got back. A fringe of dark hair flopped over his forehead, his long legs crossed at the ankles. When I rounded the corner, he flicked his cigarette onto the road and held open his arms.

He was the only person apart from Nicky who had ever hugged me, but that wasn't the same, was it? I mean, Luke, he wrapped his arms right around me and just held me in a great, protective bear hug. I'd never needed it more than I did then, either. Instinctively he knew the visit to my mum had been traumatic, although I had no intention of telling him what kind of burden we had to bear. Like most people, he'd back away and assume it was madness.

I just sank into him, loving that he stroked my hair,

soothed by the kind words he breathed into my neck. I wanted to love this man. I wanted more than anything in the world right then to be taken care of, helped, partnered. Mum and Dad had that – despite everything, their love burned more brightly than ever. You could almost see the bond.

Well, I wanted that kind of love, too. And even more than that, I wanted to give it.

After a few minutes I pulled away to look at him. His face, gazing down into mine, was a rapture of concern, his deep brown eyes glinting not with mischief this time but something else…love? He smoothed my hair back and tilted up my chin with one elegant finger. I had never been kissed before Luke came into my life. And I have a feeling few have ever been kissed the way he was about to kiss me at that moment. He did that thing, tilting his head, at first just grazing my lips, then looked directly into my eyes, waiting for the invitation. Should he go further? We were melting into each other. I nodded. And when he kissed me again, it was a hell of a lot harder. The pressure intensified rapidly. He groaned, and a hot surge rose inside me, blurring all other thoughts except the desire to have him. I'd marry him. I wanted him. His breathing became faster. Pressing me against the wall, he pushed his lean, muscular body into mine, and the fire in his eyes ignited to a blaze.

"I want you," he said, his voice syrupy, kissing me all over my face, my neck, dipping down to the throat.

I want you…

He took hold of my hand. "Come on, let's go for a walk in the park. It's not dusk yet."

I know, I was sixteen and traumatised, but I didn't

care. Besides, through Lenka I knew how beautiful loving someone physically could be, and I'd always wanted that for myself. This could be my happy ending. In time, after getting spiritual help, maybe with his strength and support I'd have a normal, happy life. After all, this was simply illusion, as my mother had said. Illusion and control…

Honestly? It was the most natural thing in the world to walk through those park gates with him towards the woods, with the amber sun dipping over the horizon. We fell into the long grass. I can still remember the desperation on his face when he entered me, the contortion of his features as he groaned in ecstasy, the pulsing of his arm muscles, the iron slenderness of his hips. And most of all, I remember the way he murmured my name, all the way through: 'Eva…Eva…oh, Eva…'

Afterwards, we lay still, panting, the sweat on our skin cooling, until the fiery ball of the sun dropped over the playing fields, streaks of crimson and rose in its wake. I curled into the crook of his arm.

After a while he lit a cigarette and passed one to me. "So how did it go with your mum, then?"

"Good in a way, but it upset me in another way."

"How do you mean?"

"Well, she has to be sedated. They wouldn't let me visit for years, so it's been a bit of a shock." I snuggled closer. "I'm glad I've seen her, though. Really glad."

"What's the matter with her, then?"

I hesitated. I didn't want to put him off. "Okay, well do you know what the supernatural is?"

"You mean witches and ghosts and stuff?"

"Well, sort of. It's to do with that, anyway. Demons.

Does it scare you?"

He laughed and kissed my cheek. "Course not!"

So I told him. After he said his mum did tarot and he'd once seen a ghost, I opened up. Omitting details regarding the World Wars or how Lenka had joined an occult order, I related quite a bit about the family legacy and what had happened in Rabenwald. It was such a relief to tell him about my mum, too, about the human spirit and to trust in God.

"So, you see," I said, "what a crazy family I have."

"That doesn't worry me. Most families have something to hide."

"What about yours? Come on, your turn!"

He took a long drag of his cigarette. An owl hooted nearby, and we both jumped.

But it was as I was laughing that his mood altered. The aura around him clouded, his face set to stone, and he sat up so abruptly that my shoulder fell back against the ground.

"You're a bit dumb, really, aren't you, Eva?"

"Pardon?"

He looked over his shoulder as I lay there on the grass. All signs of flirtatiousness, desire, and caring concern were now erased from his handsome features. The eyes were dead, the mouth sneering.

"Your mother's fed you a pile of crap, and you actually believed it. That's what's worrying. She's insane, but you believed all the shit about human light and God's creation. You must be really, seriously fucking thick."

"Hey, I didn't say I believed that or—"

"All there is, right, is what you can see and hear and touch. That's it. When you're dead, you're dead – dust!

So you might as well live life to the max – have fun, have sex with who you like when you like, make pots of money, have orgies, drive fast cars, get pissed or snort coke. Who cares what you do? There is no man on a throne in the fucking sky passing out judgement."

"I never said there was a man on a throne."

"Anyway, I'm thinking of going, taking a job in London. I was gonna tell you, but you've really busted my head in with all this talk of God and snuffing out human light. I thought you were the one! But you're nuts."

All I heard were the words 'I'm thinking of going'.

Sitting up, sobered, I stared at the side of his stony-featured face. "I thought you had a job here. Oh, please don't go! You can't do this to me!"

He laughed. "Do what to you?"

"Make me…" Shit, I was going to cry. I thought, stupidly, that he was a friend and, even more stupidly, that we were in love.

"Fall in love?"

"No."

He looked at me then and smirked. "Fuck, that's what you were going to say, wasn't it? 'Make me fall in love with you'? Eva, you're not old enough to even know what that means."

Sixteen-year-old Lenka came to mind. Oh, we *were* old enough. Our feelings were every bit as powerful as a fully grown adult's, if not more so because we leapt in with such abandon, such trust and such passion. I was really working hard at not crying. An eruption of grief was coming from the very core of my being, and I couldn't stop it.

"After what we've just done, how can you—?"

"Eva, don't be such a baby. It's only sex."

"I'm not being a baby, it's just that you've changed – you've completely turned on me."

My lower lip was weakening. Any second now, I was going to sob uncontrollably.

Those dark eyes of his were heartlessly fixed on mine. Then, just as swiftly as his rage arose, it drained away and he smiled.

"Of course, you could come with me?"

I swallowed repeatedly, confused, seesawing between hope and despair. "Really?"

"Yeah, why not? I mean, what is there for you here – a mother in a mental home, spouting religious bullshit, and a father who dumped you?"

Despite the harsh words, a glimmer of a more glamorous life flashed before me.

"Eva, can I ask you something?"

Relief was washing through me. He'd been angry because of what he didn't understand. It was as Lenka's mother had said – the Mundanes got angry. It was okay; I'd never bring it up again. "Of course."

As he raked a hand through his hair, a gossamer thread of moonlight filtered through the sylvan canopy, illuminating his features in a silver sheen. He had to be the most dazzling of men. Was he really mine?

"Well, three murders and the most incredible thought-transference abilities, yet you still haven't worked out who I am?"

That took a minute. A full minute. I stared at him openmouthed.

"You really don't know?"

He didn't seek you out, did he?
"What? I don't—"

He lunged forwards and grabbed both my arms, his accent no longer northern but cut-glass home counties. "Come with me to London and you will have everything you want – your own flat overlooking the river, more money than you can ever spend, a chauffeur to anywhere you want to go, exotic holidays and beautiful clothes. You'll have the best education money can buy so you're comfortable in the highest of circles. Eva, you know who I am! You know!"

"Der Orden der schwarzen Sonne?"

"The Order of the Black Sun here in Blighty, sweetie, but yes. Welcome to the most exclusive, elite club in the world. You have no idea how fantastic and exciting life is about to become. You will thrive. You need never be ill again, and, frankly, you've looked a bit ropey lately, so don't tell me your demons don't make you ill."

"You're not from Leeds, are you?"

That made him laugh. "Tell me what you have to do to keep the demons away, Eva. Are you going to go on murdering old ladies? And how long do you think it will keep those demons at bay for? You haven't got a couple of dozen to supply, you've got thousands!"

"So you're a Satanist!"

I couldn't help it; I started to cry.

"Eva." He pulled me into his arms as the tears burst out. It was all too much – all of it. He stroked my hair and whispered into my neck. "It's not as bad as you make out. You're just conditioned to believe Satan is bad and God is good, that's all. In reality, we all have both good and bad in us. Really, this is simply a wonderful club to be in – we have a lot of fun, and I'm asking you to join."

"Why?"

He held me away a little. "Look at it this way, then: you can either have the most incredible life with us or you can get sick and stay poor, and believe me you have no idea how bad that is going to get. A few decades down the line you are going to wish you'd made a better choice. So think about it and think hard. For a whole year, before you're even asked to attend a single meeting, you get to live in an exclusive West London townhouse with personal tutors and a wardrobe to die for. We have a female assistant all lined up for you. She specialises in the occult and can help you with that. You're going to feel and look incredible. We will take care of you, Eva. Proper care."

The thought of never seeing him again, of being left there on my own, was piercing my heart. Everyone has their weakness.

"All right," I said. "I'll come."

His smile switched back on as quickly as an electric lamp. Instantly enthused, he kissed my forehead and took hold of my hand. "Good. Come on then, let's get you home. I think you've had enough for one day."

"When will be going?" I asked as we walked back through the park. I was already picturing the new life in London, wondering what the house would be like and if he would live there with me.

He put his arm around my shoulders. "Let's go tomorrow, shall we?"

"Tomorrow? But my job, my mum—?"

"You can visit. Come on, let's go tomorrow, let's do this – strike while the iron's hot, as it were!"

By the time we left the park, it was dark. There were no stars, and the moon was obscured by brooding storm clouds. A wind had blown up, shaking the full-leaved trees in a bouncing shimmer, and our footsteps echoed on the deserted street. Coming towards us, on the opposite pavement was a woman. It didn't register immediately. In fact it was a while before the significance hit me, but by then of course, it was far too late. My mind had been on being looked after, being safe. One hand was in her pocket, the other partially hidden by the lapel of her jacket. The middle two fingers were tucked into the palm, and secured by the thumb. *The horned one…*

When we reached the end of my road, he turned to face me, dipping his head to kiss my lips. As he did so, an icy breeze fluttered against my cheeks, as soft as the wings of a bird.

"All roads lead to the Order of the Black Sun eventually, Eva. There is no escape. Not for any of us. You know that, don't you?"

***

COVERING LETTER
May 1979

My dearest Nicky,

You are the only person I can send this to because you will understand and know that I am far from crazy. You've probably wondered where I got to? I know – it's been a year! Suffice to say, the decision was a quick one with no time to say goodbye. I'm in London. Tomorrow is my initiation ceremony, and after that I can no longer be sure what will happen.

I've been writing this for a long time, months, scribbling during the hours set for 'homework'. Incredible as it is, I swear all I have written here is the truth This really is happening – all of it – and although people won't believe it, largely because they cannot comprehend other people behaving in this way, that doesn't mean it isn't true..

As mentioned, my initiation into the Order is tomorrow. I'm hoping to get to the post office this afternoon on the pretext of a medical appointment, but that could be scuppered. I'll be honest, I'm nervous. I'm not scared of dying, but I am of the punishment, something at which they excel and which will happen if I'm caught. However, I think there is a way to make it harder for them to inflict on humanity what they're planning. It will have to be at the very last second, at the moment they hand me the sword for sacrifice, because that is the way black magic works. Believe me, I have studied this, and with the advantage of Lenka's warning, I am no longer ignorant but have risen beyond ego and the importance of my own life. If it works, you'll know because their objective is another world war, only this one will be the end because of what they will use and how it will be done. I had to study biochemistry and psychology, Nicky. I will be catapulted to the top of a major television corporation within a few short years. Do you see?

The Order has infiltrated every walk of life and is already drip-feeding people so they will accept what is coming. The public is absolutely unaware of what is working in the shadows, totally oblivious that creatures such as these even walk among them. Look at the most glittering, the most successful, the richest and most powerful on a global scale – and that is where you will find them. It's a clandestine club closed to anyone other than the elite - Satan's servants are rewarded well. But the aim above all else, is to extinguish our spirit, that which makes us human. Hence the Black Sun. Always the Black Sun.

However, without me, they will lose a powerful force that's been carried through my family for generations. Don't shed a single tear. This is a good thing. I intend to take my chances with repentance and forgiveness in the hereafter, and drop the illusion that I have no choice.

Nicky, please will you look out for my mum? She's at Silverfields Psychiatric Hospital. Tell her I'm okay because I woke up just in time. And one more thing – you were, are, my dearest friend. I wish to God I had been able to follow a different path. You, though, well, you are the full sun. Shine on full wattage, Nicky, and don't ever think for one moment that you can't.

    Love,
    Eva xxx

ACKNOWLEDGEMENTS

I am indebted to Vera Slegtenhorst, who has kindly translated and proofread the German used in this manuscript. Thank you also, Vera, for constructing some creepy names for the villages. All of your help has been truly appreciated.

Also with regard to the German, thank you to Callum Harrop from Biddulph in Staffordshire.

And finally thank you as always, to my dear friend, Raven Wood, a traditional witch of Germanic and Celtic roots, who lives and practices the craft in Wisconsin, USA. Raven's crow poppet is both on the cover and featured prolifically in the text. Thank you also, for providing me with your invaluable knowledge on rites and rituals used in witchcraft, not to mention your personal insight. I am most grateful, as always, for your help. Find Raven's handmade products on: etsy.me/2L6rVih

<u>References:</u> 'Slavic witchcraft' by Natasha Helvin. Various textbooks on the Bavarian Illuminati and Kaiser Wilhelm 11.

***

MORE BOOKS BY SARAH ENGLAND:

FATHER OF LIES
A Darkly Disturbing Occult Horror Trilogy: Book 1

'Boy did this pack a punch and scare me witless…'
'Scary as hell…What I thought would be mainstream horror was anything but…'
'Not for the faint-hearted. Be warned – this is very, very dark subject matter.'
'A truly wonderful and scary start to a horror trilogy. One of the best and most well written books I've read in a long time.'
'A dark and compelling read. I devoured it in one afternoon. Even as the horrors unfolded I couldn't race through the pages quickly enough for more…'
'Delivers the spooky in spades!'
'Will go so far as to say Sarah is now my favourite author – sorry Mr King!'

***

Ruby is the most violently disturbed patient ever admitted to Drummersgate Asylum, high on the bleak moors of northern England. With no improvement after two years, Dr. Jack McGowan finally decides to take a risk and hypnotises her. With terrifying consequences.

A horrific dark force is now unleashed on the entire

medical team, as each in turn attempts to unlock Ruby's shocking and sinister past. Who is this girl? And how did she manage to survive such unimaginable evil? Set in a desolate ex-mining village, where secrets are tightly kept and intruders hounded out, their questions soon lead to a haunted mill, the heart of darkness…and the Father of Lies.

http://www.amazon.co.uk/dp/B015NCZYKU
http://www.amazon.com/dp/B015NCZYKU

***

TANNERS DELL - BOOK 2

Now only one of the original team remains – Ward Sister Becky. However, despite her fiancé, Callum, being unconscious and many of her colleagues either dead or critically ill, she is determined to rescue Ruby's twelve-year-old daughter from a similar fate to her mother.

But no one asking questions in the desolate ex-mining village Ruby hails from ever comes to a good end. And as the diabolical history of the area is gradually revealed, it seems the evil invoked is both real and contagious.

Don't turn the lights out yet!

***

MAGDA - BOOK 3

The dark and twisted community of Woodsend harbours a terrible secret – one tracing back to the age of the Elizabethan witch hunts, when many innocent women were persecuted and hanged.

But there is a far deeper vein of horror running through this village, an evil that once invoked has no intention of relinquishing its grip on the modern world. Rather, it watches and waits with focused intelligence, leaving Ward Sister Becky and CID Officer Toby constantly checking over their shoulders and jumping at shadows.

Just who invited in this malevolent presence? And is the demonic woman who possessed Magda back in the sixteenth century the same one now gazing at Becky whenever she looks in the mirror?

Are you ready to meet Magda in this final instalment of the trilogy? Are you sure?

***

THE OWLMEN

If They See You, They Will Come for You

Ellie Blake is recovering from a nervous breakdown. Deciding to move back to her northern roots, she and her psychiatrist husband buy Tanners Dell at auction – an old water mill in the moorland village of Bridesmoor.

However, there is disquiet in the village. Tanners Dell has a terrible secret, one so well guarded no one speaks its name. But in her search for meaning and very much alone, Ellie is drawn to traditional witchcraft and determined to pursue it. All her life she has been cowed. All her life she has apologised for her very existence. And witchcraft has opened a door she could never have imagined. Imbued with power and overawed with its magick, for the first time she feels she has come home, truly knows who she is.

Tanners Dell, though, with its centuries-old demonic history…well, it's a dangerous place for a novice…

http://www.amazon.co.uk/dp/B079W9FKV7
http://www.amazon.com/dp/B079W9FKV7

***

THE S⊕PRAN⊕

A Haunting Supernatural Thriller

It is 1951 and a remote mining village on the North Staffordshire Moors is hit by one of the worst snowstorms in living memory. Cut off for over three weeks, the old and the sick will die, the strongest bunker down, and those with evil intent will bring to its conclusion a family vendetta spanning three generations.

Inspired by a true event, *The Soprano* tells the story of Grace Holland – a strikingly beautiful, much admired local celebrity who brings glamour and inspiration to the grimy moorland community. But why is Grace still here? Why doesn't she leave this staunchly Methodist, rain-sodden place and the isolated farmhouse she shares with her mother?

Riddled with witchcraft and tales of superstition, the story is mostly narrated by the Whistler family, who own the local funeral parlour, in particular six-year-old Louise – now an elderly lady – who recalls one of the most shocking crimes imaginable.

http://www.amazon.co.uk/dp/B0737GQ9Q
http://www.amazon.com/dp/B0737GQ9Q7

***

HIDDEN COMPANY

A dark psychological thriller set in a Victorian asylum in the heart of Wales.

1893, and nineteen-year-old Flora George is admitted to a remote asylum with no idea why she is there, what happened to her child, or how her wealthy family could have abandoned her to such a fate. However, within a short space of time, it becomes apparent she must save herself from something far worse than that of a harsh regime.

2018, and forty-one-year-old Isobel Lee moves into the gatehouse of what was once the old asylum. A reluctant medium, it is with dismay she realises there is a terrible secret here – one desperate to be heard. Angry and upset, Isobel baulks at what she must now face. But with the help of local dark arts practitioner Branwen, face it she must.

This is a dark story of human cruelty, folklore and superstition. But the human spirit can and will prevail…unless of course, the wrath of the fae is incited…

***

MONKSPIKE

You are not forgiven

1149 was a violent year in the Forest of Dean.

Today, nearly 900 years later, the forest village of Monkspike sits brooding. There is a sickness here passed down through ancient lines, one noted and deeply felt by Sylvia Massey, the new psychologist. What is wrong with nurse Belinda Sully's son? Why did her husband take his own life? Why are the old people in Temple Lake Nursing Home so terrified? And what are the lawless inhabitants of nearby Wolfs Cross hiding?

It is a dark village indeed, but one which has kept its secrets well. That is, until local girl Kezia Elwyn returns home as a practising satanist, and resurrects a hellish wrath no longer containable. Burdo, the white monk, will infest your dreams... This is pure occult horror and definitely not for the faint of heart...

***

www.sarahenglandauthor.co.uk

Printed in Great Britain
by Amazon